D1336931

DEAD WIND

DEAD WIND

Tessa Wegert

**SEVERN
HOUSE**

First world edition published in Great Britain and the USA in 2022
by Severn House, an imprint of Canongate Books Ltd,
14 High Street, Edinburgh EH1 1TE.

Trade paperback edition first published in Great Britain and the USA in 2022
by Severn House, an imprint of Canongate Books Ltd.

severnhouse.com

British Library Cataloguing-in-Publication Data
A CIP catalogue record for this title is available from the British Library.

ISBN-13: 978-1-4483-0712-8 (cased)
ISBN-13: 978-1-4483-0843-9 (trade paper)
ISBN-13: 978-1-4483-0842-2 (e-book)

All Severn House titles are printed on acid-free paper.

MIX
Paper from
responsible sources
FSC
www.fsc.org FSC® C013056

Typeset by Palimpsest Book Production Ltd.,
Falkirk, Stirlingshire, Scotland.
Printed and bound in Great Britain by
TJ Books, Padstow, Cornwall.

For John and Carol Repsher, who shared their island

PROLOGUE

Alexandria Bay, New York

Trey Hayes arrived wearing a hoodie and sweatpants, white stripes down the sides of his thin legs. When he met my gaze, there was no mistaking the timidness in his eyes. They still shone, but weakly. He was a flashlight stuffed with dying batteries. A few blinks away from going out.

A message from his parents was the last thing Tim and I had been expecting. We'd interviewed the boy already, when he was recovered from the cold, dark place where his abductor had abandoned him. We'd taken his statement and let him get on with the process of healing, knowing it wouldn't be easy. This was the same kid, after all, who was forced to look on while a whetted knife was raised above his face. Who was missing pieces of himself he'd never get back. It could take years for Trey to come to terms with what happened to him – and if he were my child, there was no way he'd set foot in the New York State Police Troop D Alexandria Bay station ever again. But there was the message, right on Tim's phone. Texted to the number on the card my fellow investigator had handed Trey's parents that snowy day just a few weeks ago.

A request to meet.

I'd thought about the strangeness of this turn of events before leaving for work that morning. I had been monitoring the St Lawrence River closely in recent days, waiting for the ice to form. My first winter in the Thousand Islands, and I was as excited as a kid at the drive-in. I saw the first patches of ice float by as I descended the steps from my front door. They were glacier-blue in the feeble winter sunlight, so thin in places that they looked like lace, and as the river moved the ice along, broken shards collected along the shore. The pieces chimed when they collided, the sound like freezing rain tinkling against a windshield. The shoreline looked as though it was cluttered with shattered glass.

'It's you they want, Shana,' Tim had said when he got the text. 'They want you to talk to Trey.'

Flanked by his parents, the boy sat down at the table in the interview room while Tim made him a hot chocolate: sweet powder, kettle water, tiny dehydrated marshmallows bobbing on the surface. Trey took it gratefully, ran a finger around the lip of the paper cup, and licked the foam from his nail.

'Thanks for coming,' I said, not just to Trey but also his parents. His mother's mouth was a tightly stitched seam, the skin around her eyes purple.

'This wasn't our idea,' Virginia Hayes announced, fixing me with an unflinching gaze, 'and I'll be honest, I have my doubts about this.' The roots of her sandy blonde hair were growing out, and her lips were dry and peeling. Self-care had been pushed to the backburner the moment she found out her son went on a school field trip with his teachers, parent chaperones, and thirty-nine other fourth grade students, and didn't come back. 'We're here at the recommendation of Trey's therapist.' The woman's tone was grim.

Richard Hayes hooked an arm around Trey's rawboned back and splayed a hand on his wife's shoulder. 'Trey's supposed to talk about it,' he explained. 'It's supposed to help him cope.'

My eyes met Tim's where he stood by the door, and I watched his eyebrows twitch. I was starting to piece things together. Still, offloading the victim of violent crime to a couple of detectives under the pretense of augmenting his therapy seemed akin to a surgeon asking a hospital maintenance worker to take his place in the OR. Then again, I'd seen mental health counselors do some irregular things.

'Dr Tesh said it would be good for Trey to find someone he could relate to. She thought . . .' Richard's gaze hitched itself to the scar that had been carved into the side of my own face. The eternal wound that looked just like his son's. He didn't finish his sentence. There was no need.

'OK.' The word came out gruffer than I intended. 'If it's all right with you,' I said to Trey, 'I'd like to ask a few questions. About the man who took you.'

Trey's head snapped up. He had both hands wrapped around the steaming paper cup, and they started to tremble. His mother leaned toward him and gave me a look that could have cut glass, but it was too late. Trey's shaky hands upended the cup, sending a pool of scalding brown liquid across the tabletop. Chair legs screeched as Trey's parents jumped to their feet, pulling their son up with them. Tim was gone and back with a roll of paper towels before the first drop of cocoa hit the floor.

'I'm sorry,' Trey's father muttered while Virginia held the boy's face in her hands and told him it was all right, not his fault, no big deal. Working together, Tim and I mopped up the mess as quickly as we could. Three weeks. That wasn't enough time for a twisted ankle to heal, let alone for a child to bounce back from a trip to hell. *I'm going to lose them*, I thought as I dragged a sopping wad of paper towel across the table. *I can't lose them.*

I lobbed the saturated lump into the trash. *Come on, Shana. Think.*

'Hey Trey.' I gestured for the family to take their seats once more while Tim called down the hall for a replacement cocoa. 'Have you ever played Never Have I Ever?'

The game had been a favorite of mine as a kid, from grade school all the way until junior high. I wasn't sure if it was still in fashion, if Trey would even have a clue what I was talking about, but he did something with his head that I took as affirmation, so I folded my hands on the sticky table and leaned toward him with a smile.

'So, it's a really fun game, and it goes like this: I say 'never have I ever' about something I haven't done, and you tell me if you *have* done it. If you've done it, then you win. It's easy. Should we try?'

A nod.

'Here we go,' I said. 'Never have I ever eaten worms.'

Trey's eyes widened, and a smile tugged at his lips. He looked up at his mother, whose expression was already softening. 'Do gummy worms count?' Trey asked, his voice barely audible even in the quiet room.

'Yes!' I beamed at him, making sure he knew how pleased I was that he was playing along. 'That means you win the round. And then you get to ask the question. Sound good?' Trey nodded again. He was in.

'OK.' I took a breath and tried to keep my eyes on the kid. Behind him, Tim reached for his notebook. 'The first question I want to ask isn't actually about you. It's about that man.'

Trey stiffened, and his dark eyes grew wary. But he didn't shrink away from me.

'When you answer,' I told him, 'say what *he* would say if he was playing. Get it?'

Virginia shifted in her seat. This wasn't why she brought her son here, not part of the plan, and her trepidation was plain to see. Where Trey's recovery was concerned, the questions I was about to ask would do no good. If anything, they might cause Trey to regress, and that prospect made my stomach clench and a wave of acid swell in my throat. If I was going to succeed at finding his captor, though, and eliminate the possibility of more victims, more damaged psyches, more death, I had to get Trey to talk on my terms. I tried to convey this to his mother without words, a silent exchange that played out over Trey's head. Her lips were pinched tight when she pulled the nine-year-old onto her lap as if he were a toddler, but she didn't argue. She knew as well as I did the black presence that loomed over her child would never be fully vanquished until the man who'd taken Trey was found.

Here's what I know about Blake Bram: he likes to talk. When he was my captor, almost eighteen months before he came for Trey, the man wouldn't shut up. That had worked in my favor. I learned things about him that helped me. I could only hope Trey had, too.

We were already in possession of an excellent composite sketch, so I didn't need Trey to tell me what the fugitive we were hunting looked like. I'd seen him for myself, and felt sure now that if ever he got close enough for me to get a good look, he wouldn't escape again. What I was digging for with Trey was something else. Social characteristics, marketable skills, previous occupations – anything that might provide us with a clue to where Bram was hiding. Bram was at large, possibly still in the area, and his most recent victim sat right in front of me. I had to take my shot.

'Never have I ever been to New York City.'

Trey blinked. Looked up at his mom and then his dad, both of whom gave him a nod of encouragement. 'Yes,' Trey said, turning his face back to me. 'He was there. He worked in New York. He used to clean an apartment building. Like the custodians at my school.'

'Great. Great job, Trey.' It was what I'd been hoping to hear. If Bram had told Trey about New York, he might have told him much more. *This is working.* I kept my face neutral, once again resisting the urge to look at Tim. 'You know, I've been to New York,' I said. 'I used to live there.' It felt like a lifetime ago. 'Does the man work as a custodian here, too?' I held my breath, and waited.

Trey shook his head. 'He doesn't do that anymore. He didn't like it.'

There was a gentle knock at the door. Don Bogle, bless his heart, appeared with a fresh hot chocolate for Trey. Tim took it from him with both hands and carefully set it down in front of the boy.

He doesn't do that anymore. The revelation was huge, so critical I had to fight to contain my glee. When I thought about Bram, and what he might be doing now, I always imagined him smelling of floor polish and jangling with keys the way he had back in the city. I'd been calling all the apartment complexes, gyms, and nursing homes in a thirty-mile radius from where I currently sat, hoping they'd recently hired a loner with Bram's skin tone and build. I'd struck out at every turn. And now I knew why.

I had some experience with criminal profiling, and I was sure that while he plotted his next crime, Bram was operating as a functioning member of society. He didn't come from money, and would need a way to make ends meet. So Bram was working – which meant that if I hoped to find him, I needed to know his occupation. Bram had to have some kind of know-how that would be useful here. In Upstate New York.

'I know it's your turn now,' I said as Trey slid off his mother's lap into his own chair once more, 'but is it OK if I ask another one? Give you a chance to drink that before the marshmallows melt?'

I didn't wait for him to answer. Trey's face and limbs had loosened. For the moment he was happy, and I wanted to capitalize on that. I said, 'Never have I ever worked on a boat.'

It was a long shot. We had no hard evidence that Bram had been a deck- or dockhand. But he knew how to drive a motorboat. He'd stolen a skiff to transport Trey, and that wasn't a skill the man had possessed in his youth. I didn't know how long Bram had been living in New York before he started killing women, before he took me; it was possible he'd had a job at the docks, maybe done some commercial fishing on Long Island. It stood to reason that, one way or another, he'd been on the water. That he'd amassed enough experience to find steady work.

But once again, Trey shook his head.

'No time with boats at all?' I asked, deflated.

Trey took a sip from his cup and licked the bubbly foam from his rosebud lips. 'No,' he said. 'He worked with boats. Just not *on* a boat. Do I still win?'

The current of excitement started in my toes and zipped straight up through my body. 'The man told you he worked with boats?'

'We have a boat. In the summer I go tubing. So I know about marinas.'

Across the room, Tim's pen scratched wildly on the pad.

'That sounds like fun,' I said. 'So the man worked at a marina? Did he say where it was?' If I could track down a previous employer, I might be able to learn more about the work Blake Bram had done. The false identity he'd been using. Where he was working now.

Trey avoided my gaze and pinched his lower lip between his teeth. It was a no.

'Did he mention where he was living? If he had a house or an apartment somewhere?' I bit back the words *around here*. The last thing the kid needed was a reminder that Bram could still be nearby.

'No. But he went someplace else during the day.'

This we already knew from our brief preliminary interview with Trey and his parents. For much of the time Trey was held captive, he was alone. Just as I had been.

'And he didn't tell you where?' I confirmed.

A shadow passed across the boy's face. 'He said he had to be careful not to say too much. He said that would take the fun out of it.'

Take the fun out of it.

You son of a bitch, I thought, picturing Bram's face as I'd last seen it and digging my fingernails into my palms. Those words were a message, meant expressly for me. A reference to our shared past and the twisted games he'd baited me into playing when we were kids, back in small-town Vermont. They were an allusion to my efforts to hunt him down, and his to evade me. The relentless chase we'd been engaged in for months.

'Did he say anything else?' I asked. 'Anything at all?'

Trey shrugged his shoulders. 'He mostly just talked about boats. Boats, and girls.'

'Girls?' I said too quickly.

'His girlfriends.'

'Do you remember their names?'

'Some of them. Jessica. Robyn.'

I felt my brow quirk. Jessica, we knew. Jess Lowenthal had been Bram's third victim, killed in my precinct. Her body dumped at a construction site across from Tompkins Square Park. But Robyn? In all, Bram had taken three women, all of whom he'd met through an online dating site. None had been named Robyn.

Since the moment I realized who my abductor was, I'd been desperate to understand him – not just his predisposition to serial murder, whether biological, social, or psychological, but also his movements. What had he been doing all these years? Where was he hiding? In New York, his killings were well-documented. Investigators continued to search for him in the hope that they might bring closure to his crimes and give the victims' families some peace. But Blake Bram was a canny man. In addition to those victims, he'd taken me. I had been his fourth target, the only one to survive, and my selection had not been random. I believed he'd planned for a long time to reel me back into his life. Following my escape, he had tracked me to Upstate New York and pulled me into a twisted game of cat-and-mouse.

There were things I thought I already grasped about him, having known him as long as I had, but a single, powerful fear continued to dog me. I was worried the three women he killed in New York weren't the first. That the real number of his victims remained unknown.

And if that was true, if there were other girls who'd died by my wicked cousin's hand, I had to find them.

ONE

Five months later

'So how exactly is this going to work?'

I waited to ask the question until the cluster of police cruisers came into view, jogging my knee while Tim drove. We were barely five minutes past Point Alexandria and the Canada Border Services Agency we'd checked into when we made landfall on the island, but I already felt out of my depth.

'With the Canadians, you mean?' Tim shrugged and tucked a curl of dark hair behind his ear. He'd grown it out recently, embracing the lapse in regular trims, and it was damp now. Glossy. The ferry ride had been a quick ten-minute journey from Cape Vincent, New York across the St Lawrence River, but the boat heaved and rocked on the waves, the choppy water glowing pale green around us, and we'd both gotten wet. By the time Tim maneuvered the state police car from the ferry to the crumbling cement ramp and onto shore, the river was so angry the waves cuffed our windows. Water still streamed across them now.

'It'll be RCMP or OPP,' Tim told me from the driver's seat. His personal car, a gray VW Golf, had a manual transmission, so he had a habit of driving with his right hand on the gear shift even in our New York State Police-issued automatic sedan. It was where his hand rested now. 'No saying which branch of the police we'll get until we get there. Typically, the Canadians handle their crimes and we handle ours, but there are exceptions. If a resident of Jefferson County were to commit an offense across the border, for example, the Canadian authorities might take the lead, but we'd partner with them. In this case, for now, we're here to observe. But the team will be cool with that. They're a solid bunch.'

Of course Tim has a good relationship with these guys. Tim has a good relationship with everyone. Even after months of working together, I was still a little jealous of Tim's local connections, but I pushed those petty thoughts aside. We were approaching the object I'd been marveling over since we got off the ferry and turned onto the highway that bisected the flat mass of land.

'Welcome to Wolfe Island,' Tim said, eyeing me with amusement as the view before us rendered me speechless.

The wind turbine rose from the earth like a skeletal arm with three bony fingers outstretched, the land around it so level you could see the tower from two towns over. It wasn't alone. Dozens of other turbines had been erected in fields with acres in the hundreds, land that would be lush with corn and soybeans come summer. It was only April, not yet warm enough to ditch my black State Police jacket; one of the farmhouses we passed still had a pair of cross-country skis propped against its exterior wall. The day was overcast, and the vast sky roiled with gunmetal clouds. Soon it would be raining, and we needed to get to the crime scene before that happened. Before the evidence was washed away and swallowed up by the hungry spring earth.

It was part of the Frontenac Islands, this place, just across the border. I'd never been to any of the Canadian islands before, never had an urgent reason to go, seeing as my jurisdiction was limited to New York State. In my head, late at night when I lay alone in my cottage, I imagined visiting every one of the area's islands – those that were open to the public, anyway. I planned to make a game of it, see how many I could get around to on a free weekend. It would be good boating practice, and I could finally fully familiarize myself with the waters around Alexandria Bay. I would probably have picked a nicer day to get started, but like it or not my tour had officially begun.

I took a moment to quiz myself. *RCMP: The Royal Canadian Mounted Police. OPP: The Ontario Provincial Police.* I'd learned the lingo last summer when I started my new job in A-Bay, but I wanted to make sure I remembered now. It was important. I understood this was the Canadians' turf, but if my instincts were right, they were going to need our help.

Tim pulled up to a cluster of parked cars and cut the engine. Zipping my jacket up to my chin, I stepped out onto the asphalt. The Canadian authorities – OPP by the looks of things; the letters were painted in gold on the side of their black-and-white cruisers, the word POLICE on the back – had pulled onto the service road. On one side, a stand of trees. The other was all open fields dotted with jilted bales of hay. The cars sat empty, with the exception of one. When the driver saw us, he set down his smartphone and climbed out.

'Tim,' said the sergeant, sticking out his hand. He was a foot shorter than my partner, but with his patrician looks – an abundance of fair hair, an aquiline nose – the Canadian held himself tall. 'There you are. Good to see you, man.'

'Likewise,' said Tim. Then, with a nod in my direction: 'Paul Ludgate, meet Shana Merchant. She's our new senior investigator. Started last summer.'

Even as I shook Ludgate's hand and we traded greetings, my eyes scanned the horizon. I waited for the men to get the rest of the chitchat out of the way, the routine exchange of a few civilized words that precedes the horror to come, and wondered if I'd have to remind them we were in a rush. I needn't have worried. Moments later, Tim and Ludgate both looked up at the sky, heavy now with imminent rain. 'The victim's down there,' said Ludgate, nodding toward the side road, 'but we need to stay off that path until Bonetti's had a look. Hope you don't mind getting dirty.'

Without hesitation, Tim and I followed Ludgate into the field. The mud squelched under our boots, the cold making my toes tingle. Though the muck was shallow, the walk felt like wading through knee-deep water, and by the time we got to the scene we were all a little winded.

Now that I was closer to the turbine and it was no longer a one-dimensional white line against the darkening sky, the size of the thing was staggering. I'd seen wind turbines before, perched atop the mountains of Vermont up by Sutton and Eden. There were wind farms elsewhere in New York State, too. I'd never been this near to one. It was a sight to behold.

The average US turbine could be close to five hundred feet in height, the tallest topping out at eight-fifty. I'd done some reading about them during the half-hour ride from A-Bay. This one's tapered white blades were rotating with a motion that was both sluggish and perfectly smooth. I could feel them cut through the air around me, their mass like a bank of humidity pressing toward the earth. They emitted a low-frequency buzz that called to mind the unrelenting drone of a boiler room. The image unnerved me, and I quickly put it out of my mind. It wasn't the turbine we came to see, but what lay at its base.

Slumped against the steel tower's concrete platform, the victim looked impossibly small, but this was an adult we were dealing with, no question. Given the state of the skin and the rigidity of the body, I figured the crime was mere hours old. It was the coat that would have made the sagging figure visible from the road, a splash of plum against the taupe landscape. Indeed, Ludgate told us that's what led a passerby to call the police. The victim's arms hung loose, head lolling to one side.

The victim was a woman.

The group that encircled her lifted their heads at our approach, cheeks turned rosy by the brisk April wind. For a second, I wondered if this would be a case of too many cooks; if we'd step on each other's toes out here and slow everything down. Just like in rural Upstate New York, violent crime wasn't common in these parts and the team that had turned out today looked raring to go. I had to admit they appeared competent, too. In the time it took Tim and I to get here, the local authorities had made good progress. More introductions followed, and I greeted the investigating coroner with enthusiasm. She was already marking evidence to be photographed in situ before it was collected. Trying to beat the rain.

'Asphyxia,' she pronounced in a confident voice. Dr Mima Bonetti was a sweet-faced woman in her fifties who had taken the ferry over from Kingston, and she noted the petechiae rash around the victim's eyes and the marks on her neck as evidence of her judgement. 'The victim was strangled, sometime in the night. No visible scratches or bruises. Not sure about sexual assault yet.' A single raindrop glistened on Bonetti's cheek. Her curly black hair was secured in a low ponytail, and though a fuzzy strand had come loose and was flitting against her forehead, she made no move to tuck it away. She said, 'I've got a ways to go, still.'

'There's a tent coming,' Ludgate assured us as another officer snapped pictures, 'but it'll take a few minutes to set up.'

Collectively, we looked up at the sky. Everyone except Tim, whose gaze remained on the victim. The woman on the ground.

'You didn't know her, did you?' I asked it quietly, and only once the others started to talk among themselves. The way Tim was examining the woman gave me pause. There was a trace of something more profound than characteristic regret in his eyes.

His jaw tightened as he tried to tuck away his emotion. 'Awful,' he said thickly. 'She looks close to my mom's age, and she's been out here all night.' That was evident in the blue undertone of the victim's complexion – as much of it as we could see, anyway. Hanks of dark hair, damp and stringy, snaked across her bloodless face to veil her brow, nose, chin, but even without a clear view we could work out her age, give or take. Her social class, too. She'd been well-groomed in life, with good clothes and shoes that looked spendy. The exception was that hair. It was dyed a rich shade of brown and enhanced with gold highlights that couldn't have been achieved with an at-home kit, yet the roots were solid gray. They ran down the center of the woman's head like a split seam. The effect made me think of Virginia Hayes.

There was something else too, a tug that made me wonder if I'd seen this woman before. She wasn't familiar, exactly, but looking at her made my skin prickle. I'd seen too many dead women in my life. It never got easier. My gaze trailed down to her hands, palms-up on the ground. 'She wearing a wedding ring?' I asked the coroner.

'Let's find out.' With gloved hands, Bonetti wiggled the victim's own gloves – black leather with cashmere lining, expensive – sliding the fingers out one at a time. The diamond engagement ring and matching band she revealed looked like they'd been worn for a while, the white gold scratched and dull.

'She's married,' I said, surprised. 'Nobody called in a missing wife?'

Ludgate said, 'Nope. Makes you wonder, doesn't it?'

Tim peered into the victim's unmoving face once more. Casting me a blank look, he pulled back.

'Can you tell us anything else?' I asked Bonetti. 'I'm assuming there's no driver's license in her pocket, or you would have led with that.'

'Sadly, no. No purse, either. There is something, though,' she said. 'It's her clothing. Beautiful, right? The coat's a designer brand that isn't sold in Canada. I know this because I keep waiting for them to open a store in Toronto, or at least one that isn't a million miles from here. The closest is in New York City, and the brand won't even sell to you online unless you have a US billing address.' Visibly frustrated, Bonetti shook her head. 'I can't say for certain, but I think there's a chance she's American.'

American. An American woman. Killed not twenty-five miles from A-Bay.

'Thanks. That's helpful. We'll give you a minute,' Tim said. When he backed away from the body in the same direction from which we'd come, he nudged me along with him. Once he'd put some distance between us and the scene, he brought his head close to mine. 'Well?' he asked in a conspiratorial whisper. 'What do you think?'

I didn't want to be rude, was well aware several of the Canadian investigators were looking curiously in our direction, but we needed a private tête-à-tête. 'It's a big conclusion to jump to,' I said. 'The victim could be a local with friends across the border who order her clothes for her. The coat could have been a gift. She could have driven down to Manhattan to go shopping.'

'Or she could be American, abducted from her home and killed out here on the island.' Tim gave me a meaningful look.

'If she's American, this is a hell of a place to leave her.'

'Not too well-concealed,' he agreed, 'or convenient. Wherever she came from, somebody went to some trouble to bring her here.'

'And took a major gamble crossing the border into Canada. If she does live in the States – and that's a big if – either he rode the ferry with a body in the trunk or he took her through customs only to kill her right after.' *He.* I was already referring to the killer as though we knew we were dealing with a male. *Don't jump to conclusions*, I warned myself. *Not yet.* 'Why do that, though?' I asked Tim. 'The perp could have left her anywhere. The ferry only got up and running again last week. It's closed from October to late April, right?'

'Right. So maybe she was already here.' He pushed his hair back from his face. 'She could have come to the island on her own, and encountered the killer after that. There's no sign of a car, though. Stolen?'

'It's possible. *If* she's American, she had to get over here somehow, either by car or boat.'

'Not likely to be by boat at this time of year. You'd have to be crazy to go out in the channel when the water's still this cold.'

'Car, then. CCTV.' In the joyless shadow of the turbine, I felt a flicker of hope. 'The border checkpoint's loaded with cameras. We can see all the cars that crossed over.'

'That we can.'

I hadn't noticed him approach, but suddenly Ludgate was steps away from us. His clean-shaven face and neck were blotchy from the cold. 'We'll review the security footage from the past twenty-four hours,' he said, 'and work our way back from there as needed. There are two ferries – the *Wolfe Islander III*, and *Horne's Ferry*. One comes from Ontario, the other from New York, and they land at different docks. There are cameras at both.'

'We can pull border patrol records, too,' one of the other officers said once we'd rejoined the coroner. 'See if and when she crossed into Canada, and try to find out why. If you have trouble ID'ing her, that could help.'

They're a solid bunch, Tim had said of the team. I was inclined to agree. Above us, the blades of the wind turbine continued their silent rotation, and I felt the sting of rain.

Tim didn't talk to me again until we were back in the car, the engine running and heat from the vents warming our damp faces. Instead of looking at me, his head was twisted in the direction of the turbine. Of the woman on the ground, just a purple smear in the dark field once more. His eyes, which I'd studied so carefully since joining the Bureau of Criminal

Investigation, were active, moving over the bleak countryside. 'What is it?' I asked. 'What's wrong?'

Tim swallowed once and licked his dry lips. 'She's older, isn't she? Than what he normally goes for?'

The air around us grew still. Under my jacket, my muscles tensed. *He.* Tim hadn't used his name. He didn't like the way it tasted any more than I did. We both knew who he meant.

It always came back to him.

'Yeah,' I said. 'She is. The others were all under thirty.'

'Not Trey.'

With the exception of Trey Hayes and a rookie cop Bram shot to escape arrest, his victims – his targets – had all been young women. Unlike our Jane Doe, all were unmarried. 'You know Trey was different,' I said. *Bram killed those women to get my attention. Trey's kidnapping was about keeping it.*

'This feels different, too. I don't like it,' said Tim.

'I'd wonder about you if you did.'

'I'm serious, Shana.'

'So am I. Don't worry,' I said. 'We'll deal with it.' *Just like we did before.*

'We'll deal with it.' He took one last look at the mud-covered landscape, still months away from going green. 'Jesus, Shane,' he said, his nickname for me laced with irritation.

I just shook my head. My yearning to deny the obvious parallels was deep as bone. I longed to believe this crime was unrelated, disparate in every way. In actual fact, the killing had our fugitive's MO written all over it.

And it was way too close to home.

TWO

'It's him.'

I raised my eyes from my keyboard to find Tim watching me.

'It's him,' he repeated under his breath. 'I know it. I've

been thinking about it nonstop since we left the island. It's definitely him.'

I leaned back in my folding chair and trapped a thumbnail between my teeth, tapping at it with my incisors. I'd been thinking about it, too. There were aspects of the crime that fit, and others that made no sense at all. But Tim was right. The similarities were indisputable.

It had been noisy when we got back to Alexandria Bay, not the phones-ringing-off-the-hook kind of ruckus I used to get in my old precinct on the Lower East Side of Manhattan, but the disruptive chatter of New York State troopers coming and going from the patrol room where they did their reports. It was the noon hour, too, a busy time of day. Normally, my team would try to meet the troopers on duty for lunch. Today, the station was all business.

Barracks, I reminded myself. As a member of the State Police, I was supposed to call the station the Alex Bay barracks. Tim had told me troopers used to live in the buildings where they worked, and informally, the term barracks had stuck. Even after all these months residing and working in town, I still had a hard time getting used to that.

The basement of the barracks was where I'd decided to situate our lead desk. With a homicide investigation, it's standard procedure to set up temporary headquarters somewhere close to the action, which in this case meant closer to Wolfe Island. I'd considered Cape Vincent – tag line: Where Lake and River Meet. The picture-perfect village, its main drag crammed with souvenir stores, gift shops, markets, and cafes, sat on the water's edge, right where the St Lawrence River merged with Lake Ontario. It was a stone's throw from there to the crime scene, and I could have used a school or firehall to set up shop. But Cape Vincent was less than thirty minutes from A-Bay, and I liked the idea of sticking with home base. The barracks had a finished basement, and I'd have easy access to my investigators. It was as good a place as any to get down to brass tacks.

With me and Tim were Don Bogle and Jeremy Solomon who, while waiting for my briefing to commence, were arguing the merits of A-Bay's fine-dining restaurants. Their wedding

anniversaries, five years for Bogle and two for Sol (summer
venue rates could be prohibitively expensive) were weeks
apart, and each of them had a different go-to spot. I smiled
as I listened to them bicker.

'Bay Point Grill is always solid, and their steaks are the
bomb,' said Sol, to which Bogle snorted.

'If you call that fancy, then the diner might be more your
speed.'

'What's *your* speed,' Sol countered, 'a tux and a table at
Chateau Gris? You'd be out of your mind to eat there.'

I had my own opinions about what they should do, since
I'd recently discovered Calliari's had a weekday deal on wine
and was open year-round, but I kept my thoughts to myself.
I had bigger perch to fry.

I'd been about to fill in the team on the homicide and start
delegating assignments when Tim pulled his chair flush
against mine, ready to discuss what was both my least favorite
subject and the object of my obsession. Blake Bram. Everyone
knew his name now. He was the bogeyman under the bed, as
much a myth as a man. That Bram was my cousin remained
a heavily-guarded secret, but everyone in town knew what
he'd done to Trey Hayes. Bram had disappeared after we
located Trey. At least, that's what he wanted us to think. After
what he'd done, and the groundwork he'd laid, I knew better
than to assume he wasn't coming back.

A lot can happen to a person over the course of nineteen
months. In that amount of time, you can meet someone and
get married. A kid can go from drooling on a play mat to
streaking across a playground. It can feel like a lifetime. It
can go by in a wink.

In nineteen months, I went from being a well-adjusted
detective with the NYPD, to a victim, to someone's fiancée.
I was none of those things anymore, but I wasn't the person I
used to be before Bram, either. I'd become someone entirely
new, consumed by a fevered need to find him. Just like he'd
been consumed with finding me.

'Let's think this through,' Tim said in a voice both hushed
and heated. 'If this death is Bram's doing, it has a purpose.
Trey's abduction was Bram proving he could infiltrate your

life here. Daring you to come after him. The phone call he made to you after we rescued Trey was more of the same. Bram was watching to see how you'd react, how much you'd engage with him. If he did this, on Wolfe Island, it's a message.'

What Tim was describing, I'd feared since I broke out of the prison Bram fashioned for me in an East Village basement. The idea that he might use murder as a means of sucking me into his orbit followed me like a jinx. He'd done it before with Becca, Lanie, and Jess, the three women he killed in New York, and again when he took young Trey. Of the five of us, only Trey and I had escaped, and only because Bram allowed it. Yes, I'd managed to decipher his clues, but he'd designed them for that very purpose. So that I stood a chance. If he was responsible for killing the woman whose body lay on Wolfe Island, what could it possibly mean?

'Are you going to call New York?'

Tim watched me closely as he asked it, assessing my demeanor with all the subtlety of two tanker ships crossing in the channel, horns blaring. It seemed like a lifetime ago that I'd first worked with detectives in the neighboring Seventh Precinct to investigate the crimes committed by Bram. After everything that transpired with Trey's abduction, I'd reached out to tell them Bram had come upstate. I'd been in close contact with both the Seventh Precinct and my own, fondly referred to as the Fighting Ninth, ever since. I had shared the composite sketch Tim and I commissioned from a forensic artist in Albany with the teams on the Lower East Side, along with information relating to Bram's latest crime. If this murder was his doing too, the investigative task force needed to know.

The thought tilted my stomach. *Need to know* was a concept I'd struggled with in recent months. Tim and Mac were still the only two people aware of my deeper connection to the man who called himself Blake Bram. In the fall, prior to working my first homicide case in the North Country, I had kept secrets from them too. After Vermont, though, I told them everything there was to know about my childhood with Bram when he was still Abraham Skilton, not limited to his socio-pathic behavior and the scar he'd engraved on my face. They alone understood that Abe and Bram were different people now, that Abe ceased to exist back when my cousin fled our hometown as a teen.

Even so, if my lieutenant discovered I was withholding information pertinent to an active case, there was a chance that I could be demoted. If Trey's family found out, they might have grounds to file a civil suit. Was I being selfish? Yes. Irresponsible? Definitely, and I had a hard time comprehending how I let myself get in so deep. Wasn't my prime concern as an investigator to protect human life and keep the peace? Preserving my own reputation wasn't part of the oath. Morally, my behavior was reprehensible. That's how it would look on the outside, anyway. What people didn't grasp, and what kept me from spilling my guts even now, was that I knew what my cousin was capable of.

I couldn't shake the feeling that telling my supervisor and the team back in New York would set Bram off. If I turned up the heat, he might panic and respond with an act that was even more extreme. I'd known him better than anyone once. I had to trust my instincts.

'If we're wrong about this,' I muttered through unmoving lips, 'if Bram's not involved at all, we'll only slow New York down. They're still following leads related to the false identity he used for that janitor job. Let them focus on that for now. As soon as we have something solid, they'll be the first to know.'

Tim eyed me warily, but nodded.

The air in the room shifted, and I felt a breeze slither in down by my feet. A moment later, Sheriff Maureen McIntyre swept through the basement door. Her short, layered hair swooped upward at the ends, and she pushed it back from her face as she walked. It was a face set in concentration. Mac had recently started wearing glasses, and the lenses reflected the fluorescent lights overhead in a way that made me uneasy. I couldn't read her expression.

'Sheriff,' said Tim, ever formal, always by the book. 'To what do we owe the pleasure?'

'Pleasure,' Mac replied drily, 'is a cold beer in a hot shower.' I wasn't sure whether or not to laugh, and could sense Tim felt just as befuddled. 'Shay,' said Mac, turning my way. 'Got a sec?'

There wasn't much Mac and I couldn't talk about in front of Tim. It hadn't been easy to open up about the effect my abduction had on my mental health, but the outcome was a tight-knit team of three. I couldn't imagine what Mac needed to tell me in private here at work.

Unperturbed, Tim excused himself and I followed Mac upstairs to the interview room, where she shut the door behind us.

'What's up?' I asked, unable to wait any longer. Whatever it was that she had to tell me, it was pinching the corners of her mouth.

She spoke in a clipped tone, like she was delivering unwanted news and knew better than to drag it out. 'I just came from getting coffee at the Bean-In. Carson is engaged.'

The revelation hit me in waves: I was confused, then shocked, then confused all over again. Dr Carson Gates was no longer part of my life. Once I worked out the magnitude of his duplicity, splitting from my former fiancé was a given. His deceit had made it easier to accept that the man for whom I'd relocated to an unfamiliar rural town had left me utterly alone. After that, even the fact that we shared a tiny village didn't make it any harder to move on. I saw Carson every now and then, on the other side of the Price Chopper produce section, or waiting in line at the sub shop on Fuller Street. Beyond the requisite nod of acknowledgement, we didn't talk, and that was how I liked it.

Mac's treatment of this new information gave me pause. *Carson. Engaged. Should I be upset? Did Mac expect me to be? Was it weird that I wasn't?*

I slid my fingers into the pockets of my pants and hooked my thumbs onto the belt loops. 'Good for him,' I said, doing my best to mask my frustration. I wasn't bothered by this news-flash, not rankled in the least. What bugged me was that Mac assumed I'd have trouble shouldering it. How could my friend and mentor think me so fragile?

'Shana,' Mac said with a meaningful look. 'He's engaged to Kelsea Shaw.'

My gaze traveled to the closed door.

Tim Wellington is no weakling. There's a sanguinity to the man, though, that makes people reluctant to disappoint him, and I'd go so far as to say he's sentimental when it comes to matters of the heart. None of that played a part in Mac's decision to tell me about the engagement first. That call was entirely about Tim's history with Carson.

'That's a coincidence, right?' I said. 'It can't have been intentional.' At the same time, my mind was blaring warnings. *It's only been five months. Out of all the women in town, Carson picked Tim's ex.* Tim's relationship with Kelsea had been brief, ending in late November after Tim and I got back from Vermont, but that wasn't the point. Tim and Carson had grown up together. Carson's knack for manipulating psyches came from years of practice. And Tim had been his guinea pig.

'It'll be fine,' I said when Mac didn't reply. 'Tim's mature enough to know this isn't an attempt by Carson to bait us.' Even as I said it, though, I had to wonder if that was true.

'I thought maybe the news should come from you. Since you both have experience with Carson,' she said.

Since we both let him control us, Tim as a child and me as an adult.

'It'll be fine,' I said again, willing it to be so. 'I'll talk to him. Thanks for letting me know.'

'Sure thing. And you?' She lifted an eyebrow and squinted, the skin beside her eyes gathering into delicate pleats. 'You OK?'

'Look,' I said, 'if Kelsea wants to take *that* on, more power to her.'

'Power. Interesting word choice where Carson's concerned.'

'He'll always have it. Just not over me and Tim.'

Mac said, 'Ever heard the saying: "If the devil is powerless, send him a woman"?'

I laughed much louder than intended. 'I hope Kelsea knows what she's getting into.'

After Mac left, I looked for my chance to tell Tim about Kelsea and Carson, but there was work to be done, and the timing wasn't right. The day dragged on until our shifts were over, and by then I'd decided to wait. I hadn't processed the news enough to share it, and wasn't sure how Tim would react. I told myself there was plenty of time, and elbowed it out of my mind.

It was a five-minute drive down Route 12 from the barracks to my place, four if I had a heavy foot, which I did. After weeks of house-hunting in the surrounding villages and growing increasingly disheartened by Mac's insistence that room and board in the winter months was virtually nonexistent, I'd lucked out. The owner of a pizza joint in town came in to report a series of bad checks he'd received from a supplier. He'd been livid, going on about respect and trust and how he was loath to lease out his newly vacated riverside rental, so disillusioned was he by humankind. I took down his statement and dropped a few hints about needing to find a new place. Before I knew it, the house was mine.

Located at the very end of East Riverfront Road, the rental cottage could fit on a postage stamp, just six hundred square feet with a garage on the bottom and one bedroom, a bathroom, and a kitchenette above. It was right on the river, though, and included a dock and a small boathouse. At first, I found the proximity of that boathouse unsettling – memories of my case on Tern Island lingered – but *my* boathouse didn't smell of rotting fish or belong to a family of sociopaths, and after a month of sleeping with a thin blanket and thinner walls at the motel in town, I was in no position to be particular.

The advantage of having so few personal belongings was that I'd managed to unpack in a matter of hours. Every item had an assigned home. My keys went in the decorative I Love NY dish gifted to me by my brother before I moved from Swanton to the city. This sat on a bookshelf-slash-entryway console packed with Harlan Coben thrillers and police training books, above which hung a flag of Vermont. My jacket had a place on a loon-shaped hook by the door, a souvenir from a visit to Sackets Harbor, right next to the fleece-lined plaid shirt I put on after slipping off my shoes. I felt a bit like Mr Rogers, coming home alone. Sloughing off the formality of the day and settling in for the night. The notion made me wonder all over again about the extra cardigans hanging in Fred Rogers' closet, some of which looked as though they could belong to a woman. A mystery wife, maybe, who was never seen.

Wife. That's what the woman on Wolfe Island was to someone. Someone who, according to the Canadians, hadn't yet reported her missing.

Wife. It's what I would have been to Carson, a role that would now go to Kelsea. I didn't envy or resent her in the least. If anything needled me where Carson was concerned, it was the idea that someone was about to bind themselves to that man for life.

In the living room, I reached for my laptop and sunk down onto the couch. It was time. I looked forward to this nightly routine like a blood draw: it hurt a little, but had to be done. The act always left me tender and bruised, but I did it anyway, for the greater good.

Holding my breath, I clicked on the email folder I'd titled *Bram*.

It was filling up, home now to a couple dozen email messages in addition to my own notes. Some of these were to-do style reminders about avenues I still needed to pursue. *Car rentals. Grocery store. Laundromat.* I'd been working every angle I could think of, even calling on Adam Starkweather, a psychological profiler I met years ago in the city. Adam was the one who taught me the concept of organized and disorganized dichotomy, and how to identify character traits based on the nature of the crime. Criminals who map things out tend to be antisocial but relatively sane, while those who kill in a frenzy, leaving behind blood and prints, are often younger, or mentally ill. Adam's voice had a way of going brittle when he talked about the criminal mind, as if the people who suffered at the hands of the disturbed individuals we studied were never far from his thoughts. He was a broad-shouldered, keen-eyed Forest Whitaker type who held sway over the whole department, but it wasn't his power that impressed me so much as the way he was in total command of his work.

I leaned on his teachings every time I worked a case. As grateful as I was to Adam for his wisdom, though, I kept my link to Bram a secret even from him. *A runaway, just someone*

I'm trying to track down, I'd said when I phoned him up a few weeks prior, feeling a kick of guilt when he spent an hour of his invaluable time jogging my memory about pre-imposed offense behavior. As long as I was able, I had to hold back the fact that Abe Skilton and Blake Bram were one and the same.

By no means was I convinced this was the right thing to do. My priority – *everyone's* priority – was to find Bram. We were all doing our part, and I'd convinced myself mine was to combine the understanding of criminal psychology I'd honed in New York with my unique knowledge of my target's background so that I could get to Bram first. I wasn't concealing his true identity to safeguard my cousin. My worldview wasn't so warped that I could justify that. I was simply using what I knew about our shared past to chase him down myself. The man was my kin, our connection innate. I honestly believed I stood the best chance of finding him. And I wanted to have as much control as possible over what happened when I did.

Besides Adam, there was a list of contacts in the folder that ranged from bank managers and motel owners to IT specialists and old classmates from the training academy. Anyone and everyone who might be able to help. I'd added a lot to the research file since that interview with Trey Hayes, when the child told Tim and I what he knew about the man who took him. Like Trey's therapist, I'd found the kid to be reticent – it hadn't been long before he shut down completely – but one tip still made the fine blonde hairs on my arms stand on end.

Bram had worked at a marina.

I wasn't sure at first whether I could trust Trey's account. Tim, Mac, and I already knew that Bram and Trey had holed up in a rental cabin on the river, right here in Alexandria Bay. When Trey told us Bram had worked by the water, I wondered if *work* was code for Bram's most recent crime. It wasn't until Trey started going into greater detail about his abduction that I realized I'd hit pay dirt.

'It was bumpy,' the child said. 'He had this rough blanket, like what my mom used to protect the floor when she was painting the kitchen, and he made me lie down under it.'

A handyman on Heart Island, the place from which Trey was taken during his field trip to historic Boldt Castle, had remembered seeing that tarp and the lumpy shape beneath it. It was how we'd managed to connect Bram to the stolen boat. To track it to the cabins at Dingman Point and, eventually, to locate Trey.

'My head kept banging on the bottom of the boat, and water sloshed in,' Trey said while his mother rubbed circles on his small, dark hand. 'It wasn't because he was a bad driver. He told me that. Boats float lower in freshwater than saltwater. He wasn't used to it.'

Growing up in Vermont, at the edge of Lake Champlain, boating should have been as natural to both Bram and I as driving a car. Most of the kids we knew had been operating motor-powered vessels long before they had a license, the knowledge having been amassed over innumerable fishing trips with their dads. The Merchants weren't boaters, though, and neither were the Skiltons, so my cousin Abe should have been clueless about water-based recreation. Evidently, that had changed.

The mention of saltwater was my best lead yet.

What I wanted, more than anything, was to saw Bram open like a cadaver on an autopsy table and pore over what I found inside. I was desperate to know everything about his life over the past fifteen years. I didn't believe, and never really had, that the murders in New York were his first – not when he was already bludgeoning small animals at the age of nine. My holy grail was a kill map: a chart of all my cousin's crimes. But in order to draw it, I needed to know where he'd been.

All over the East Coast, marinas were closed for the season, and had been for months. There was no way Bram could have been working on the water over the winter. So, I'd changed course. Used what I learned from Trey to find out what Bram was doing *before* New York, and unearth as much about the bastard as possible.

I could only hope my plan would prove out.

After rereading the messages I'd received in recent weeks, I checked my inbox. I'd called and emailed our composite sketch of Bram to every marina up and down the coast of New

Jersey and both sides of Long Island, and I'd reached out to places in Massachusetts and Rhode Island, too. The way I saw it, it was likely Bram became proficient at boating within shooting distance of Manhattan. I had recently started to investigate Connecticut.

Just 300 miles of shoreline and roughly seventy-five more marinas, yacht clubs, and shipyards to go.

I opened window after window in my browser, populating them with Google searches, spreadsheets, maps. It wasn't long before the fan on my laptop began to whir. As the heat radiating from the underside of its shell began to warm my upper thighs, I reached past it to the coffee table onto which I'd propped my legs. *A place for everything, and everything in its place.* That was my policy in my new home. From the tray that held the TV remote and the latest copy of the local paper, I picked up a pack of playing cards.

The deck was a few months old and had never been used. Mac and I had put our regular games of Bullshit on hold; if Bram was stalking me, I didn't want him to see us spending time together outside of work for fear that she'd become his next target. The only thing distinguishing the playing cards in my hand from the others in the souvenir shop where I bought them was that I'd peeled off the protective cellophane.

It was the photos on the back of the cards that interested me. I studied them every night without fail. The cards depicted local landmarks, familiar sights like the Lost Channel and the Thousand Islands International Bridge. One of them showed Boldt Castle on Heart Island. The site of Bram's last crime.

Tonight, thinking about what I'd seen on Wolfe Island, I didn't just flip through the deck. Instead, I set my laptop aside and fanned the cards out over the table. I arranged them in a series of neat rows and scrutinized every image. Bram had a deck just like this. It was currently in an evidence locker at the station, but it had been in my purse for a while. Somehow, he'd managed to stash it there. That's how close he came to me. How close I'd been to finding him.

I knew there were no wind turbines on the cards I'd been analyzing all these months. I knew – and yet, I had to look again. I leaned over the table and felt my hair, kinky from the morning on the ferry and my unconscious habit of coiling loose strands around my fingers, tickle my cheeks.

Islands and bays, historic landmarks and quaint corners of A-Bay village. No turbines. No Wolfe Island.

I got to my feet, and walked to the door.

There was just the one, both entrance and exit, and it opened onto the deck with a staircase that descended from the second-floor living space to the ground. I'd splurged on some Adirondack chairs, dreaming of the day when Mac, Tim, and I could sit out here together without having to worry that a psychopath was poised to attack. I'd positioned them in a way that allowed me to watch the sunset on the water. Tonight, I went straight to the railing.

At this time of day, it wasn't uncommon to see a bat rocket across my field of vision. At the moment, though, the air was still. The clouds had dissipated over the course of the day, and the setting sun gave the river a glittery sheen. It was narrow here, in the area known as Swan Bay. I had a clear view of the mobile home park and its multiple boat docks on the other side.

If I had one problem with the Thousand Islands, it was this: the place welcomed all manner of residents with open arms. Manufactured homes wrapped in vinyl sat minutes away from island estates worth millions. You could see an honest-to-goodness castle from the windows of a hotel that offered nautical-themed rooms and served an egg-and-home fries breakfast dish called the Tater Tanker.

Every Fourth of July, the town flooded with luxury SUVs, a rainbow of plates from Pennsylvania, Massachusetts, Ontario, Quebec. The population would swell from just over a thousand all-year residents like managers and teachers, cashiers and cooks to more than 15,000 boaters and vacationers. The variety of real estate and lodging A-Bay had to offer both factions was a good thing for everyone but me. It made it easy for Bram to find a place to hide.

Somewhere in the distance, a boat started up, the oscillating drone of the motor echoing across the bay. It occurred to me, not for the first time, that if I could see the trailer park, its residents could see me.

There were moments when I was sure he was tracking me, when I felt his presence like an icy chill. I imagined his cold gaze trained on my face and the corner of his mouth gliding up into a sneer. How much did he know? Had he already followed me to my cottage on the bay? It would take minimal effort to trail me from the barracks. Bram was good at being invisible.

Was he here now?

Eventually, I retreated back into the warmth and comfort of the cottage, my mind whirring with questions. If it was Bram who killed the woman on Wolfe Island, why had he chosen that particular location? Was there a message I was missing, just like Tim said? Did Bram intend for the incongruity between this homicide and his past crimes to show me how ill-equipped I was to take him on? I didn't think so. I understood how things operated between us, the games he liked to play. He'd spent his childhood concocting mysteries for me to solve. He liked to test me. The cards were a taunt, a jeer from a bully aimed at a mark who'd reached her breaking point. But their significance didn't end there.

The cards weren't just about what Bram had done.

They were a clue to what he would do next.

THREE

The morning brought a warm front that obscured my river view with mist. It looked as if the St Lawrence was steaming softly, set on a low simmer. It was an apt metaphor for how I felt when I checked my inbox yet again before dragging myself into the shower. The pressure to find Bram was rising. My blood was starting to boil.

I knew the moment I got to the lead desk there was news about the body on Wolfe Island. Tim had coffee waiting for me, poured into the biggest mug he'd managed to find in the cupboard of the break room, and he'd called in Sheriff McIntyre. That was my assumption, anyway, but after taking

my first sip of the scalding, slightly bitter brew, I realized it
was Mac who wore the grim expression, and Mac who spoke
first. Once again, she had the corner on big news.

'She's one of ours,' the sheriff said. 'Not just an American,
but a local. She's from Alexandria Bay.'

A chill twirled up my spine. *One of ours.* We'd been
anxiously waiting for word on our victim from Paul Ludgate,
hoping he'd have some luck determining who she was. The
woman was found on Canadian soil. The theory that she was
American had seemed like a long shot. It never occurred to
me she could be from our own town.

'Who—' Tim began, but my questions reached Mac first.
'How'd they ID her? Was she reported missing?'

'Oh, yes.' There was something peculiar about the set of
Mac's mouth again. I'd gotten to know her expressions pretty
well, and this one was unnerving.

The explanation for that came when she told us the
woman's name.

'Hope Oberon?' I repeated. 'Are you serious?'

'Yep. She had a meeting scheduled with her lawyer yesterday
and didn't show. The coroner sent me some photos from the
scene. No question about it. It's her.'

'Dammit,' said Tim. 'That poor woman. I thought she looked
familiar.'

'She did to me too, a bit,' I said, thinking back to the crime
scene, that tingle of knowing. 'All those photos in the paper,
I guess.' It didn't surprise me that neither of us had been able
to place her. Violent death can bludgeon a person's physical
characteristics, stealing all the things that make them who
they are. The way a smile glides to the right, or how someone's eyes taper when they're pleased. Such traits are scrubbed
away, leaving behind only the semblance of a human being.
A Halloween mask forgotten on a deserted, leaf-plastered
October street.

Mac told us Hope's car was found abandoned just off I-81,
not far from Perch Lake. 'I already sent a tech out there to
process it. I can't believe it,' she said with a sorry shake of
her head. 'And with just two weeks to go until sentencing.'

Mac had spent months working on the investigation that

ultimately saw Hope Oberon – along with three other respected Watertown city officials – charged with misconduct and corruption. All had been respected members of the community that Mac had sworn to serve and protect. She'd shared lunches with them over the years, and actively shot down rumors on their behalf when, last fall, the townsfolk started to gossip. When it was determined that they were guilty, Mac refused to believe it. She worked overtime trying to exonerate them, only to discover the case was airtight. I wondered how she felt about Hope after all that, whether she still saw the woman as a colleague or simply as a criminal. The regret on Mac's face suggested it was the former.

The Case was how Mac referred to the burden she'd been carrying since October. Even now, the controversy was polarizing; for every local who wanted to see the accused slapped with the maximum prison sentence, there was another appealing for leniency and urging prosecutors to show compassion. Reporters lambasted Watertown for fostering a 'culture of corruption', and branded the city employees as the Fraudulent Four. A local artist illustrated a cartoon for the paper that depicted the group as Marvel characters, wherein The Thing, the Invisible Woman, the Human Torch, and Mr Fantastic combined their powers to rob town hall. Because of Watertown's proximity to Alexandria Bay – they were separated by fewer than thirty miles – A-Bay and its residents made their opinions on the matter known. As the face of Jefferson County's law enforcement, Sheriff McIntyre bore the brunt of the complaints even while embarking on the taxing process of rebuilding a community in chaos.

I hadn't followed the case too closely, though it was a big enough story that news outlets outside the Thousand Islands picked it up, too. From what I could gather from Mac, who talked of it often, the con had been related to a development project, the offenders a city manager, a city clerk, a member of the Planning and Zoning department, and Hope Oberon, president of the Watertown development council herself.

Bribes in the tens of thousands were exchanged to ensure the development council received a favorable ruling from the zoning board. Public opposition toward the plan was strong, and that had been the problem from the start. I didn't fully understand why community groups, land trusts, even other agents of local government were so opposed. What Hope Oberon wanted was to introduce a new source of energy to the area. If approved, it would generate more than 300 megawatts of power.

The project was a wind farm.

'Well, shit,' I said, running a hand through my hair. It was still damp from the shower. The morning was off to a running start.

'Yeah. There's a connection there, obviously,' said Mac. 'What I don't get is why this happened now. The development project's a non-starter. Hope was indicted – they all were. Everyone involved in this crime against the city is weeks away from going to prison. And *this* is the moment someone chose to take Hope's life?'

'It's weird,' Tim agreed. 'But her body was dumped next to one of those turbines. Looks to me like she was being punished. I mean, the message is pretty darn clear.'

'Almost too clear,' I said. 'Whoever did this went out of his – *their* – way to draw a line back to the project.'

'And that line cuts through Canada. To get to the wind farm, the killer had to cross the border. It's a colossal risk,' said Mac.

'So why take it?' I asked. That was the question, the one we all pondered as I spun a pen in semi-circles on the surface of the table around which we now sat. 'Hopefully we'll have some answers soon. Ludgate says his team already eliminated more than half the people who crossed the border on Monday. They're working through the list of visitors, ID'ing drivers and making sure their stories check out. He'll call when he knows more.'

For a moment, we were all silent. Then Tim said, 'There is some good news in this.' His tone reminded me of a parent trying to cheer up a child. *Chin up, kid.* 'At least we know this has nothing to do with Bram.'

I nodded absently. Now that we knew who the victim was, along with the relevance of the location where she'd been found, it did seem less likely that Bram was involved. Hope Oberon was a prominent figure, a fixture in the local community. She'd already been publicly disgraced once, and now, again, her wrongdoings were laid bare, the turbines a harsh reminder of her crimes. It was hard to imagine her death wasn't related to the life she'd chosen to live, and try as I might I couldn't picture Bram risking exposure by taking his crime spree to Canada.

So, not Bram. How did I feel about that? I put the question to myself and waited for my gut to answer. Did I wish I could see the situation through Tim's hopeful eyes, and accept his reassurance that this was good news? Sure. Knowing Bram probably wasn't behind the homicide should have come as a relief. But as messed up as it was, I couldn't help but feel the relief would only come when he made his next move.

There wasn't much that kept me up at night. Like any investigator with several years on the job under her belt, I was a longtime, box seat ticket holder to violent crime. Like anyone with a career that demands as much from the soul as from the body and mind, I had taught myself to compartmentalize. It worked, most of the time. Until my mind floated down the river to Deer Island, where we'd found Mac's little dog Whiskey, whom Bram had snatched and wounded as a reminder that he was everywhere. That no one was safe who thought him gone.

At least if Bram was the one who killed Hope, I would have known what he'd been planning.

'Something else that's good about this,' I said, eager to sidetrack my own thoughts, 'is Mac. Your knowledge of that corruption case is going to be invaluable,' I told her. 'You've been immersed in it from the start, and watched it evolve over all these months. The players, what they did – you could give a TED Talk on the Fraudulent Four. How well did you know Hope? Enough to help us get a handle on her life?'

Mac sighed deeply, and traded a secretive glance with Tim.

Since arriving in A-Bay, I'd adjusted to being the odd man out. Maureen McIntyre was born in Loudonville, just outside of Albany, but she'd worked in Jefferson County for the better part of twenty-five years, graduating from road patrol to the BCI before being elected sheriff. As for Tim, he was born and raised within ten miles of where we now sat. Both understood the area, its history, its people. It was one of the reasons they'd been hit so hard by the Watertown officials' deceit.

'Everyone knew Hope,' Mac told me. 'And not just because of the scandal.

'She was friends with my mom,' said Tim. 'Just acquaintances really, they weren't meeting for coffee or anything.' He tacked that last part on as if concerned I might judge his mother for consorting with a criminal.

'Her family's roots go deep around here,' added Mac. 'Which means we have to act fast if we want to keep the rumor mill in check. The husband?' she asked, turning to Tim.

'Best place to start,' he agreed. 'We don't want him hearing the news of Hope's death from a neighbor. Or worse, a reporter.'

Mac said, 'I've got to get back to Watertown. Fill me in later?'

I assured her we would, and saw her out. Neither Mac nor Tim mentioned potential suspects. For my part, I wanted to get the visit with the family out of the way first. Clear my head and heart before digging any further into the gory details. I couldn't speak for why Mac and Tim were tightlipped about possible perps, except to say their reluctance was likely connected to the corruption case. The community had already been hit with upsetting news, and there was more on the way.

But Hope's premature death would be the least of the locals' problems if we found out one of the Fraudulent Four wasn't just a crook, but a killer.

FOUR

According to our records, Hope Oberon's home was on Iroquois Point just a few minutes north of the village. There were maybe a dozen houses on the small island, which could be accessed from the mainland and Carnegie Bay Road by bridge. It wasn't hard to imagine the homeowners congregating for barbecues in the summer, or singing Christmas carols together outside their beautiful waterfront homes. The way the houses were arranged around a patch of public beach reminded me of a summer camp I once attended on the shores of Lake Champlain. My cousin and I had gone together, but we only lasted a few days. He was teased so mercilessly I'd called my parents and begged them to pick us up.

The Oberon house was a ranch with cedar shingles, a gooseberry-red door, and a small detached garage. Nothing lavish, but it looked well-kept. There was classical music playing when we pulled up, and it seeped out through the open front window, which someone had cracked to welcome the lush spring breeze. As with my rental cottage, the house had a deck out back that presented a 180-degree view of the river. When, in the sunroom, we broke the news about Hope, Maynard Oberon turned toward the back windows overlooking the water – emerald green today, and flat as glass – and dragged a hand over his cropped silver hair.

We'd caught Hope's widower as he was getting ready for work. A cup of milky tea sat steaming on the coffee table, infusing the air with the scent of bergamot and honey. He was having a hard time looking directly at us, which I took as a sign of resistance to the horrific news we'd brought to his doorstep. More than once, his shiny eyes drifted toward the hall. Tim offered to call a clergy member or family friend, but the man shook his head and slumped into a chair. Tim immediately handed him his tea, an act of kindness that flooded my belly with warmth.

Death notifications are the most difficult part of my job. I've seen every possible response from the loved ones of victims, had people faint and shriek and fleck my face with spittle. I've witnessed the most ungodly keening, wails so black and raw that, if I listen hard, echo in my ears even now. I never tap dance around the news I've come to break, or use words like 'lost' or 'passed away'. That might sound cruel, but inviting a person to hold out hope when all hope is gone is crueler.

And Hope *was* gone. There was no changing that.

Maynard Oberon had a fleshy chin that I guessed was a genetic predisposition, because apart from that pocket of fat beneath his jaw he looked incredibly fit for a guy in his mid-fifties. No spare tire here. The word that came to mind was *mascular*. Henrietta, my brother's kid, was about to turn fourteen, but the funny things she used to say when she was little had become family lore, and *mascular* – a cross between muscular and masculine – described Hope's husband perfectly. He had a thick neck and a jaw like an anvil, and the sleeves of his T-shirt were taut as rubber bands around his upper arms. There was a set of free weights in the corner of the living room, where I imagined he worked out while enjoying his river view.

'Who did this?' he asked, his energy sluggish from the shock. 'Who the hell would do something like this?'

It was too early, and we still had a lot to learn. 'I wish I could tell you that,' I said. 'We hope to have some answers for you soon.'

'We used to go there, you know. Wolfe Island.' His gaze dropped down to his tea. 'We've always spent time in Canada, trying out different spots, but there's a restaurant on Wolfe that Hope and I really like. We've been going there for years. We just ate there last summer.'

'When was the last time you saw your wife, Mr Oberon?' I couldn't get past the fact that he hadn't reported her missing. That was more than a little strange.

'It's Pope, actually,' he said softly. 'Oberon is Hope's maiden name. She kept it after we got married, for obvious reasons.' *Obvious is right*, I thought as I scrawled *Hope Pope* inside my head. With as much tact as possible, Tim took out a pen and started to scratch at the small notebook he carried with him at all times. I had one just like it in the pocket of my jacket, filled with all manner of cryptic writings.

'Monday,' Pope told us. 'I saw Hope on Monday afternoon.'

It was Wednesday morning.

Maynard Pope hadn't seen his wife in almost two days, and he hadn't done a thing about it.

In the early stages of a homicide investigation, my objective is always twofold: retrace the victim's movements in the days and weeks preceding death, and evaluate the life they left behind. I was accustomed to looking for unusual behavior.

Here it was.

'Why didn't you report her missing?' I asked. Tim had checked with the Alexandria Bay PD after our victim was identified, and there hadn't been any calls made to their office, either.

Pope spoke in a voice barely louder than a whisper. 'It isn't unusual for us to go a few days without seeing each other. Hope doesn't really live here anymore.'

'Hope doesn't live here?' I hadn't noticed any items belonging to a woman when we first entered the house, but I scanned its interior again, this time with fresh resolve. In the kitchen, which was open to the living room, a rack of beautifully patinated copper pots dangled above the island alongside crispy bouquets of dried lavender. A section of the countertop that ran below the cupboards was cluttered with candles, tubs of protein powder, and bottles of prescription medication. On the living room wall, a framed photograph of a girl aged seven or eight hung in a place of honor above the fireplace. The child had fiery red hair, a shy smile, and Hope's clefted chin. With the exception of the large number of men's shoes and boots by the front door, there was nothing to indicate the place was Pope's alone.

Pope said, 'She spent most of her time in Watertown. She was renting a studio apartment there. Council members are required to live within the city limits. Hope had to move when she got the job.'

'So Hope's primary residence was in Watertown?' That didn't make sense. If Hope was a resident of Watertown, it should have been Mac's detectives at the Watertown Troop D station taking the lead on this case. Why had Mac assigned it to us? The sheriff lived and worked in Watertown, too. She had to have known Hope was a resident.

But Hope hadn't always lived in the city. It was possible her connection to Alexandria Bay was what incited McIntyre to go against standard protocol and kick the case over to us. There was another conceivable reason for her decision, though, one far more complex. Even if this homicide had nothing to do with Blake Bram, the town had been on high alert ever since Trey's abduction. Local reporters were quick to connect the man who snatched him with the killing spree in Manhattan a year and a half prior, and word had gotten out that I'd been searching for Bram in my previous job. The more I considered the situation, the more convinced I was that Mac's choice was all about optics. She was betting that putting me front and center on Hope's homicide would put minds at ease.

Pope's neck had gone scarlet and the tops of his ears looked shiny and hot. 'I know it sounds strange, us not living together,' he said. 'But working in local government was Hope's dream.'

'Why didn't she do it here in town,' Tim asked, 'where she lived?'

'She would have loved that. She kept hoping a position would open up, but small towns have a small staff, and she never got a chance to break in. When she heard about the job in Watertown through a friend last year, she jumped at the chance. Natalie had just left for college – Syracuse University – so the timing was perfect. Natalie's our daughter. Oh, God.' He sank lower in the chair and dropped his head into his thickly knuckled hands.

'And you couldn't move to Watertown with her?' I said.

Pope shook his head. 'I need to be close to the restaurant.'

Tim had told me about the restaurant on the drive over. Hope's husband was the owner of Chateau Gris, the swankiest eatery in town. Fancy was a relative term in the North Country; even taking into consideration the rich folks who summered in the Thousand Islands, there wasn't much demand for fine dining up here. Chateau Gris managed to stay open year-round, though. I hadn't eaten there yet, but it was known for its specialty meats and charcuterie, coupled with the kind of mainstream French fare that didn't have to cost a fortune and felt accessible to the masses: *soupe à l'oignon, salade Niçoise,* and for those truly special occasions, a snappy *crème brûlée.*

'So you last saw Hope on Monday,' I said. 'Do you remember what time?'

'She came here around four. I had a little food from the restaurant for her, some meat and produce left over from the weekend – we're closed on Mondays and Tuesdays, and I wasn't sure it would keep. She came to pick it up and stayed about an hour. We talked about what to get Natalie for her birthday. Jesus. I don't know how Natalie's going to handle this. After everything that's happened with her mom.'

I gave a sympathetic nod. 'Did you see her or talk to her before that? Over the weekend, maybe?'

'I brought over her dry cleaning on Saturday.'

'To Watertown? That was kind of you. Round trip takes almost an hour.'

'Hope didn't like to go out in public,' Pope said. 'The looks and comments she would get . . . you wouldn't believe it.'

'Is that why she didn't move back here after losing her job?'

Pope looked momentarily taken aback. 'Yeah. I've been doing her errands and groceries since the fall so she could stay inside, here or in Watertown.' Even his eyes had a tinge of pink to them now. 'You know what happened there, I guess.'

Tim started to affirm that yes, we were all well aware of the scandal, but I cut him off.

'We know what's been reported,' I told Pope, even though Mac was a fountain of knowledge and Tim, a long-time local, had followed the case pretty closely, too. I wanted to hear the husband's take. Get a full account straight from the source. 'Did that come as a shock, finding out what Hope did?'

The question made him bristle. 'What difference does that make now?'

'We're just trying to understand her,' Tim said gently, leaning toward him. 'Her life, her family. Who she was.'

'Mr Pope, we're going to be leading the investigation into your wife's murder.' I thought of the turbine out on that rugged, windswept island and added, 'We don't believe this was a random attack. I know how hard this must be. We're not here to interrogate you. If you could clear up a few things for us, just enough to get us started, it would really help.'

Pope got to his feet – the guy really did cut a commanding figure – and I watched him make a slow turn of the room. The word *investigation* can strike terror into the hearts of witnesses. Even those who live the most guiltless of lives don't generally love the idea of detectives clearing off the dust and peeking through their windows. I gave Pope all the time he needed to think it over. To make him think he had a choice.

'Yes,' he said at last, settling back into his chair with a sigh. 'Yes, what Hope did shocked me. She finally had the job she'd always wanted, and she threw it away. She threw everything away.'

I knew from chatting with McIntyre that countless reporters had pressured Hope Oberon to reveal why she did what she did. Allusions were made to the similarities between Hope and Rita Crundwell, who while working as Comptroller for the tiny town of Dixon, IL had embezzled almost fifty-four million dollars in what was said to be the largest case of municipal fraud in US history. Like Crundwell, Hope had deceived the residents she was meant to serve. She tried to con her colleagues into going against the city's wishes, and put her own desires before those of the people she'd been hired to represent. I initially thought the comparison to Crundwell was a stretch, but after Mac explained the extent to which Hope's deception had unsettled Watertown, I saw the reference for what it was: an attempt by the press to vilify and malign a woman whose story was selling papers by the bundle.

'Why do you think she did it?' I asked Pope. 'As her husband, you must have some idea.'

When he finally met my eyes again, something – disappointment, or maybe distrust – flitted across his face. I didn't doubt that Hope's behavior was hard on Natalie Pope, despite the fact that she'd been living in Syracuse, but what had Hope's husband been through these past months? What must it have been like to learn his wife and the mother of his child was a palm-greasing criminal?

'Do we really need to talk about this?'

'It could be relevant to her death,' said Tim.

After a beat, Maynard Pope nodded and reached for his mug of tea once more.

'It started about a year ago, when she first met with Green Wind Renewables. They're the company that wanted to expand to this region,' he said. 'Hope was president of the economic development council, so she and Sejal Basak – the city manager – took the meeting. The others only got involved later.

'She told me about the idea of bringing a wind farm to

these parts right away,' Pope went on. 'She was excited. Green
Wind was committing to donating almost eight hundred
thousand dollars to the local community, and Hope and her
colleagues would be able to use that money for whatever they
wanted. She had this dream of building up tourism, turning
Watertown into more of a vacation destination. It's not right
on the St Lawrence like Alexandria Bay, but Black River runs
through the downtown core, and she wanted to beautify that
area. There's a hotel there she had big ideas about fixing up.
It didn't go as planned. There was too much opposition,' Pope
told us. 'Citizens of Watertown, mostly, but regional council
members, too.'

When his pause stretched beyond five seconds, I said, 'But
she was determined to make it work.'

'I didn't think she'd take it so far. It was a bad decision. I
know that. *She* knew that – and she felt awful about the way
she went about it. Some people around here don't believe that.'
There was a bitterness to his voice, a tang that made his mouth
pucker. 'All anyone talks about is how Hope was the ringleader
and the bribes were all her idea. Hope and her crimes. It was
totally blown out of proportion. Nobody seems to care that
she meant well, that what she did was ultimately for the good
of the community. She did it for them. For them, and for
Harve.'

'Harvey Oberon was a great mayor,' said Tim. 'The best
A-Bay has ever had.'

In a flood of heat, blood rushed to my cheeks. 'Harvey
Oberon?' I repeated, trying to make sense of what I was
hearing.

Pope's lips skated into a smile. 'Hope's father. And thanks
for saying that,' he told Tim. 'Harve *was* a great mayor. In a
way, that was the problem. He set the bar very high.'

Tim nodded knowingly. Still looking at Pope, I said, 'Sorry,
I'm not from these parts.'

Pope studied me. I couldn't help but feel his impression of
me had suddenly changed. 'Hope took that job in Watertown
because she wanted to make a splash. To do something
important, like Harvey did here. He was hugely popular when
he was in office. When Hope went into municipal government

too, she felt a lot of pressure to succeed. Harve's pretty much a local legend.'

'He sure is,' said Tim. 'I was sorry to hear he's not well.'

My body was so rigid it hurt, yet I forced myself not to look at Tim for fear that my face might betray me. Hope Oberon was the daughter of Alexandria Bay's former mayor? Why the hell was I just learning about this now?

I thought back to the conversations I'd had with Mac about the corruption case. They'd occurred off-duty, outside of work, when we were shooting the breeze as friends. I hadn't pressed her about the particulars, would never have thought to ask about the Fraudulent Four's personal lives or family make-up.

There had been that moment at the barracks, though, when Mac and Tim traded a glance.

Next to Tim, on the couch across from Maynard Pope, I fumed in silence. These were the kinds of details that built the framework for a suspect list and led investigators to criminals hiding in plain sight. We'd been in a rush this morning to notify the family, but Tim and I had a good ten minutes in the car, and he was well aware my knowledge of local politics was limited. I couldn't understand why he'd held this information back. But dammit, he had.

I'd worked hard to connect with the man who for all intents and purposes was my partner. It hadn't been easy, especially early on, when the pain of my abduction was still fresh and my therapist-turned-fiancé was using my trauma to convince me I was incapable of doing my job. I'd managed to get past that and regain control of my mental health, and in the process I'd come to trust both Tim and his investigative skills. We were supposed to be a team.

A memory came back to me, of Tim and I debriefing post-Tern Island, after we'd driven to troop headquarters in Oneida to explain to our lieutenant how the case had gone so horribly wrong. *We're a team*, Tim had assured me, and I believed he meant it. But a lot had happened since then. Things between us had changed.

'How's your father-in-law doing?' Tim asked. If he'd picked up on my anger, he didn't show it.

Again, Pope's gaze drifted. Something wasn't right about the way the hall kept drawing his attention. It was morning, not yet ten, but the windowless hallway was dim. From where I sat, I could see two doors. One was open a crack, weak light bleeding onto the hardwood. The second was shut tight. If I strained to listen, I could just make out a whisper of sound, rhythmic in its cadence.

'People say Alzheimer's can be managed,' said Pope. 'That it's possible to slow down the symptoms of the disease. He takes all the pills the doctors tell him to, but it's like Harvey's mind is reverting to that of a little kid. At first, he was just scatterbrained. He'd put the milk in the pantry with the cereal and forget to brush his teeth for a few days. That kind of thing. Then, one day, he went out for a walk and couldn't remember where he lived. This was before he moved. Luckily, a neighbor found him and got him home safe.'

'The stress of Hope's trial can't have helped things any,' said Tim.

'No, it hasn't. The last few months have been rough. I'm not sure how I'm going to tell him about this without sending him into a death spiral.' At the prospect of breaking the news of Hope's murder to his father-in-law, Maynard Pope looked even more depleted. He slid a hand up his neck, spread his fingers, and gripped the back of his skull.

'He's going to need more attention soon,' the man went on. 'A full-time nurse or . . . something. I've been having to watch him more closely lately, to make sure he's taking care of himself. I mean, we're right on the water here. It's not safe.'

Another glance at the hall.

'Harvey,' I said, turning my head toward the hallway and that closed door, 'he's here?'

'The apartment in Watertown's on a busy street, and there was no convincing Harve to leave A-Bay. He loves this place – and the hospital's just eight minutes away.' He shrugged and splayed his hands in an expression of defeat. 'This is how the chips fell.'

'Would you like us to speak to him?' I asked, softening my voice. I felt guilty for jumping to conclusions, supposing something sinister was going on behind that door. *This is my life now*, I thought. I didn't know how to take things at face value anymore. Every day, without exception, I expected the worst. 'We could call that chaplain . . .'

'No. I'll tell him. It's better if it comes from me. He's sleeping now anyway. Christ.' Once again, he shook his head. 'You know, when Hope was charged, part of me hoped Harvey would be too far gone to understand his daughter was going to prison. I know that sounds awful, but it's true. These past few months have been bad enough. The way people talk about our family now, you'd think we're all criminals.'

For a few moments, no one said a word. Through the large windows displaying a lawn that sloped down to the river, I caught a glimpse of a turkey vulture high in the sky. It looked weightless as it hovered, its wings buffeted by an invisible wind as it circled the space above the marshy spring grass.

'Mr Pope,' I said, 'when you saw Hope on Monday, did she say anything that struck you as odd?'

'Odd how?'

'Just . . . off. Would you say she was acting normally?'

'She was a little down, I guess. But that's par for the course lately.'

'Can you think of anyone who's particularly angry with Hope?'

Now Pope, too, was staring out at the bird. Together, we watched it spot some tiny creature down below, pin back its tawny wings, and dive.

'Everyone's angry with Hope,' he said, turning his attention back to me, 'including the people she worked with. Freddie and Jim. Sejal. That was the hardest part for her, I think. She and Sejal used to be good friends.'

'But they were all involved.' *Guilty* was the word I wanted to use. *The Fraudulent Four.* All of them were complicit. 'They were in it together, right?'

'Yeah,' Pope replied roughly. His demeanor had changed, his reaction to my new line of questioning verging on hostile. 'And yet, they tried to pin it all on Hope.'

'Did she ever receive any threats?' I asked. 'Voice or text messages, maybe? Letters?'

Pope shook his head. 'Not that I know of. Around here, everyone's happy to spout venom out in the open. I hear them talking; I know what they're saying. Gossip. Nasty stuff.'

That didn't sound like the A-Bay I knew, but I nodded, doing my best not to stoke his anger. Pope's expression had grown stormy.

'We'll leave you now,' I said, reiterating my condolences. Handing him my card and offering again to connect him with a grief counselor, a proposal that was promptly rebuffed. 'We'll likely need to speak again at some point, OK? And if you think of anything unusual about Hope's behavior . . .'

Plainly relieved to learn we were leaving, Pope promised to let us know if anything came to mind.

Tim and I stepped over the well-worn front doormat into the chilly morning air. It was always a few degrees cooler by the water, which three weeks ago had still been topped with slabs of ice. Tim had parked next to Maynard Pope's Chevy Tahoe in the shadow of the pines and peeling birch trees that surrounded the house and shaded the garage. I suppressed a shiver as I buckled myself into the car.

The second Tim closed the driver's side door, I pounced. 'Why didn't you tell me?'

It took him too long to cock his head. I could see right through his mock confusion.

'Harvey Oberon,' I said. 'His status in town. His condition. Why didn't you brief me before we went in?'

Tim's mouth moved ineffectually. 'It was a death notification,' he said. 'It didn't occur to me, I guess. Do you think it's important?'

So we were still ignoring it, then. The current of tension that ran beneath every conversation we'd had since we got back from Vermont. The way he'd been holding himself at a distance. 'Of course it's important,' I said, suddenly spent. 'The fact that her father's a former bigshot in local politics, a field she worked in herself, seems pretty relevant, don't you think? Hope's behavior angered a lot of people. And not just in Watertown.'

Tim looked down. Brushed something off the side of his

shoe. I watched his profile as he came to realize our pool of
suspects just got a lot bigger.

I said, 'Talk to me about Harvey Oberon.'

Heaving a sigh, he looked straight ahead through the windshield. The vulture, having finished off its victim, was long
gone. 'Everyone who grew up around here knows Harvey. My
parents used to talk about him like he was some kind of god.
He's well-liked. Popular. Even after his terms were over, he
was still involved in all kinds of town beautification initiatives.
The Oberon family's a big deal in these parts.'

Jesus. 'We need to talk,' I said before I could think it through.
'We can't pretend you're not still pissed at me.' Was *that* why
he hadn't told me about Harvey? Was this Nice Guy Tim's
passive aggressive way of getting back at me for the secrets
I kept from him last year?

He bowed his head, but I could see his jaw shift beneath
the skin. 'Look, I didn't think to mention it, that's all. There
was other stuff on my mind. Bram—'

'Bram has nothing to do with this. This is about us.'

We'd had our share of moments like this one in recent
months. I knew that maintaining our congenial dynamic, effortless rapport, and professional kinship – all the things we'd
toiled for almost nine months to build – was too much to ask,
but for the most part we'd managed to keep up appearances.
Then Tim's hand would accidentally brush against mine on
the way to the car, or the smell of his go-to brand of gum
would remind me how he'd tasted outside the motel next to
Otter Creek the night we almost caught Blake Bram, and I
would shut down again, and feel him do the same.

If I had my way, that kiss wouldn't have been our last. My
reasoning for rejecting Tim didn't make me happy, but it was
sound. Bram had made it clear I was under surveillance. He
knew when I temporarily moved in with Mac, and exactly
when he'd find her dog alone in the house. I couldn't distance
myself from Mac and Tim completely – we worked together
every day – but I sure as hell wasn't going to offer them up
as a sacrifice, or let Bram see I had a new love interest he
could leverage to get at me. So, I'd done what I had to: pull
back, get a place of my own, push Tim's advances aside. I

couldn't bear the idea that the next house Bram visited could be his.

'I don't know what you want from me, Shana.' I could smell that gum on Tim's breath even now. 'I've done what you asked. I left it alone. Doesn't change how I feel.'

Same, I wanted to say. *I feel it too, and it hurts like a knife in the sternum.*

What I did say was: 'Let's visit Hope's accomplices. Talk to the father.'

Tim's nod was heavy and resigned. I put the car into gear. We knew how to sit together in silence, at least. There was that.

But it was still silence.

FIVE

My passport hadn't seen so much action in years.

Hope Oberon's remains had been transported to Kingston, Ontario, directly across from Wolfe Island. Skipping lunch – it's never wise to kick off a visit to the morgue with a cold cut sub – we left the station before noon. The call from the tech who'd processed Hope's sedan came in just as we arrived at the hospital in Canada.

'Fibers,' he said with enthusiasm. 'We've got a couple of samples. They're natural, probably sisal. They were down in the footwell.'

'You thinking rope?' I asked.

'Could be. Strange that they'd be on the driver's side,' said the tech, 'but it's possible your perp stored a rope down by his feet. I've got some more work to do. I'll keep you posted about prints.'

'Thanks,' I said as we pushed through the door to the Kingston Health Sciences Centre.

The forensic pathologist, a large Filipino man who wore a plastic apron over his scrubs and whose face was strapped with a surgical mask and goggles, was prepped and ready when Tim and I walked in. The forensic tech and photographer were there too, along with Paul Ludgate, representing the OPP. We were a big group, but even without us the huge autopsy suite, which reeked of formalin, would have been a busy place. With its multiple stations, all bright lights and sterile steel, the place hummed with energy.

On the Kingston–Wolfe Island ferry ride over, Tim had told me he'd attended post-mortem examinations before. Within five minutes of stepping into the room he was breathing quickly, his skin pasty and slick with sweat.

'Focus on the music,' I told him under my breath. It pumped from an invisible speaker, and while the alternative rock cover of the lively George Michael single 'Faith' felt at odds with the activity of the day, the song would help distract Tim from the view. His eyes were red, but he drew himself up to his full height and nodded. Later, when the pathologist made his first incision, we both pulled in a breath and forced ourselves not to look away from Hope Oberon's marbled, blue-tinged skin.

The first autopsy I ever attended was in New York, and I had the good fortune of being there with a more experienced investigator who, rather than laughing at my discomfort, was willing to show me the ropes. I arrived with a jar of VapoRub and was preparing to dab some under my nose just like Clarice Starling in *The Silence of the Lambs* when Reynolds caught sight of me. He whisked the ointment from my hands under the amused gaze of the forensic pathologist, and tossed it in the trash.

'I was told it helps,' I stammered, shamefaced. 'With . . . the smell.'

'Better just to get used to it. It's like diapers,' said Reynolds, who I later learned was a new dad. 'The odor's practically lethal, but you have to buck up and take it.'

Something else I learned that day: gallows humor makes autopsies a lot more bearable.

Eventually, Tim's stomach seemed to settle, and we all fell into the routine of cataloguing what we saw and talking through the deceased's injuries. Hope's body, laid out in front of us, bore no cuts or scratches. I saw no indication that her wrists or ankles had been bound by rope. There was still much to be analyzed, and it was possible we'd find fibers matching those in Hope's car on her clothing, but none of us felt confident she'd been trussed up on her trip to Canada.

One thing we knew with certainty was that the coroner's initial assessment was right: Hope Oberon had been strangled. There were bruises on her neck from the assailant's fingertips, and subconjunctival hemorrhaging in the whites of her eyes that presented as blotches of crimson. The official cause of death was decreased cerebral oxygen delivery due to tracheal occlusion. According to the pathologist, it took thirty-three pounds of pressure to fracture a trachea. It was likely, therefore, that the killer held Hope down and used extreme force to snap the cartilage.

In other words, somebody gave this attack everything they had.

Once the body had been stitched back together and flipped over to facilitate fingerprinting, we thanked the team and went on our way. Ludgate promised to keep us abreast of any new developments, and Tim and I did the same. Monday evening, between six p.m. and midnight. That's when the pathologist believed our victim had taken her last breath. The few DNA samples he was able to recover would be crosschecked with criminal databases in both Canada and the US, but given the significance of the locale where Hope was found, none of us believed we were looking for a serial offender. At least not one who was already in the system.

What we did know was that whoever killed Hope was able-bodied, determined, and mighty pissed.

There was a fact that had been nagging me since the moment Mac revealed Hope's identity, a detail that stuck in my teeth like the razor-edged hull of a popcorn kernel. When it came to Hope's crime, she hadn't worked alone. By all accounts she'd been the ringleader, but there were three others involved in the scandal, and their scheme had been exposed. Given the apparent connection between the murder and the wind farm, the logical place to begin our investigation was with Hope Oberon's accomplices.

Except. The Fraudulent Four had been indicted nearly five months ago. Their crimes weren't violent, and since all four individuals were first-time offenders, they'd been released on bail. For the moment, they were free – but only provisionally. I'd dealt with enough criminals to know they'd be required to check in with their lawyers on a regular basis; Hope had missed just such a meeting on Tuesday. They were also prohibited from leaving the country. That included taking a trip to Wolfe Island.

Needless to say, I was eager to speak with the surviving Fraudulent Three.

According to the state database, Sejal Basak, Freddie Keening, and Jim Hathaway all lived within fifteen minutes of each other. After hearing Maynard Pope speak of Hope's relationships with her co-conspirators, Tim and I set our sights on Basak. The woman's home was an eighties construction on Riverglade with a brown roof and tan siding, but the spacious inside had been meticulously updated. In her mid-forties, tall and sturdy with a hooked nose and garnet highlights in her dark hair, Basak seemed surprised to see us. It was late afternoon, and from the basement I could hear the ruckus of several young children at play, home from school and full of beans. When, over sickly-sweet coffee, we told Basak about Hope, she eased the basement door closed, held her hands to her smooth cheeks, and wept.

She'd been hired by the city shortly before Hope, and confirmed that they'd become close friends. Tim asked about her job as city manager, and Basak told us it had involved everything from labor relations to financial analysis. I followed that up with a question about her criminal charges. Basak spoke in the hushed tone of someone deeply ashamed.

'I don't know what I was thinking,' she said. Her accent was Indian English, her cadence simultaneously lyrical and clipped. 'Hope made it sound harmless. I should have known better. But all that money – for the community,' she added hastily. 'So much money, to be pumped into the city. I didn't think there was any harm in encouraging the zoning board to vote in such a way that would benefit us all. Hope was very convincing,' she added, almost as an afterthought.

'How close were you with Hope, Mrs Basak?'

She coughed, her voice thick with tears. 'Very close. Hope and I used to be good friends.'

Until word got out about their crimes, and Hope's accomplices pinned them on her.

I said, 'All four of you were due to be sentenced the week after next, is that right?'

Her gaze lingered on the basement door. There was no mistaking the longing in her eyes. 'Yes,' Basak replied. 'For the sake of my children, I pray the judge will be lenient.'

'Where were you on Monday evening, Mrs Basak?'

'I was here,' she said, as if there could be no other answer. 'My husband and children will tell you. The neighbors, too. I can't show my face anywhere now. I'm here with my family every day. Always.'

The air felt different in Watertown, on that wide street with its jumbo lots and swimming pools, and when I stepped outside the beige house I felt momentarily lost, like I'd been dropped into some other subdivision altogether. 'If it checks out, that alibi puts Basak in the clear,' I said as we walked to the car, but Tim wasn't listening. He'd taken a call from Sol, a trio of lines appearing between his brows as he listened to the report. After sending Sol and Bogle to check out Hope's apartment, where everything appeared to be in order, I'd dispatched them to interview Freddie Keening and Jim Hathaway. Now, blocks away from us, my investigators were delivering news that made Tim frown.

Like Sejal Basak, Keening and Hathaway had apparently displayed convincing shock and regret over Hope's untimely passing. According to Sol, both said it was Hope who'd initiated the ploy that had cost them their jobs and reputations. They claimed to have been in their homes for the past forty-eight hours. Laying low. Bogle and Sol had even canvassed their neighborhoods and found several witnesses who confirmed what our suspects told us.

In the end, all three former officials had sound alibis.

The possibility that Hope's co-conspirators might, in fact, be innocent caught me off-guard, and I turned that inconvenient truth over in my head on the drive back to A-Bay. I had convinced myself one of them found a way – by boat, perhaps, despite Tim's warning about the cold water – to get to Wolfe Island. I hadn't expected our most promising lead to die on the vine. The victim had been deposited next to a wind turbine exactly like the ones Hope wanted to bring to Watertown. If the others weren't involved, it seemed to me we were looking for one of two things: someone else who had a score to settle with the fallen city council president, or somebody shrewd enough to use Hope's misdeeds to throw local law enforcement off the scent.

I hoped it wasn't the latter.

SIX

Ravenous couldn't describe how I was feeling by the time we finished with Basak, and my stomach rumbled loudly all the way back to town. Still, when Tim asked if I was interested in debriefing over a bite to eat, I hesitated. I'd trained myself to exist in a permanent state of hypervigilance, my eyes forever scanning the rear-view mirror and sizing up the people around me. I hadn't noticed any potential threats, but that was hardly a guarantee of safety. So far, I'd been mindful of abiding by my self-imposed rules. They were designed to keep my friends safe. And yet, there were moments when the idea that I couldn't live my life on my own terms made me see red.

'I have demands,' I told Tim firmly. 'We sit indoors, away from the windows. And we make it quick.'

He raised an eyebrow, but acquiesced.

Tim navigated our unmarked sedan into the downtown core, which consisted of four square blocks next to the river. We found parking directly across from The Dot on James Street. 'It's no Chateau Gris,' he joked, car doors slamming in unison, 'but it'll do.' The restaurant was an institution in town, a relic from the fifties that still sported a gold-and-orange neon sign with the words 'Cocktail Lounge' flashing underneath. In the summer, its outdoor patio pulsed under a seasonal banner that advertised wine slushies made with a fruity mix from a local vineyard. Inside, the place was dark and moldering. In other words, perfect. We picked the gloomiest corner and concentrated on our meals – chicken Caesar for Tim, caprese panini for me – like they held all the secrets of the world.

'So where do we stand on suspects?' Tim asked as he stabbed a hunk of romaine doused in bacon-studded dressing.

'If Hope's accomplices are off the hook, I'm not sure. We need to talk to the people who knew her best. Get a list of names from the husband.'

'We can cross-reference that with what my mom knows about Hope's circle of friends,' said Tim.

Every now and then, there were still moments when working in A-Bay felt like starring in an episode of *Murder, She Wrote*. I would never have imagined there was a place less than four hundred miles north of New York where everyone knew each other's business and homicide detectives sourced intelligence from their moms . . . but if Mrs Wellington could serve as an objective informant and help us better understand Hope's personal life, I wasn't opposed to the unorthodox technique. Tim had gotten very good at leveraging his local connections and knowledge of the townsfolk for the purposes of the job. So far, it had served us both well.

'We really need to talk to the father, too,' I said.

I sensed him stiffen. 'That's gonna be tough. I hear Harvey's pretty far gone. That's why I figured it was best to notify Maynard about Hope's death instead.'

'Hope and Harvey were close, though?'

'Sure.'

I popped the last bite of panini into my mouth. I hardly remembered tasting the sandwich, yet it was already gone. 'Close enough that she might have told him if she was being threatened?'

'Maybe, but—'

'Then we need an interview. Tomorrow? After Pope's had a chance to break the poor man's heart?'

Tim still looked reluctant, but he knew as well as I did that an interview with the former mayor and father of the victim was inevitable.

He'd been right to suggest that we debrief. It was important to examine what we'd learned, and determine where we stood after our first full day on the case. For the moment, though, Tim was fed and relaxed, and I had his undivided attention. I wasn't sure how soon I'd get another chance like this. I waited until he reached for his soda, and went for it. 'Mac heard some news yesterday. I'm just going to come out and say it, Tim. Carson and Kelsea are engaged.'

Mac's band-aid approach had worked for me, and I hoped it would soften the blow for Tim, too. He was chewing a cube of grilled chicken, and my newsflash slowed the movement of his jaw. He swallowed the dry mouthful with difficulty, squinting as it went down. He nodded.

'Had you heard?' I asked, nonplussed by his response. Or rather, the lack thereof.

'No.' Tim reached for his ice-cold Pepsi, the cubes tinkling against the glass. His gaze was steady. 'I'm just not all that surprised.'

I knew what he meant. Carson Gates could be a paradox; God knows he'd kept me on my toes when we were together. At the same time, his penchant for head games was wholly predictable, as Tim and I were both well aware. Mere months ago, *I'd* been Carson's fiancée, and Kelsea had been Tim's girl. I hated to think the opportunity to raise our hackles might have factored into Carson's decision. I also wouldn't put it past the man to relish in our stupefaction.

I'd met Dr Carson Gates in the city, September of 2016. I had come to him a broken woman, suffering from PTSD and resigned to completing my obligatory trauma therapy as quickly as possible so I could get back to the precinct. Ten months later, I was living in his hometown upstate, listening to him tell me I was too emotionally feeble to ever work again. I exposed his tear-down job eventually, but not before my anxiety and self-doubt made me bumble my first case on the new job and almost got an innocent man killed.

For Tim – or Timmy, as Carson insisted on calling him – this negative influence stretched all the way back to childhood. Carson had been Tim's closest friend. Or so Tim was led to believe.

'You're right,' I said, dragging my own soda toward me. 'If he picked Kelsea to get under our skin, so what? He can't antagonize us if we don't let him.'

'Exactly,' said Tim. 'Screw it. Screw *him*.'

I snorted mid-sip, and fizz shot up my nostrils. 'When I took this job, I did hope you and I would have something in common.'

'I'm guessing this isn't what you had in mind.'

I waited for the absurdity of the situation to wheedle a smile out of him, but Tim only poked at the colorless chicken on his plate. 'I found out Carson was moving back to town through my dentist,' he said. 'Did I ever tell you that? Carson and I went to high school with her, and like every other girl I knew back then, she was hopelessly in love with him. If memory serves, Carson led her to believe he'd take her to prom only to ask her more popular friend instead. She told me about his homecoming and his hotshot detective fiancée while drilling out a cavity.'

The hotshot detective fiancée being me. 'A cavity, huh? The irony,' I scoffed, thinking of my rotten ex. 'No wonder you had your doubts about me when we met.'

'My point,' Tim said, 'is that Carson's right back to his old tricks. Wait. You didn't think I'd be upset about Kelsea, did you?'

I shrugged. 'Not really. Maybe.'

'Well, I'm not.'

I didn't buy it. Tim seemed troubled.

'There's something I should have told you about Kelsea,' he said after a beat. 'She asked me about Carson. Right after we found Trey.'

'After we found Trey?' *Right before Tim and Kelsea broke up, then.* I studied his face, but it gave nothing away. 'What did she say?'

'She wanted to know if it was true Carson had treated the only woman who ever survived one of Blake Bram's attacks. She knows, Shana,' Tim said, 'and I have no idea who else she told.'

Anxiety bloomed inside my chest, and I felt my pulse quicken. People knew I'd investigated Bram's crimes in the city. Those who followed his murder spree closely might even be aware one of his victims managed to escape. The fact that the sole survivor now lived in A-Bay and was employed by the state police was a secret I'd worked incredibly hard to protect.

Mercifully, my name had been omitted from the news reports. But Dr Carson Gates had been my therapist. He knew exactly what happened to me in that basement, and that there were no limits to Bram's malevolence. He no longer provided counseling services for the New York City Police, but patient confidentiality was a core tenet of Carson's profession. Despite my lack of faith in him, it hadn't occurred to me that he could betray my trust a second time, in such a vile way.

Maybe it should have. If he wasn't entirely morally bankrupt when we were together, he certainly was now. Carson had breached client confidentiality and boasted about his work with me to Kelsea, which could cost him his license. That she might now be spreading the news around town could cost us all much more.

The locals talked about Bram like he was some kind of dark legend, dreadful and fascinating. In A-Bay, he had reached icon status. Breakfast conversations at the diner were shot through with awestruck mutterings about his sins, and his name was whispered by children in the schoolyard. Spoken through cupped hands, as if they were experimenting with a swear.

The door to the restaurant opened, setting off a bell that jangled my nerves. With my heart in my throat, I was halfway out of my chair before I realized the customer was a bow-legged man in his seventies who couldn't have been taller than five feet. Slowly, aware of Tim's stare, I lowered myself back into my seat.

If people thought Blake Bram was a curse that could be prayed away, they were sorely mistaken. If they hoped conflating him with monsters and nightmares would slake his thirst for notoriety, they were fools. Filling others with fear didn't satisfy my cousin. It only made him want to terrify them more.

Bram may have put me through hell for eight days, but my

cousin was nothing if not protective. If Carson was using Bram to elevate his status with his fiancée – or worse, with the whole town – Bram would find out.

And he wouldn't like it one bit.

SEVEN

It was not yet seven a.m. on Thursday morning when my mobile phone rang. The noise yanked me out of a disturbing dream about an island. No longer connected to the earth, it floated freely down the river as I looked on from the mainland. When it passed me, I saw it wasn't made up of soil and rock but heaps of women's lifeless bodies, a bloated tangle of bluish limbs. In my confusion, and my haste to catch the call, I knocked a tumbler of water off my bedside table, breaking the glass and flooding the floor next to my bed.

'I didn't wake you, honey,' said Felicia, 'did I?'

I blinked a few times before ducking into the bathroom for a towel, taking my aunt with me. I dreaded unanticipated conversations like this one. Ever since I was in my teens, I'd worried that, someday, I'd get a call from a tearful member of my family announcing something awful had happened. That the boy who left home at the age of sixteen had come back with fists flying, prepared to exact revenge on the people who'd driven him away. It was a distressing thought, made no less punishing by the knowledge that my cousin had grown more violent than any of us thought possible, and that it was his mother who was calling me now.

'Fee,' I said, dropping to my hands and knees to mop up the lake by my feet. 'What's going on?'

'I'm sorry to be calling so early, but I wanted to catch you before you left for work. Have you got a sec?' Aunt Fee asked.

'Sure.' I sank down onto the bed with the cold, wet towel in my arms. Still uneasy.

It took a second for her to speak again. 'I did something,' she said, a note of excitement in her voice. 'I haven't told

your mom yet – or Crissy, for that matter – but I will. I wanted
to talk to you first. You understand this stuff, so I know you'll
appreciate it. What I'm trying to do, that is.'

'OK.' I wasn't following. 'What did you do?'

She drew a breath. 'I hired a private investigator. A PI to
help me find Abe. We're going to find him, Shana.'

The past few months had been rough on my aunt. She may
not have been in touch with my Uncle Brett for almost two
decades, but learning of his death dislodged some discomfiting
family memories. It didn't help that I'd come around asking
questions, trying to help solve a homicide that was outside
my jurisdiction and that I had no business working given my
personal connection to the victim. I should have known it
would all start Aunt Fee thinking about Abe again. Wondering
what ever happened to her youngest child. Her only son.

At the same time, I'd been hoping she might finally be
ready to let him go. That thinking again about his troubling
behavior as a kid would convince her his departure was for
the best.

Apparently, I was wrong.

'Fee—'

'I know what you're going to say. You're going to tell me
it's a waste of money. A mistake. If Abe wanted to reconnect
with me – with *us* – he would have done it a long time ago.
That's what you're thinking, right? I've considered all of that.
Really, I have.'

'Then maybe—'

'But Shana, there's something else we have to consider, too.
Abe's been gone for fifteen years, and in all that time, nobody's
heard a word from him. He's never called, or sent a letter, or
shown up at my door. And because of that, I'm afraid. I'm
afraid something happened to him, honey, just like it did to
Brett. And if it did, if he's gone, well . . . I have to know.'

Her voice was shaky now. I didn't want to upset her further,
but this couldn't happen. I couldn't let it. The kind of PI my
aunt could afford was likely a bargain basement sleuth with
allusions of being Nero Wolfe, but what if he wasn't? The
man might get lucky. He might figure out that, somewhere
along the way, Abe Skilton assumed a new identity and began

slaughtering women. Worse still, Fee's bloodhound might discover I'd narrowly escaped becoming one of them.

'I understand where you're coming from,' I said as I rose from the floor and headed for the kitchen. Tucking the phone against my ear to free up my hands, I started fixing the coffee. I was going to be late. 'But there are a lot of untrustworthy guys out there who are all too happy to take your money, and who have absolutely no intention of delivering anything of value.'

'Oh, I know,' Aunt Fee said, 'that's why I hired a woman.'

'A woman.' A woman, following Bram. Intentionally trying to find him. The idea of it made me feel ill.

'I called a few of the references she gave me, and she seems to be effective. She specializes in missing persons and has a sixty-percent success rate.'

'Is that right.'

'Yes! I've already given her everything I could think of to get her started – pictures, Abe's social security number, handwriting samples. It's all very old, of course, but she's optimistic that it'll get her on the right track.'

So it was done, then. The wheels were in motion. A woman, a PI who couldn't begin to fathom what lay at the end of the road she was following, was actively looking for Bram. And my aunt Felicia was ready to cheer her on every step of the way.

It hadn't been easy, reconnecting with Fee while knowing, and holding back, such a horrifying secret about her son. Every now and then my aunt made a cameo in my dreams, and afterward, her witchy gray-blonde hair and washed-out eyes would dominate my thoughts for days. I'd played out the scenario, the one where I told her Abe was now Bram and Bram was an abomination, a hundred times in my head, and it always ended the same way. Fee, her daughter Crissy, and my own family were left eviscerated. The information I'd concealed from them was a knife with an obsidian blade, and it would flay every one of them alive.

But this wasn't just about protecting my family. The games I'd played with Abe when we were kids were ours alone. That's the way he wanted it, the way it had always been. He trusted me to keep those little mysteries from our families, and I had, for much the same reason that I continued to fleece them as an adult. I didn't trust my cousin not to punish me – and all of us – if I betrayed his trust.

'I'd like to help you, Fee,' I said, because there was nothing else I could do. 'I'll be honest: I think this PI of yours may be facing an impossible task. But maybe we can work together somehow. Maybe I could help her. Do you think . . . would she be willing to share what she finds with me?'

'Oh Shay, I was hoping you'd say that! I have to confess, I've already told her who you are and what you do, and she said she'd be happy to pass along whatever information she finds.'

Fee promised to email me the private eye's contact info, and said she'd tell the woman to expect a call. 'You never know . . . if you combine your skills, you just might find something.'

'Maybe,' I said, listening to the coffee maker gurgle and gazing out the window at the river.

As long as I get to Bram first.

EIGHT

When investigating a crime, there are always moments that raise my antenna and make me go: *Wait. Hold on. This isn't right.* I've learned to bird-dog incriminating behavior and latch onto it with teeth bared. It's this level of aggressiveness that moves an investigation forward, and ultimately delivers that first glimpse of the person who might well be a killer.

With Hope Oberon's homicide, that moment happened when the call we'd been waiting for from the Canadians finally came in.

Early morning in the barracks was an assault on my senses, the smell of aftershave applied with a heavy hand and shampoo clinging to hair still shower-slick competing with printer toner and coffee breath, spring damp permeating the basement walls. I wiped my watery eyes as Tim put Paul Ludgate on speaker and we leaned in. The OPP had managed to obtain a full record of border crossings from earlier in the week, and there was no indication Hope Oberon had entered Ontario via the ferry checkpoint in the past few days. Ludgate had looked into the ferry from Kingston, too, with the same outcome. Hope didn't check in.

But her car – the same one we'd just found abandoned near Watertown – did. It rode *Horne's Ferry* from Cape Vincent to Wolfe Island at seven p.m. on Monday night, and returned on the ferry's last trip of the day, just half an hour later.

'But she wasn't driving,' I confirmed.

'Right. She must have been in the car, though, concealed in the back seat or trunk,' Ludgate said. 'We have video footage of every car that comes off that ferry, and there's no question it was hers. The driver was a man, and the passenger seat was empty.'

'So we might have surveillance footage of the killer,' I said, my skin atingle.

'Not only that – we have his full name and passport number, too. Val Giovanni mean anything to you?'

'Giovanni,' Tim said. 'Why do I know that name?'

Ludgate said, 'Maybe because he's your neighbor. We've done some poking around on our end, and Giovanni appears to reside near Watertown. He's some kind of environmental activist.'

'An environmental activist,' I repeated, thinking of the wind farm. Taking it all in. 'So as of now, Hope's husband is the last person to have seen her alive, and that was Monday at around five p.m., before she left for home. The coroner put the time of death between six and midnight, and we think she was on the ferry – possibly already deceased – at seven. The perp must have intercepted her on the way from A-Bay to Watertown, then. Watertown, where this Val Giovanni lives.'

'He had to work fast out there on the island,' said Tim. 'Just half an hour to get her body to the turbine and make it back for the last ferry trip. When does the sun set these days? Before eight, yeah? So it wasn't even dark out yet, and our perp's unloading a body in a wide-open field. Why take that chance? This keeps getting stranger and stranger.'

'It's a hell of a thing,' said Ludgate.

I was inclined to agree.

After Ludgate hung up, Tim and I didn't waste any time tracking Giovanni down. He did indeed live near Watertown, and he worked in the small city too, exactly twenty-six minutes from the State Police parking lot according to the map on my iPhone. I got to searching the internet while Tim took the I-81 south.

'His name's all over these articles about the corruption case,' I said. '*Hope's* case. Jesus, Tim. He was protesting the wind farm.'

The man had earned so many mentions in the news he was practically a local celebrity. 'Some of these stories refer to him as an anti-windmill activist. I didn't even know that was a thing.' But it clearly was – and Giovanni's brand of activism appeared to have a radical bent. 'Here's an article about some protestors who set fire to turbines in France,' I said as I scrolled. 'In the Netherlands, some anti-wind-farm groups come to rallies armed with grenades. Not to say all protestors are violent, but in Europe at least, things are getting dicey.'

It seemed possible that Giovanni was of the same mind as his European counterparts. According to numerous online reports, he'd been charged with disorderly conduct at a rally against a proposed landfill in 2014. That same year, he was arrested for chaining himself to a cement truck while fighting a construction project that would have involved filling in a small natural pond. He'd been in Canada recently, too; I found his name in the caption of a newspaper photo, which put him at a climate strike in Ottawa last summer. What kind of man were we dealing with, here?

'So Giovanni was against the wind farm,' said Tim, tilting his head in my direction without taking his eyes off the road, 'which suggests he could have had a beef with Hope.'

'Looks that way. The theory that her killer's someone who took issue with the project does make sense.'

'There were definitely protestors out and about as soon as news of the proposed wind farm broke, and they got a lot of press coverage. I remember one story said something about wind farms making people sick.'

'Gimme a sec.' I typed those keywords into my phone's internet browser and rearranged my legs in the passenger side footwell. 'Looks like there's a theory that wind farms can lead to health problems. Some people who live near them report headaches, tinnitus, anxiety, sleep deprivation. They claim it's like a jet flying overhead, except the sound is never-ending.'

The idea of that made me cringe. Having seen the turbines up-close, it didn't surprise me that sleeping through the noise might be tricky. The vibration in the air was almost enough to wake the dead. 'But Giovanni's quoted as an environmental activist,' I said. 'I thought they liked green energy?'

'From what I've read, there are a couple of issues at play when it comes to renewable energy like wind and solar power. Wildlife is a big one,' said Tim. 'Apparently the turbines can impact wildlife behavior, especially that of birds. Putting them up can mess with migration patterns. The ground around the turbines needs to be cleared, too, so that means disrupting the habitat of grassland species. There was some concern about this stuff back when the wind farm went up on Wolfe Island, what, eight or nine years ago.'

'I'm seeing the terms "ecological sanctity" and "visual pollution" used a lot on environmental blogs, too. Well, whatever his motive, the guy was in Hope's car the night she was killed.' Allowing myself a small smile, I added, 'I think we've got ourselves a new suspect.'

We found Giovanni at his place of work, an environmental services company called Greener Care, and intercepted him as he was returning from a visit to the vending machine. Clutching a foggy bottle of unsweetened ice tea, and under the watchful eye of his colleagues, he wasted no time professing his innocence even as we read him his rights, invited him to contact a lawyer, and escorted him back to the barracks.

With his dull gray ponytail, scraggly beard, and fisherman sandals worn over black socks, Giovanni looked like an aging hippie. In the presence of his attorney, I asked if he was aware Hope Oberon was deceased. I'd sent out a news release about our homicide investigation the previous day, after returning from the autopsy. If the local papers hadn't glommed onto it yet, they would soon.

'I read about her last night,' Giovanni confirmed. 'Shame.'

'Tell us how you know Hope,' said Tim.

Giovanni fingered the place where his glasses met his ear and glanced nervously at his lawyer. 'Who *doesn't* know Hope? She's been all over the news for months.'

'So have you,' I said. 'You were actively protesting her wind farm proposal. That right?'

A shrug. Giovanni's shirt was stained around the collar, stiff with dried sweat. He moved; it didn't. 'I wasn't the only one.'

'Maybe not, but your voice was the loudest. Where were you on Monday between five p.m. and seven thirty, Mr Giovanni?'

'Monday.' His eyes widened in thought and he puffed out a breath. You'd think I was asking the guy to solve for x. 'I finished work at five and went straight home.'

'Alone?'

'Yes. No.' Hands flapping on the table. 'I was alone, but I played this game with some friends. An online game. They'll tell you.'

'An online game.'

Giovanni took a breath, as if preparing to talk for hours. 'Wingspan,' he declared. 'It's a tableau builder game – that's a style of board game where you have cards in your hand and you choose which ones you want to play out on a tableau to build your board. Each card gives you powers that you can leverage when it's your turn to play.'

I opened my mouth to interrupt, but Giovanni kept going.

'It's a great game, big in Europe. Bird-themed. I'm into birds. Everybody has their own bird habitat that's divided into three zones – forest, meadow, wetlands – and you can play bird cards into the different zones where they would go in real life, and there are food resources and it's all accurate with this beautiful art straight out of an Audubon book, and—'

'Mr Giovanni,' I said. 'Explain to us how this game serves as an alibi.'

'Oh,' he said, glancing once more at his attorney, who looked at odds over her client's rant. 'Well, I was online from six until ten. Monday is our game night, me and these three buddies of mine.'

Giovanni was lying. Had to be. Border patrol put him in Canada at seven p.m. 'So you played this online game with your friends from six to ten. You're sure about that.'

'Right. Yes.'

'That's interesting,' I said, 'because according to the Canada Border Services Agency at Point Alexandria on Wolfe Island, you were in Ontario on Monday evening.'

Giovanni blanched. 'What?'

'I have to advise you not to say anything more,' his attorney, a squat woman with sleek hair cut short, said through a scowl.

But Giovanni didn't listen. 'That's . . . no. That's wrong. I was at home playing Wingspan.'

'Your passport says otherwise.'

'My passport?' He shook his head. 'I haven't used my passport in months. Not since I went to Ottawa last summer.'

I looked at Tim, who was sitting beside me. There was a pile of papers upside down on the table in front of him, images Ludgate had sent to the lead desk. Tim flipped them over and slid them across the table.

'These are stills from the border surveillance footage recorded on Monday. From where I'm sitting,' said Tim, 'that looks like you.'

The ponytail. The beard. The slightly hunched shoulders and overall looseness of a big man who's lost a lot of weight. Giovanni's eyes scanned the photos, and widened.

'What the . . . no. That's not me. I mean, OK, it looks a bit like me, but it's not, I swear. I was at home. Ask my friends.'

I've been lied to by plenty of suspects. It's usually easy enough to tell when someone's backpedaling, or inventing details on the spot. Fidgeting, deliberately maintaining eye contact, glancing at the door – all are signals of anxiety and blatant desperation. These attempts at subterfuge are hardly sophisticated, but a skilled liar can do a lot better. A master of deceit can avoid the urge to touch their face even when stress engorges their nasal tissues and makes their nose itch. Val Giovanni looked uncomfortable, but his hands were on the table. Either he was good at telling stories, or there was some truth to his claim.

'If it wasn't you, how do you explain these photos?' I asked.

'What you've got here is an image of a bearded man whose face is partially hidden by a hat,' said the attorney. 'As far as evidence goes, it's weak.'

'That man isn't me,' Giovanni said again. 'My house – I never lock the door. I live on the outskirts of town, no neighbors for miles. Anyone could walk right in.'

The thought made me shudder.

'Are you suggesting your passport was stolen?' said Tim.

'I don't know. It could have been, couldn't it? I haven't seen it in months. If you take me home, I'll look for it. I'll prove it to you.' Giovanni's voice was pleading. 'I didn't go to Canada. You can ask my friends. I was with them online. I didn't kill that woman.'

I crossed my legs and leaned back in my chair. Last year, shortly after I moved to A-Bay, Mac told me about a guy she once met who worked as a border patrol agent up in Cornwall. The man had no shortage of stories to share about what was evidently an interesting job. Within his first six months on duty, he'd confiscated guns, porn, bacon, a narwhal tusk, and six endangered lizards native to the Middle East. Even more enthralling, at least to me, were the countless botched attempts to cross the border using stolen passports. Agents were trained to detect imposters by studying facial features like jawlines and ears, which don't typically change over time. With a decent disguise and the right build, though, someone might be able to pull off an impersonation. Giovanni had long, stringy hair. His beard covered the bottom third of his face. I'd seen Bram completely transform his looks using little more than a prosthetic nose and colored contact lenses. I hated to admit it, but any motivated criminal could do the same.

Still, if we were anywhere else, I might not have believed Val Giovanni's claim. These days, many border checkpoints used advanced technology like biometric verification. The Canada Border Services Agency boasted bilingual agents, ground sensors, AI-powered radar and high-resolution camera surveillance. Travelers were thoroughly questioned, their vehicles routinely searched. But crossing the longest undefended border in the world in the Thousand Islands? That was different. Americans could cross by boat at Rockport to visit the waterfront pub, where they might encounter a part-time border guard but could just as easily find a sign telling them to call a reporting center and check into the country by phone. The same was true of Brockville, Kingston, Cornwall, and any number of towns along the river. Up here, the honor system was the default setting, and people could be trusted to do the right thing.

On Wolfe Island, border patrol consisted of a three-season hut steps from the ferry slip. When Tim and I had crossed, I'd stayed in the car. With our passports in hand, he'd stepped up to a horizontal sliding window that reminded me of the drive-up ice cream shop I used to visit as a kid. The whole process had taken less than five minutes.

Was it possible someone could have stolen Giovanni's passport and impersonated him at the border?

It was.

'Wait here,' I told our suspect and his attorney, motioning for Tim to follow me into the hall.

'What the heck?' he said as soon as I'd closed the door to the interview room behind us.

I raked my hair back from my face, fingers snagging on knots. Mid-morning, and already the day felt endless. 'I know. That alibi of his . . . what do you know about – what was it? Online tableau games?'

'A little?' Tim shrugged. 'My stepbrother's a gamer.'

'Could the people Giovanni played with verify he was home during the game?'

'If he was playing with people he knows in real life – as opposed to random players from all over with obscure usernames – it shouldn't be that hard to substantiate his statement.'

'Is it possible he could have been playing while en route to Canada?'

'I think it would depend on the game. When J.C. plays, he uses Discord,' Tim said. 'It's like an instant messaging service that has voice and video functionality. Pretty much all the serious gamers use it. J.C. stays online with his friends the whole time, chatting about the game and what each player is doing. I don't know anything about Wingspan, but if it's like a real-world board game, and Giovanni uses something like Discord, it might be tough to participate while actively strangling someone.'

'Let's call these friends of his,' I said, 'before we take this any farther. If there's actually a chance someone stole both Hope's car and this guy's passport, we've got our work cut out for us. I know what you're thinking.'

'A murder,' Tim said. 'The theft of a vehicle. A disguise. Shit, Shana, are we absolutely sure this isn't Bram?'

I had been sure, but now? Now, I was starting to wonder. If this was Bram's doing, if he'd plucked this conspicuous victim from the heart of Jefferson County and discarded her body in a whole different country, then he was taking our game to another level.

And I'd have to play even harder to win.

NINE

I had to wonder whether Paul Ludgate knew what he was getting into when he agreed to collaborate with the BCI.

'I'm texting you a phone number,' he said when I called, and to his credit he'd kept his voice impassive when I told him our theory about the passport, the hypothetical disguise, the unknown perpetrator who may or may not have snuck into Canada in the black of night. I felt considerably less stupid when I got through to the border agent who'd been on duty Monday. When I pressed him on the highlights of his shift, the agent – new to the job at the sleepy Wolfe Island post, and just a few months out of training – sheepishly confessed it was possible the man who checked in was not, in fact, the passport's owner. It was getting dark, the agent said. It had been raining, and the traveler had a hood pulled up around his face. It was tough to tell – and anyway, who would steal a passport to get onto boring Wolfe Island?

I was pretty sure I'd never see that border agent again.

In the meantime, Tim had dug into Val Giovanni's alibi and found it checked out. While Hope Oberon was abducted, killed, and ferried to Wolfe Island, our one and only suspect had been online with three real-life friends, playing the virtual version of Wingspan. Just as Tim had predicted, the group used Discord to converse throughout the game, and Giovanni's buddies confirmed he'd been chatting the entire time and never missed a turn. Tim and I had no choice but to let Giovanni go with a warning to stay close to home. Not an hour later, he phoned us to report he couldn't find his passport anywhere.

I was frustrated, and disheartened. Every path was a dead end, each avenue blocked. Homicide cases involving dumped bodies were rarely closed overnight, but something about this one made me leery. Somehow, I felt like I was being played. I'd assigned Tim to act as lead desk case agent, and he'd consolidated the team's findings, but the findings were slim. Sol had tackled the list of Hope's friends, while Bogle took depositions from witnesses on *Horne's Ferry*. Across the border, Ludgate continued to collect statements from residents of Wolfe Island. The wheels were still in motion; it just didn't feel like we were getting anywhere. The call from Felicia that morning hadn't helped my mood. I couldn't stop thinking about the fact that a PI was investigating Bram. In my personal life as in my job, the pressure was on.

When my cell phone rang after I'd been staring at the photos of the crime scene for more than an hour, I jumped to answer it.

'I remembered something,' Sejal Basak told me when I picked up. 'It might not be relevant.'

Swiveling to face my computer and quickly navigating to Hope's case file, I said, 'We'll take any information you have.'

'Well . . .' There was a quiver in the woman's voice. 'Hope mentioned something. Someone had been bothering her recently.'

'Bothering her?' I leaned back in my chair. 'How do you mean?'

'She received some letters. Two, I believe. They were mailed to her office. They were . . . not kind.'

I had so many questions – who were they from? What did they say? Where were they now? – but I could sense the woman's hesitation, and I didn't want to scare her off. 'Were the letters threatening, Mrs Basak?'

'I only heard a few lines, just what Hope read to me, but yes, I would say they were meant to be threatening. They were about the project. The wind farm.'

Never once did Mac talk about the corruption case without mentioning the opposition faced by the Fraudulent Four. The way she described it led me to picture an angry mob wielding pitchforks and flinging flaming torches through the doors of town hall. After visiting Wolfe Island, I could appreciate why some residents were reluctant to welcome the development project with open arms. Turbines had their benefits, but they were also a blight on the landscape, and in an area that relied on tourism dollars, that left many residents rankled.

Basak went on to paraphrase the contents of the letters. If her memory was accurate, the threats were alarming. The sender singled Hope out, calling her a greedy bitch. Telling her not to sleep too soundly.

'He signed both letters the same way.' She dropped her voice. '"Blow me".'

Great, I thought. *Our suspect has a sense of humor.* 'He? The sender was a man?'

'Yes,' she said. 'His name is Val Giovanni.'

I held very still. *But Giovanni's clean. We sent him home. He's gone.* 'You're sure about that.'

'Absolutely. He claims to be an environmentalist, but we all think of him as a protestor. A pest. He came to city hall a number of times in an attempt to divert the project and intimidate us.'

Holy hell. 'When was this, exactly?' I asked, frantically typing notes.

'Last year. The first one came in late August, the second a few weeks later. There was a lot of buzz about the project at that time.'

'And where are the letters now?'

'I don't know.'

'Do you know if Hope talked to the police?' I'd investigate this myself after our call, connect with the officers in Watertown to see if she'd filed a report, but I liked to ask the witness first. It was a way to gauge how much I could trust them.

'I don't think she did,' Basak said. 'We were nervous about calling attention to ourselves.'

Oh for two. 'OK,' I said, tamping down my frustration. 'Can anyone corroborate what you're telling me? About Giovanni's behavior, or the existence of the letters?'

'His behavior? Anyone at town hall can tell you about that. He would stand outside with a big sign, oh, two or three times a week. He wasn't subtle. But the letters . . .' Her voice trailed off. 'I don't know who else Hope told. Her husband, possibly. I know she was very close with her father, but he's not well.'

'What about friends? Do you know who else she was close to?' The list we'd received from Maynard Pope had been short.

'I'm sure she had friends,' Sejal Basak said, 'before. After everything that happened though . . .' She drew a shaky breath. 'I can't speak for Hope, but there are many people in my life I once considered friends who won't talk to me now. They won't even take my calls. Something like this, a scandal, it pushes people away.'

When I was a kid, my family was burdened by its share of scandals, too. Uncle Brett, Bram's father, was always getting into mischief, racking up fines for unpaid parking tickets, disorderly behavior, public intoxication. I was mortified by his behavior which, even if my parents tried to hide it, inevitably reached me through my classmates at school. In a village the size of Swanton, or even a small city like Watertown, folks looked after their own and watched their backs, and wayward behavior wasn't treated as an anomaly so much as a virus. You had to be quick to distance yourself from the diseased, or risk infection.

Nobody had reported Hope Oberon missing when she disappeared for two whole days, not a friend, a neighbor, or even her own husband. Her crime had set her apart from both the communities to which she had ties.

Sejal Basak was right. Scandals pushed people away.

They might even lead to murder.

TEN

V al Giovanni's house was on the outskirts of Watertown, not far from Perch River. It must have been a farmhouse once, might even have been considered historic, but someone had covered the original clapboard with aluminum siding that was now the color of a heavy smoker's front teeth, and the rest of the property had long since gone to pot. I didn't know how much land Giovanni actually owned, but there wasn't another mailbox for miles. I tried to imagine living that way, in a house so isolated and exposed. Not a soul around to hear your scream.

Tim and I spent the drive reviewing what we knew about Giovanni, his activism, and his connection to Hope. By the time I stepped out of the car onto a patch of parched grass – there was no driveway to speak of aside from two long ruts of petrified mud that jostled our car like a ride at the county fair – I was buzzing. The guy was a serial picketer, associated with protests all over Jefferson County. He had threatened the victim. He may have had an alibi defense, but his passport was in Ontario the day Hope was murdered, and we still hadn't made sense of that. Yes, we lacked the evidence to hold him, and yes, Giovanni had been sent home. By no means was I convinced he was innocent.

My intention was to bring him back to the barracks for questioning. I wasn't expecting him to decline the opportunity to call in his attorney again.

'I have nothing to hide,' the man said, waving us through a living room cluttered with the kind of Mission-style furniture that had filled my grandparents' house, all nicked cherry wood and vertical panels reminiscent of the bars in a prison cell. The walls were adorned with thrift shop paintings, flocks of geese flying over golden fields and navy lakes. Giovanni might be a liar, but he'd been honest about his love of birds, at least.

In the man's dated kitchen, the countertops were littered

with compost bins and mason jars from which various seedlings spiraled. More plants hung from the ceiling above the windows, and the sills were crammed with pots of herbs that, together, cast an unsettling green glow over the room. The house smelled of rotting fruit, at once sweet and revolting. Giovanni sat down at the kitchen table, folding his arms across his sunken chest, and Tim and I pulled out two chairs to join him.

'Just a few more questions, if you don't mind,' I said. 'Why don't you start by telling us a little more about your relationship with Hope?'

The man sighed heavily and scratched at his beard. The gray smudges under his eyes were nothing new, but there was a slightly sour odor wafting from his body now that suggested he hadn't showered. 'There was no relationship,' Val Giovanni said. 'I knew about Hope because of her affiliation with the town council. Because of what she was trying to do.'

'Did you ever meet her in person?'

'Meet her? No. I saw her around now and then.'

'Around town hall, you mean?'

His eyes darted to the left. 'I guess.'

Tim said, 'Mr Giovanni, we've received reports that you were threatening Hope Oberon. We're told you sent her several letters.'

'Who told you that?' Before we could answer, he said, 'I didn't *threaten* her, just gave her some advice she didn't want to hear. As in let that damn project lie.' Whether because he was on his own turf or because we'd failed to make a murder charge stick, the man seemed bolder today, almost cocky.

'A witness told us you called her' – here, Tim made a show of checking his notebook – 'a greedy bitch. You also told her she shouldn't sleep too soundly at night. That right?'

'Two simple truths. She was charged with corruption. Hard to argue that's not a display of greed. And only someone completely cold-blooded could sleep after committing such a heinous crime against the community.'

'The community,' I said, remembering all the news features on Giovanni, his objections to the development plan. 'Why don't you tell us about your qualms with the wind farm.'

'Look around.' He said it with a derisive snort. 'This part

of the county's covered with pristine wetlands, the perfect breeding ground for bald eagles and black terns – birds that are threatened and endangered and need all the help they can get. Wind farms negatively impact biodiversity. Ask any birder! You won't have trouble finding one, they're all over this place. At least *some people* appreciate the importance of preserving wildlife. At least *some people* get it.'

There it was, at last: the anger Giovanni had publicly displayed toward the wind farms swooped in like a bird of prey with talons splayed.

'So you were opposed to the project because you wanted to protect local wildlife,' I said.

'Yes, and that's reason enough. Look.' He lifted his large hands, hands that could easily control a panicked, struggling woman. 'I believe in clean energy. Wind farms are great, in theory, but they don't produce nearly enough power to justify endangering all those birds. Studies show wind farms kill more than three hundred and twenty-eight thousand birds in the US every year. Nobody should support an initiative that does that. I'm just the only one with balls enough to say it.'

'So you made your feelings clear. But Hope wouldn't back down.'

'She was a stubborn woman, wouldn't listen to reason. She came to regret it, though, didn't she?'

A chill rolled over me. 'Meaning what, Mr Giovanni?'

He blinked at me as the significance of what he'd said sunk in. 'Hope and her crooked pals were caught out, that's all. They should have listened when I told them a wind farm was a bad idea.'

It wasn't a threat, not really. But it was close enough.

'Environmental issues are important to you, aren't they?'

'Of course,' he said. 'They should be important to everyone.'

'Tell us about your job again?' I held the man's gaze.

'I'm in environmental protection.' Giovanni sounded slightly defensive. 'I work for a major environmental restoration company, assessing the environmental impact of fires and various forms of contamination to prevent water and air pollution. But I'm sure you already know that.'

In fact, we knew something more. Before leaving the

barracks, Tim had called Giovanni's boss. As a job description, *environmental protection* was exceedingly generous. Giovanni worked for a clean-up crew, removing mold from old buildings and scrubbing out neglected air ducts.

'So you're an expert in environmental clean-up. That's a handy skill set for a murderer. Wouldn't you say so, Tim?'

'How do you mean?' Tim asked, the question unsophisticated, and right on cue. We didn't play good cop/bad cop, per se, but our interrogation technique was designed to throw suspects off-kilter. To gain their trust before cutting them off at the knees.

'I mean,' I said, 'if someone wanted to hurt Hope, I can see the appeal of tapping into those capabilities.'

Giovanni blanched.

'What she's suggesting,' said Tim, 'is that you have an accomplice. Someone who did the dirty work per your instructions while you were online with your friends. And if that's the case, the question you have to ask yourself is whether it's worth risking your freedom to protect the real criminal here.'

Val Giovanni looked from Tim to me and back again, and for a second I thought we had him. I was so sure he was going to crack that I was already imagining what it would feel like to tell Lieutenant Jack O. Henderson, my direct superior down in Oneida, we'd solved the case in record time. There was something I hadn't counted on, though. Giovanni wasn't the reckless, lawless criminal I assumed him to be. He was vigilant, and lightning-quick. And he was wise to our tricks.

A scowl of disappointment passed over his face. 'Look,' he said coolly, 'I know what this is. It's hardly the first time the police have had it out for me. I'm not the only conservationist around here, but I'm the loudest voice, so I'm the guy they target.' With a look that implied he had resigned himself to our stupidity, he shook his shaggy gray head. 'I know what you think when you look at me, a bachelor playing online board games. Living all the way out here to be closer to the birds. Hope Oberon is dead, and because I disagreed with her politics, you're sitting in my kitchen accusing me of murder. I didn't like her. I didn't like what she was doing. But I didn't kill her, and you'll never find anything that proves I did.

'So go ahead,' he went on. 'Find my so-called accomplice. Considering that I spend all my time with three gamers who don't even live in the state and the rare Orange-crowned Warbler I've been tracking for weeks, I wish you the very best of luck. In the meantime, I don't think I'm going to answer any more of your questions. In fact,' he said, rising from his chair and planting his feet on the linoleum floor, 'I think I'd like to call my attorney after all.'

ELEVEN

ase crumbles. Killer goes free.
        I could see the headline in my mind, how those bold black letters would shout our defeat from the front page of tomorrow's *Watertown Daily Times*. I didn't like the look of it one bit.

The rich aroma of freshly-brewed coffee that pervaded the barracks when Tim and I returned to the lead desk did little to lighten my mood. Even when I discovered a plate of home-made Snickerdoodles sitting unattended in the break room – Sol's wife Monica loved to bake – and wrapped two up in a paper napkin, my lips remained firmly planted in a frown.

'I hate this.'

'You can't be talking about that snack in your hand, so let me guess,' Tim said. 'Is it the fact that we were foiled not once but twice by our only suspect, and that our case against him is for the birds?'

'You win. Yay,' I said with zero enthusiasm. I bit into a cookie, let it melt onto my tongue and chased it with a sip of scalding coffee. 'I want a do-over.'

Tim flipped open his notebook with a flourish. 'OK. What do we know about our killer?'

'We know we're looking for someone strong enough to fracture a trachea.'

'It's also still likely the motive was somehow connected to the wind farm and Hope's crimes, right?' Tim snatched the second cookie from my napkin with a crooked grin. 'I wonder how Green Wind Renewables feels about all of this.'

It took a second for me to place the reference. In my head, I'd conflated Hope with the wind farm so fully I'd almost forgotten she was just the middleman. 'What do you mean?' I asked.

'Well, what Hope and the others did wasn't great PR for them, was it?' said Tim. 'Now, the focus will shift to her murder. The papers will still cover Sejal, Freddie, and Jim, at least as far as their sentencing is concerned, but Hope's death will trump all that. Pretty soon, the corruption stuff will be a footnote at best.'

I blinked at him. 'You're right. Hope's murder totally reframes the story. Green Wind's finally out of the spotlight.' As horrible as they were, the events of the past three days had worked in the development company's favor.

It was a long shot. I had a hard time imagining a renewable energy company putting a hit on a potential client, but I pushed my half-eaten cookie aside and opened a new browser window on my computer anyway. 'The closest regional development office is in the Capital District. Let me see who I can get on the phone.'

Ten minutes later, we had an appointment to meet a senior product developer with Green Wind in Albany, New York, and I was taking my coffee to go.

It was raining when we left A-Bay, fat, lush drops that burst against the windshield like fun-size water balloons. It kept up all the way through Utica and into Schenectady as the greening trees whipped by our windows, a blur of jade and brown. 'Home sweet home,' I said with a half-smile.

'Good old Albany,' said Tim.

Every New York State Trooper attends basic school in Albany. Not all of them graduate. Tim and I had both stuck it out, enduring the brutal and relentless training, drills, and paramilitary lifestyle for the full twenty-six weeks. We'd missed each other by a few months, but our experiences at the New York State Police Academy had been very similar. It was nice having someone to reminisce with on our two-hundred-mile trip south.

'I must have done a million push-ups while I was there,' I told him as I watched the wipers swish back and forth, catching on the glass every time. It was pleasantly snug in the car, and I relaxed into the passenger seat. 'My arms ached so badly at night that I could barely lift my toothbrush.'

'You must have been jacked back then. Not that you're soft now or anything. Not at all. Sorry,' Tim said, his face aflame. 'Geez.'

I laughed and hoped he wouldn't notice the flush that suffused my own cheeks. 'Did you like living here?' I asked. Recruits stayed in the dorms for the majority of the week, Sunday night through Friday afternoon, but for the remaining forty-eight-plus hours, we were free.

Tim's hand was on the gear shift again, and he tapped his index finger as he drove. 'It's a good city. Don't you think?'

'Sure.' What was good about the city to me was that it wasn't Swanton, and it was a long way from my cousin. 'It was a means to an end, I guess. I always had my sights set on New York.'

'What was *that* like?'

We rarely talked about my previous home. Tim was sensitive enough to avoid it. There was a trace of awe in his voice, though, and I wondered how long he'd been waiting to ask. Tim was of the same breed as my friends and family in Vermont, Mom and Aunt Fee and my old friend Suze, all of whom had been born into a village no bigger than a thumbprint and never had the inclination to leave. I'd read once that more than seventy percent of Americans live in or near their place of birth. The idea of staying put for so long struck me as claustrophobic, but I knew Tim didn't see it that way. For him, residing where he was raised wasn't about a lack of ambition or even fear, but loyalty and devotion. If it came down to it, I knew he could navigate a bigger, badder pond no problem. I did worry when I first moved to little Alex Bay that Tim might resent me, or realize taking a job ten minutes from his childhood home had limited him professionally. It didn't take long for me to see that simply wasn't true. Tim was passionate about his work and community. He valued his family. There was something to be said for fidelity like that.

'Manhattan was wild,' I told him as we navigated Albany, passing strip malls and historic tree-lined avenues as we neared the Hudson River. 'I guess I would describe it as chaotic. All those people, sharing the same grid of streets yet moving in completely different directions. It felt a bit like being in a room overflowing with those dollar-store wind-up toys, with everyone bumping into each other all the time.'

'I get that,' he said. 'Every time I go I feel like I'm running a gauntlet. It's just so jammed.'

I thought about Tim's cabin on a wide-open expanse of river, and smiled. 'It is, but there's a kind of intimacy to living in such close proximity to strangers.'

'I guess.' He wrinkled his brow. 'But did you ever really feel . . . I don't know . . . safe?'

I had – right up until the night I walked into an Irish pub and woke up in an unfamiliar basement boiler room. That's what Tim was really asking about: not my life in the city, but my brush with death. I suspected that after hearing me tell of my abduction he equated New York with danger. Yes, there were people all around, yet that night none noticed that one of their own was in trouble, not even when Bram stuffed me, drugged and spinning, into a car and whisked me off to hell. Tim had a hard time imagining a thing like that could happen where he lived. I couldn't bear to remind him something very similar had transpired with Trey Hayes on an island much smaller than Manhattan.

When I didn't answer him, Tim transferred his hand from the gear shift to the steering wheel. After a second, he said, 'Do you feel safe now?'

'I'm not worried you're going to steal my lunch money, if that's what you mean.'

'You know it's not.'

I blew out a stream of air and stared down at my lap. 'Yeah.'

'We never talk about it,' he said, 'but Bram's still out there somewhere, and he's following you. Christ, Shana, he called you at the barracks. He knew exactly where you were.'

I would have gladly taken a dozen calls like that one if it helped us get closer to finding out where Bram was hiding, but we had no way to trace a mobile phone without the help of a network operator, and there hadn't been nearly enough time for that.

'I'll be honest,' I told Tim as we passed city hall, its medieval-looking tower piercing the cloudy sky. 'I'm starting to get used to the feeling that I'm constantly being spied on.'

Tim shot me a disparaging look. 'Come on Shane, this is serious. You should be able to feel safe. It's a basic human right.'

'For most people, maybe. For me . . .'

He started to speak again, but I lifted my hand. 'We went over this in Vermont, remember? I'm always careful, always watching.'

'OK,' he said. 'But if you change your mind, I could keep an eye on your place. Or if you wanted to stay at mine for a while—'

'We're here.' I bent toward the rain-lashed windshield and squinted at the tidy brick-and-stone building up ahead.

With a sigh, Tim parked the car.

On LinkedIn, Janice Stanton-Smith touted herself as 'a passionate project developer who enjoys meeting landowners across the Northeast'. In person, she was a spindly woman with heavy make-up, overprocessed blonde hair, and an ill-fitting polyester suit. Tim and I joggled the water from our jackets before shaking her hand. We'd found parking only half a block down the street and dashed from the car, but spring rain showed no mercy.

'I was very sorry to hear about Mrs Oberon,' Stanton-Smith said as she showed us to a small glass-walled conference room. When I asked how she'd heard about Hope's death, she explained she'd set up a Google Alert to deliver news about Watertown's criminal investigation to her email. 'We're all very upset about it, as I'm sure you can imagine.'

'Bad PR,' Tim said with a knowing nod. While he spoke, I gave the office the once-over. Through the glass I could see a man at one of the desks, his broad back to us, head down. Apart from him and the woman we'd come to see, the place was deserted.

'Bad everything,' Stanton-Smith said through pursed lips. 'I was surprised when I heard from you, actually.' She licked her teeth. 'You're aware the investigation into the behavior of those city officials showed our company had nothing to do with their crimes?'

'We're aware of the outcome of that investigation, yes,' I said. 'So you had no knowledge that Hope, Sejal Basak, Freddie Keening, and Jim Hathaway tried to purchase political influence?'

'None whatsoever. I was shocked to hear Hope was the mastermind behind it all. She seemed like a good person.' Stanton-Smith tucked a limp strand of hair behind her ear and sniffed. Her nose was too small for her face, so much so that I wondered if she'd had rhinoplasty. Her LinkedIn profile had said she once worked in luxury commercial real estate, a world rather more glamorous than the one she'd landed in.

'Can I ask how you ended up in renewable energy?' I said.

'Oh. It was because of my family, really. My husband took a job in Albany. I used to lease office space, but I didn't have any contacts here, so I thought I'd try something new. Green Wind was hiring.'

'Was it you who approached Hope, or the other way around?'

'I reached out to her. I'd read about the wind farm on Wolfe Island.' She paled as she said it, but powered through her dismay. 'I hoped people would be amenable to something similar in Jefferson County, that they might already be used to the idea what with those turbines nearby. Hope was really excited about my proposal.'

'It sounds like you made her a generous offer. Close to eight hundred thousand to bolster the local community, is that right?'

'There are immense benefits to wind energy,' Stanton-Smith said, sliding effortlessly into her sales pitch. 'Villages, even small cities like Watertown, get tax credits from wind energy production. It can become a new source of revenue for munici-palities, and that has a direct impact on taxpayers. More revenue means counties don't have to raise taxes to pay for operations. Landowners stand to make more money, too. We lease the land from them – the ones who consent, which the vast majority do – and they get an annual land lease payment that spans the life of the project. Hey, farming is farming, right?' I could see every one of her bleached teeth when she smiled; the woman was as slick as a car salesman behind on his monthly quota. 'Harvesting the wind isn't much different from harvesting crops, and if you have a bad year, well, wind isn't affected by drought or abnormally cold winters. It's always there. It always delivers.'

'Sounds like a no-brainer,' I said pliably. 'But not everyone felt that way, huh?'

'There are always a few outliers.' Her smile had slipped, and by the tilt of her mouth I suspected she was downplaying the opposition she routinely faced. 'There are advantages, and lots of them,' Stanton-Smith said, 'but I won't pretend there aren't drawbacks, too. Most people underestimate the size of the turbines. It's hard to imagine how big they'll be until you see them in person. The compensation we offer to the communities that host our renewable energy projects, which usually take the form of donations to community-focused initiatives, help people come to terms with it all. Unfortunately, even with that sizeable donation, Hope and the others couldn't convince the city council to vote in favor of the project.'

'Were you angry about that?' Tim asked.

'Angry? No. It was frustrating to put in all that work for nothing, but it happens. Not every deal goes through.'

I said, 'I bet you wish this deal wasn't quite so high-profile, though.'

'It wasn't great for our image when word got out about the misconduct, if that's what you mean.'

'And now?' I asked. 'What does Hope's death do to Green Wind Renewables' image?'

The fluorescents in the conference room weren't especially bright, but the inclement weather outside had darkened the windows and intensified the light. I could see the line where Stanton-Smith's make-up ended and her sallow skin began, along with every fine hair on her cheek. That included the single, stiff, white whisker protruding from underneath her chin. The woman had no place to hide. 'Time will tell,' she said, 'but if I had to guess? People will forget. There are too many benefits to pass up, and wind power's only going to get more popular.' Stanton-Smith bit her lip and looked at us askance. 'Is it true Hope was found next to a turbine?'

There was a spark of excitement in her eyes that I didn't like. 'Mrs Stanton-Smith,' I said, 'can you tell us where you were on Monday evening between five and eight p.m.?'

'Me?' Her false eyelashes fluttered. 'Monday. Well, I was home – but then I went to my yoga class, over on Delaware Avenue. I'm there every Monday from six to seven. I never miss a class. You can ask my instructor.'

Six to seven. No chance the woman could have made it to Watertown, let alone Wolfe Island.

'Why do you ask?' Stanton-Smith said warily.

'Standard procedure,' I told her. 'We think there may be some connection between Hope's murder and the wind farm project.'

'What kind of connection could there be? The project was dead in the water the minute the officials were caught out. What's done is done. Why on earth would anyone care about it now?'

The woman was right. The turbine project was over; even Val Giovanni had packed up his dissent and gone home to his birding. It didn't make sense that someone would still be angry enough about the proposed wind farm to resort to murder.

There was another explanation, one that continued to hound me. Maybe the turbine was a diversionary tactic. An attempt to misdirect us and derail our investigation.

Maybe our killer had dragged Hope all the way to Canada simply to throw us off track.

The question, of course, was why?

TWELVE

'Can you teach me to drive a boat?'

I didn't ask it until we'd passed Douglas Crossing and were minutes from home, but I'd been carrying the question around with me for a lot longer.

'You want me to give you boating lessons?' Tim said from the passenger seat. I'd offered to relieve him of his driving duties, and he'd all but dozed off.

'It's a reasonable request.' The ice on the river had melted, making it safe for boaters once more. I hadn't seen many on the water yet, but the ferries were up and running, so it stood to reason other vessels could be, too.

'I'm surprised, that's all. I always thought boats made you nervous. Why the sudden interest?'

'They don't *make me nervous*, I just don't know much about them. And it's not that sudden,' I said. 'I live next to the river now. The troop has a police boat. Summer's coming, and there are homes all over the islands, and their owners might need our help. Boating feels like a basic life skill around here, and my abilities are seriously lacking.'

In fact, I'd been fretting over my dearth of experience with the river ever since the day last year when Tim, Mac, and I followed Bram to Deer Island only to watch the boat he'd stolen skate into the channel and out of reach. Learning from Trey that Bram had worked at a marina made me feel ill at ease. I was a landlubber, which put me at a disadvantage here – and when it came to my cousin, I needed the playing field as level as I could get it. This was a deficit I couldn't afford anymore, not if Bram was comfortable enough on the water that he might use it as an avenue of escape again.

'I have a little runabout,' said Tim. 'Nothing fancy; I take it out fishing sometimes, or just to tool around. If you really want to learn, I could teach you.'

'Can you teach me this weekend?'

'It takes more than one lesson.' He said it with a laugh, his gray-blue eyes alight. 'But sure, we can start this weekend.'

'Great. I want to be ready for anything. When he comes back.'

His face hardened. 'I know. Hold on. My phone.'

The call was from Tim's mother. I focused on the road while he talked, trying to pretend I wasn't listening in. Our shifts at the barracks were fairly regular; we followed an on-call schedule for weekends and after-hours, but otherwise we were on duty every day from eight to four. My own family only phoned within that window if it was an emergency. Tim didn't seem alarmed by the call, though. He sounded composed as he talked, though he did fiddle awkwardly with his left earlobe.

'Sorry,' he said earnestly once he'd hung up. 'I wouldn't normally indulge her like that during work hours, but she's still upset about Hope's death.'

'This must be hard for her. You said your mom and Hope knew each other?'

'A bit, yeah. Hope's death hit close to home. I'm sure a lot of people in town feel the same way. First that business on Tern Island, then Trey, and now this.'

It had been a tough few months for Alexandria Bay – and it all started with the corruption scandal. 'Did you manage to calm her down?' I asked.

'I'm not sure. She doesn't like that we haven't made an arrest yet.'

'I don't like it either.'

'That makes three of us, then,' said Tim. 'She wants me to go over there for dinner tonight, so at least I've got another shot at putting her mind at ease.'

'Do you do that often? Go there for dinner? It's not a trick question,' I said when he looked unsure about how to answer. 'You're lucky, is all. I'd give anything for regular meals with my folks.' I envied Tim his uncomplicated life. But that wasn't fair, was it? His life may have been simpler than mine, but it wasn't without complications. Case in point: the uncertainty between us.

'Yeah?' he said. 'Why don't you come along?'

'What, to your mom's place?' I couldn't hide my surprise, and worried my reaction had offended him. But Tim just shrugged his broad shoulders.

'Why not? You could help me reassure them. You're my superior. They'll listen to you.'

'I – wow, I don't know. Are you sure they'd be OK with that?'

'Of course,' he said, looking slightly abashed. 'You're my partner.'

All in all, it hadn't been the best of days. We'd hit a dead end at every turn, and where the investigation was concerned, it wasn't just Tim's mom who was on tenterhooks. It wouldn't be long before reporters, my supervisor, and the general public demanded to see some progress.

Beside me in the car, Tim felt sturdy and warm. We'd been in Albany for hours, navigating the city and visiting Green Wind's offices. There was no way Bram could have followed me there and back, and no reason to think he'd been tailing Tim. I weighed the idea of a home-cooked meal and the chance to meet Tim's family against the prospect of returning home to my cottage alone. To another night of scrutinizing that same impenetrable deck of cards.

The choice, as it turned out, was easy.

THIRTEEN

I didn't know much about Tim's family beyond what he'd told me in Vermont, but I'd gotten the sense they were a happy, boisterous bunch, and I knew the moment we walked into their Cape Cod-style home that my hunch was bang on. Present at the Wellington house, the same one Tim had lived in from age eight to twenty-two, were his mother, Dori; his stepmother, Courtney; and Haitian-born Jean-Christophe, the youngest of Tim's two stepbrothers. Tim's father had moved to St Petersburg, Florida a few years ago, and his sister was raising a family in New Hampshire while their second stepbrother was a college freshman in Michigan. The remaining Wellingtons greeted me like a long-lost relative.

'It's hard to believe it's taken this long for us to get you out here,' Dori said as she pulled me into a heartfelt embrace. She looked great for sixty, with slightly wild blonde-gray hair parted down the middle and cut in a bob. Her eyes were green and clear. Tim must have gotten his dark coloring from his father, but he had his mom's toothy smile. It was cozy in the dining room, a colorful space decorated with vibrant, tropical-themed artwork that Tim said Courtney had picked up on her travels to the Caribbean. The table was laden with two deep-dish lasagnas that hissed from the heat of the oven, two different kinds of salad, and a basket heaped with steaming dinner rolls.

Like me, Tim came from a family of good cooks. Even before his mom and dad divorced and Dori got together with Courtney, he'd grown up with Sunday roasts and flaky butter-crust pies. According to him, Dori loved Chinese food, but there wasn't a takeout place for miles, so once a month she made a feast of fried rice, breaded shrimp, and homemade egg rolls. When she motioned for me to pass my plate for a helping of tonight's equally mouth-watering meal, I didn't hesitate for a second. My forearm flexed in response to the weight of the noodles and meat. Balancing slabs of the stuff on a bent spatula, Dori delivered lasagna to the other waiting plates. When we'd all been served, we raised our glasses to the chefs, and dug in.

'This is delicious, thank you,' I said. 'Feels just like home.'

'We're so glad,' said Courtney. 'How are you two holding up?' In contrast to Dori, Courtney's hair was straight and long, dyed a peachy shade of strawberry blonde. She had small blue eyes set close together and a general roundness that I found appealing. 'This must be incredibly hard for you under the circumstances, Shana.'

Reflexively, my eyes flicked to Tim where he sat across the table. I was confident he wouldn't have told his family about Bram, but I didn't know how much they knew about my suspension. I'd been on probation for several weeks following the Tern Island case – time, it turned out, I badly needed to get my head straight. I held his gaze, trying to parse his expression. Apart from the steady scraping of Jean-Christophe's fork and knife against his plate, the room was quiet.

Opting for ambiguity, I said, 'It's been a busy few months.'

'The Tern Island case and abduction were bad enough,' Tim added, 'but this homicide is really putting us through our paces.'

'Tim tells me you knew Hope, Mrs Wellington?' I said as I ate.

'Please, call me Dori. We were in school together, but Hope was a few years younger than me. Courtney knew her better than I did.'

'I met her when I moved to town from Massachusetts,' Courtney explained. 'Hope's daughter, Natalie, is the same age as my eldest son Tyler. They were pretty good friends, so Natalie came over to the house sometimes. J.C. had the biggest crush on her.'

'*Mom*,' Jean-Christophe grumbled, which made Tim grin. At almost eighteen he was as tall as Tim and nearly as muscled, but J.C. still looked at his brother with the unalloyed devotion of a doe-eyed kid.

'Hope was a nice woman,' Courtney went on. 'Kind. Generous.'

Dori put a hand on Courtney's arm. I put down my fork.

'I'm sorry,' I said. 'I'm sorry this happened to her.'

Courtney nodded and lowered her eyes. Dori said, 'How's the investigation going? Tim doesn't tell us anything.'

'That's not true, Mom,' he said, reddening. 'Anyway, a lot of stuff is confidential.'

'But we can tell you we're doing our absolute best to find the person who did this,' I put in.

'I'm sure that's true,' said Dori. As she spoke, Courtney's gaze flitted to mine.

When I accepted Tim's dinner invitation, his family's relationship with our homicide victim had been the last thing on my mind. I wasn't here to interview anyone, and I certainly didn't plan on upsetting them while they fed me the best dinner I'd eaten in months. At the same time, it had dawned on me that this was an opportunity to obtain some much-needed information. If Tim could leverage his family's knowledge of A-Bay and its people, maybe I could, too.

'We're still in the fact-finding phase of the investigation,' I said, washing down a bite of lasagna with a swallow of dry red wine. 'We're trying to understand what Hope was like. Her personality, her life.'

I shifted my eyes to Tim. *OK?* I asked without saying a word. I could feel Jean-Christophe watching us closely, his own curious gaze moving back and forth between us. After a moment of consideration, Tim gave a small nod. I turned back to Courtney.

'I don't suppose you could help us with that?' I asked.

'Me?' Courtney's lips twisted. 'Oh.'

'You don't have to,' Tim said quickly. 'We don't have to do this if it's still too raw.'

'It would be cool to help, though, Mom.' J.C. was invested now, his attention redirected from his plate of food to me.

'You did know her,' Dori told Courtney. 'Maybe you know something that could be useful.'

'I'd like to help, I really would,' Courtney said. 'I'm just not sure what I can tell you that's of any value.'

'What we usually look at is behavior. Something different, out of the norm.'

To my disappointment, Courtney said, 'I hadn't seen her in quite a while. Maynard – him, I see all the time. But not Hope.'

'She was living in Watertown,' I said.

'She was – but she spent a lot of time here, too. Until word got out about what she'd done, anyway. I'd been trying to work up the courage to ask Maynard how Hope was doing.' Courtney's face fell. 'I couldn't do it. I convinced myself it would make him uncomfortable, but honestly? I chickened out. Now I wish I hadn't been such a coward. At least then Hope would have known I was thinking of her.'

I remembered what Maynard had said about the townsfolk's reaction to the scandal. *Hope and her crimes.* 'I understand she had a rough time these past few months,' I said.

'Oh, it's been awful. People who've known her for years, who I thought of as her friends, snubbed her on the street and said horrible things behind her back. What she did was wrong' – here, Courtney gave J.C. a meaningful look, taking advantage of the teachable moment at hand – 'but I was shocked by how quickly everyone turned on her. When our kids were in school, Hope ran the book fair, led the PTO, introduced monthly outdoor movie nights – the list goes on and on. I don't know how she found the time to do so much, because she helped out at the restaurant, too. That woman was a real powerhouse. She even worked with the board of ed to reinstate the defunct home ec program, and gave high school kids with culinary aspirations a chance to intern at Chateau Gris. I work at the school, so I know how involved she was.'

'Wow,' I said, genuinely impressed. 'She sounds like a chip off the old block. Her father was ambitious, too, right?'

Both women chuckled. 'That's true,' said Dori. 'Hope was a lot like her dad.'

'Sounds like she interacted with a lot of people over the years,' I said, thinking of the extensive list of activities Courtney had rattled off. 'Any scuffles you can think of? Jealous parents who wanted their own chance to shine?'

'Oh gosh, no. Everyone was grateful for Hope's help.'

'What about her relationship with her family?'

Courtney's smile was melancholy. 'Natalie and Maynard are great. The other mothers and I joked that Hope hit the jackpot with him – looks, brains, *and* he does all the cooking. Not that he's my type, of course.' She nudged Dori's arm and snickered while Tim and J.C. stared in horror. 'That man's a catch, though. A good dad, too. Huh.'

'What is it?' Tim leaned forward. Suddenly, Courtney looked far away. After a moment, she blinked and smiled.

'I was just remembering something Maynard used to do. It was the sweetest thing; I'll never forget it. A few days a week, he would drive Natalie to school – this was back when she was twelve or thirteen, shortly after the kids and I moved to town and I started teaching there, though of course it could have been going on for longer. Maynard would park the car at school, they'd get out together, and he would stand there and watch Natalie go inside. Every five steps or so, Natalie would turn around and wave at him, and Maynard would wave back. Five more steps, another wave. By the time she got to the door, they'd have done their little routine seven or eight times. It was adorable.'

'Adorable,' I echoed, though I had trouble imagining my niece doing the same thing. When Hen was that age, my brother would complain she'd sooner eat dirt than acknowledge him in public. Alexandria Bay only had one school, and it was pre-K through Twelve, which meant kids as old as eighteen could have been watching Natalie and her dad.

'Poor Natalie must be gutted,' Courtney said. 'At least she wasn't in town to see what Hope had to go through these last few months.'

I said, 'It must have been hard on Maynard, too.'

'It was the kiss of death. What she did, it upset people way more than I would have expected. I mean, we don't even live in Watertown. It shouldn't matter that much. But I guess her crime felt like a personal affront, and now Maynard's paying the price.'

It took me a second to understand what she was getting at, but then a memory floated back to me, of Sol and Bogle debating where to go for their anniversary dinners. Sol had said Bogle would have to be out of his mind to eat at Chateau Gris. 'The restaurant. Are people reluctant to go there now?'

'More like boycotting it,' said Courtney as Jean-Christophe passed his empty plate for more lasagna. 'The place has been empty as a drum for months.'

I nodded. Under the circumstances, the reaction made sense. 'I hear Hope's father's kind of legendary around here,' I said, changing course.

'I told Shana about his stint in office.' Tim tossed me a hangdog look.

A nod and smile from Dori. 'That's true. Harvey used to be our mayor. This was decades ago, but he's still remembered. He made a lot of improvements during that time, really changed things for the better around here. He rebuilt and widened the public docks to attract more visitors, beautified the golf course . . . the list goes on.'

Just like Hope's. 'Impressive,' I said.

'It is,' Dori acknowledged. 'We've always had tourists in the summer, all these wealthy homeowners back for a week here and there, but for stuff like shopping and dinners out, they tended to go to Canada. He really spruced up the downtown area, though, and kept helping out long after he left office. I'm sure I heard somewhere that Harvey gave Maynard a hand with opening Chateau Gris. I wouldn't be surprised if he ponied up some cash to get it running. I had my doubts about that place at first – it seemed a bit too swanky for these parts – but until recently it was doing really well. Due in part to Harvey's influence, I'm sure. That man is a force of nature. It's a shame, what's happened to his mind. I wish you could have seen him in his heyday,' she told Tim and I.

Harvey Oberon's litany of accomplishments seemed to be never-ending. Dori went on to speak of summer festivals and family-oriented events that had since become traditions. It was all for the good of the town. 'Did Tim tell you Harvey used to play Santa Claus?' Dori asked. 'With the exception of this past year, when everything was blowing up with Hope, he'd been doing that for, oh, almost three decades. He had all the kids in town convinced he was the real deal, that the rest of the year he was just undercover. He even wore a ring engraved with *Santa* to convince them.'

I laughed. 'That's amazing.'

'It really is. And of course, there were the parties.'

'Parties?'

Her face lit up. 'You don't know about the parties? Back in the late seventies and early eighties, Harvey threw some real ragers.'

'The up-all-night kind.' Courtney said it with a knowing wink. 'This was before my time here, but from what I've heard, Harvey had Dori dancing on the tables.'

'Oh Lord! Oh please,' Dori gasped, practically in hysterics. Across from me, both Tim and Jean-Christophe looked aghast.

'Boys,' Dori said, laughing some more, her cheeks pink and high. I liked this woman. 'I promise you that's an exaggeration. Those events did bring out the wild side in people, though. There were times when I was asleep on my feet and Elliot practically had to carry me home. Hold on, I have pictures!'

Tim's mother shuffled over to a cabinet in the living room and started rifling through the low shelves. When she got back, she held a photo book that looked as heavy as a cement block.

'They started before the kids were born, when Elliot and I were newlyweds. We were regulars for a few years before Catherine and Tim came along. They were a real treat. A luxury,' Dori told us as she flipped open the photo book. 'Harvey lived to entertain. Look.'

Reaching past plates and full water glasses, over the wooden salad bowls and open bottle of wine, Dori handed me the book. The pages were plastered with photographs of a hand-some young couple in party clothes, Dori's hair done up like Dynasty's Krystle Carrington with frosty blonde highlights and wingy bangs. Elliot, Tim's father, sported wide lapels and fitted brown slacks. If not for the outfit and wooly mustache, he would have looked exactly like Tim.

'Wow,' I said, captivated. 'These are outstanding.'

'The parties were, too. In the beginning, Harvey rented out the country club. Oh, how we danced. Sometimes the guests would spill out onto the golf course. Gosh, I remember those nights so clearly, the humid summer air and the cool grass under my feet.'

There were pictures of those moments in the book, Dori and Elliot and a group of their friends barefoot on the putting green, their mouths hinged open in laughter. Dori waved at me to turn the page. 'It was the island parties most people remember, though,' she went on. 'Those started later. Harvey had some friends who owned private islands. I don't know if he paid for everything or if the owners chipped in, but we're talking the works: food, booze, even live entertainment. The way the music and voices would echo across the water . . . you can't imagine how magical it was.' Dori looked over at Courtney with a dreamy expression, and Courtney gave her partner's hand a squeeze. 'Harvey would hire college kids home for the summer to work as servers and ferry guests back and forth from the mainland. One year he had lobsters and littlenecks flown in from Maine for a clambake. It was wild, just wild.'

'No kidding.' I paused to study a snapshot of Dori arm in arm with two other women around her same age. By the looks of their outfits and fuchsia fingernails, we were in the eighties now. In the background, beyond trees tinted blue by the camera's flash, the moonlit water glistened.

I met Tim's eyes across the table, and smiled. I'd been reading up on the history of the area, and Dori's stories had me spellbound. These bashes of Harvey's sounded like a modern take on the epic Golden Age gatherings of old. Blues and jazz bands playing on rocky island terrain. Partygoers in pastel polo shirts mingling inside the mansions that made up

Millionaire's Row, built by department store magnates and railway tycoons. I'd learned some of the homes in the area harbored actual nightclubs and dance halls, though many of those were shuttered in the fifties due to illegal gambling. It was fun to imagine that, decades later, they were put to use again by a mayor with a penchant for throwing lavish affairs.

'That's Harvey's wife,' Dori said, pointing to a woman with straw-colored hair cut into a feathered wedge. 'She was quite a bit younger than him, closer to my age. Diane wasn't much for crowds. More often than not, she didn't show up. I got the sense she'd indulge her husband now and then but really preferred to stay home with Hope. Harvey was this loud, larger-than-life guy, but Diane was much softer.'

'What happened to her?' I asked. 'I know Harvey lives with Maynard Pope now.'

'Oh, she passed away a few years ago. Heart disease,' Dori said. 'She was only in her mid-sixties.'

'Maynard said Harvey and Hope were close. I wonder if losing her mother is part of that,' I mused.

'Most likely. Although I think they always had a strong bond.'

'I can vouch for that,' added Courtney. 'Hope and Harvey were together all the time. She even used to bring him around to the school to talk to Natalie and Tyler's class about how to be good citizens and upstanding members of the community.'

In the context of the scandal, Courtney's words – *upstanding members of the community* – hung in the air like a miasma. Hope had tarnished the Oberon family's sparkling reputation and alienated her family from the people her father loved, all in one fell swoop.

'I can't even imagine,' Dori said, reading my thoughts. 'Hope went from perfect daughter to pariah. I hope people go easier on her family now.'

Now that she's gone.

'You must think this place is really something,' Courtney said grimly, reaching for her wine.

'I'm from a village of sixty-five hundred,' I said simply. 'There's always more to small towns than meets the eye.'

'And they always have their share of colorful characters.

You and Tim should swap stories,' said Dori. 'Compare notes about your local heroes – and the ne'er-do-wells, of course.'

'Yeah,' Jean-Christophe said. 'Since Tim was one of them.'

Instantly, Tim's expression clouded. His eyes were hard, his voice harder. 'J.C. Don't.'

'If you think Harvey's a legend,' the boy said through an expansive smile. 'You should hear about my bro and Carson Gates.'

I felt my stomach drop.

'J.C.,' Courtney hissed under her breath.

'Oh, Shana,' said Dori, eyes wide. 'I'm sorry.'

'*We're* sorry.' The glare Courtney gave Jean-Christophe was almost lethal. It took a long time for the kid to realize what he'd said, but when he did, he dropped his gaze and didn't look at me again.

'Tim did tell us about you two,' said Dori. 'The break-up, and all. I'm sure you don't want to talk about him.'

'It's fine. Don't worry about it,' I said.

'And I'm *sure* she doesn't want to hear about Carson's behavior in high school,' added Courtney.

I didn't have to look at Tim to know he was mortified. Mortified, and furious with his brother. But J.C.'s claim that Tim and Carson had been troublemakers in their youth wasn't news to me. I'd heard the story of their friendship straight from Tim, back when I still had plans to marry Carson Gates. That was how I'd discovered my fiancé's favorite hobby had been humiliating and entrapping Tim. The worst of the stories I'd heard involved a porta potty set aflame. That stunt of Carson's had landed Tim in jail, and had required a lawyer and a good chunk of Dori and Elliot's savings to resolve.

Reliving those experiences made Tim irate. Close to fifteen years had gone by since he banished Carson from his life, and he hadn't been happy to find out his childhood frenemy had moved back home. But it was thanks to Tim that I learned, not a moment too soon, my fiancé was a manipulative bastard who preyed on the weak. Who went after Tim when he was an innocent kid, and me when I was a broken woman.

Harvey Oberon might have been a legend, but Carson was just a disgrace.

FOURTEEN

It was late when I left Dori and Courtney's, and dark as a Canadian winter. The moon was concealed by a curtain of cloud, and there weren't as many streetlights in town as I would have liked. I kept an eye out for wildlife as I drove home. It was the season for fawns, and I'd already seen several white-tailed does on the side of the highway, their downy-soft bodies struck down and left to rot. It pained me to think of their young abandoned. I didn't want to be responsible for taking a life tonight.

Even with J.C.'s awkward mention of Carson, my time with Tim's family had been a delight. I was grateful for the chance to get to know them, and pleasantly surprised that Tim and I could spend an entire evening together without a single clumsy interaction – at least not one related to our unresolved attraction. The food had been excellent, right down to the fresh berries with yogurt that Courtney, a diabetic, served for dessert. Turning onto the gravel drive that forked off East Riverfront Road and meandered toward the St Lawrence and my rental, I realized I was in the best mood I'd been in for weeks.

I pulled up to the building and stepped out onto the damp ground. There was only one way to open the garage door, and that was with a grunt and some muscle, but I'd grown accustomed to the routine. In no time, the car was inside and I was climbing the staircase to the cottage door, thinking of the threadbare T-shirt and flannels I kept under my pillow and how good it would feel to pull them on and melt into bed.

There was a sconce next to the door that, at nighttime, limned everything with a sunny yellow glow, but I rarely remembered to turn it on before going out. Like the roads, the deck was dark. It hadn't been long since the rain passed through, and the air was so swollen with moisture I could feel a haze of damp on my cheeks, cool and soothing. It had been warm at Dori and Courtney's, and stuffy in my car, so I stood on the deck for a moment and let the mist roll over me. Looked out at the glittery black water, and breathed it in.

It wasn't until I turned around that I noticed my front door was open. A sliver of shadow, darker even than the night, stretched onto the hardwood inside. The metal latch on the jamb was mangled, and there were marks up and down the door near the knob. I'd seen dints and scrapes like them before. They were made with a crowbar. A tool that doubled as a weapon. Property crime was practically unheard of in town, and I still hadn't gotten used to the fact that most residents didn't lock their doors. I'd kept up my old habit of double-checking the bolt every time I left home, making the cottage a hassle in a sea of easy targets. This wasn't a random break-in. This was something else.

Most investigators don't carry their sidearms when off duty, but I'd been keeping mine close, in a holster on my belt, since the day I realized Bram had followed me upstate. I withdrew the Glock 30 and contemplated what to do. I could call Tim and the troopers, or I could chance a peek at what awaited me inside. I couldn't do both, though. Not without putting myself in danger.

With the toe of my boot, I nudged open the door.

It was cold in the house. Quiet. I could see almost every inch of the place from the doorway, and I didn't sense a presence inside. Nothing appeared to have been disturbed.

Beating back my fear, I stepped farther into the living room. No sound or movement of any kind. With my heart in my throat, I dove for the wall and slammed on the light. I did the same in the bedroom and bathroom, blinding myself in the process. When the green stars that clouded my vision finally faded, I found myself staring at an empty house.

I lowered my weapon, and that's when my gaze fell on the kitchen counter.

The box was small, no more than four inches in length and half of that in width. It was the kind of box you'd use to gift someone a delicate necklace, maybe a fine fountain pen. The lid was tied on with a strand of butchers twine. All of it sat atop a tiny envelope about the size of a card from the florist.

The last time I'd received an envelope from Bram, it

contained a bloodied tooth that had been forcefully extracted
from Trey's mouth. I could still feel it in my hand sometimes,
hard and light against my palm. I reached for my phone and
took photographs of the objects that had no business being in
my kitchen, and then, from the pocket of my State Police
jacket, withdrew a pair of gloves. Only when I'd snapped them
on did I reach for the envelope.

The flap wasn't sealed. I withdrew the card. It was plain
white, and displayed a handful of words scribbled in black
pen.

I know how much you like a real dessert after dinner.

Shaking in earnest now, I reached for the box. Untied the
twine, and lifted the lid.

A single pre-packaged Swiss Roll, coated in cheap chocolate
and oozing cream. A harmless supermarket snack cake.

It chilled me to the bone.

The plastic covering crinkled in my hands as I picked up
the cake to reveal what was hidden underneath. It was a playing
card, from the same kind of deck I'd been studying for months.
The photograph was black and white and depicted an antique
boat gliding through the shallows. Three passengers sat inside,
all wearing bathing caps. *Eel Bay from the Narrows*, the caption
read. The card meant nothing to me, but I was willing to bet
it held meaning for Bram. The last card he'd played had
symbolized the abduction of a child. I couldn't imagine what
he was planning now.

I turned my back on the box, slumped against the lower
cabinets, and slid down onto the floor.

There were things Bram knew about me that no one else
had ever learned, and my love of Swiss Rolls was one of them.
They'd been a favorite childhood treat, the antithesis of my
father's chef-caliber baking. So achingly sweet they made
my teeth hurt. Bram and I would dip into my allowance to
buy snack cakes from the gas station, and devour package
after package sitting in the scratchy grass next to the Missisquoi
River. I knew my parents wouldn't approve. I hadn't even told
my brother Doug.

That was a long time ago, and my tastes had changed. *I'd*
changed. But this gift meant Bram had been watching tonight.

He knew where I was. He even knew what Tim's family and I had eaten for dessert.

Tim's family. *Oh, God.* I covered my mouth with both hands and willed Dori's lasagna to stay down. By going to Tim's family's place, I might have put them in danger. I'd led Bram directly to their door and all but invited him to weigh up the happy scene inside. I'd grown complacent. Focused all my energies on Hope's case, as if Bram might wait his turn.

Well, he wouldn't wait. I saw that now. Bram was done waiting.

He was back.

FIFTEEN

'*F uck.*'

Tim rarely cursed. But then, his face was rarely as contorted with rage as it was when he finally lowered himself onto my couch. Although I'd told him over the phone the cottage was all clear, he drew his sidearm upon arrival and conducted a thorough second search. He'd done the same with the trees around the perimeter of the house and was sweaty as a result, breathing hard through his angular nose, pulse throbbing under the slick skin of his neck.

To his credit, Tim didn't flinch when I broke the news that I was still looking for Bram. I think on some level he knew it even before I did. I'd been pursuing my cousin since before his riddles led us to Swanton. In a way, I'd started prior to leaving New York. I was always wary, heedful of where he might pop up next and who he'd be when he did. It was only a matter of time.

'So he breaks in here,' Tim said, grudgingly holstering his weapon, 'and he leaves you a Swiss Roll? What the hell does that *mean*?'

'It means he's watching me, that he's *been* watching me, probably for a while now.' I forced myself to draw a breath. While my own heart rate had finally returned to normal, the shock of knowing Bram had been in my home jangled my nerves something fierce.

'If you're about to tell me you can handle this on your own,' Tim said, 'I'm leaving.'

'Don't do that. Let's think this through.' I crossed the room to join him. 'Bram already knew where I worked. Now he knows where I live, too. It was bound to happen. He tracked me to Mac's place in the fall, remember? Maybe he followed me here one day, or overheard me talking to someone in town.' I'd been careful, but it wasn't inconceivable that I could have dropped my guard. Hell, I'd done it tonight. 'Point is, we know for certain he's still in the area. That gives us the upper hand.'

'Does it?'

I told him about Felicia's PI, how I hoped to get some information out of her. 'Up until now, we've been flying blind. We didn't know what Bram was plotting, or where he'd turn up next. We were completely at his mercy. That's not the case anymore. This PI is coming at things from another angle – she isn't looking for Bram, she's looking for *Abe*. People like her fly under the radar. Some even break the rules. She might unearth something useful. And then there's this.' I reached across the coffee table for the playing card, which I'd slipped into a zip-top bag so I could get it to a fingerprint analyst in the morning. 'These games he plays, they're designed to give me a fighting chance. We have a shot now, Tim, because we finally have a clue.' I held up the card. 'What do you know about Eel Bay?'

Tim sighed. 'Eel Bay is a large cove west of Wellesley Island, between the state park and the Canadian border. It's a popular swimming hole for boaters during the summer. The locals don't use it much, on account of the eels.'

'There are actual eels?'

'It's pretty shallow, which makes it a good breeding ground. Legend has it the eels swarmed the bay in the summer months, and Native Americans speared and cured them to eat in the winter.'

I rubbed my temples. At no point in our childhood had Bram and I had any contact with eels. I wasn't looking forward to revealing this to Tim, not after my speech about having the upper hand, but I was done keeping secrets from him, and the obscurity of the card was troubling. 'The last time one of these playing cards turned up, I didn't understand that it was a message, and Bram took Trey from Heart Island. Eel Bay has some kind of significance. We can't just sit here waiting to find out what it is.'

'So we'll keep looking for him,' said Tim. 'You work your contacts at the marinas and collaborate with that PI, and I'll call around to the local hotels to see if anyone matching his description has been renting a room.'

'That isn't enough. Whatever plan he's devising, we need to intercept it.'

'How, though?'

How do you read a killer's mind?

When Abe and I were kids, he was always open about what he was thinking. Oh, he hid things from me, most notably the grisly riddles he concocted for my enjoyment, but with everything else my cousin was an open book. He was a talker, and that hadn't changed. Trey Hayes and I could both attest to that.

I remembered one evening in June or July when my parents took us for ice cream at a little country store not far from my house. Aluminum buckets on either side of an outdoor seating area overflowed with brightly colored petunias, and two plastic soft-serve cones dangled from the awning next to the door. As we licked our frozen treats – pistachio for me, vanilla with chocolate sprinkles for Abe – I asked if he wanted to play a game. Never Have I Ever was our go-to, largely because it was a challenge; we were together so much that we really had to dig for a fact about the other we didn't already know. It wasn't easy, flushing out those surviving secrets like pheasants from a brush. Both of us relished the hunt.

'I'll go first,' I told him that day. 'Never have I ever picked my nose in public.'

Abe laughed into his ice cream and pretended to wind a finger up his nostril.

'Never have I ever eaten a worm,' he said.

'I haven't,' I told him. 'But I would.'

Proud as a peacock, Abe said, 'I would, too. I'd eat something way grosser. Sheep intestines. Slug phlegm.'

I'd glanced down at my ice cream and almost gagged. 'You wouldn't.'

'You don't know what I can do, Shay,' he said, deadpan. 'If you did, you'd win this game every time.'

'I know what to do,' I told Tim.

There was a strong possibility he'd try to warn me off my plan. *It's dangerous*, Tim might reply. *He's* dangerous. But Tim had also once told me that, together, we could make Bram stop.

Meeting his uneasy gaze, I said, 'We flush him out. He called me at the barracks last fall, remember? He wanted to talk, to take whatever the hell he thinks our relationship is to the next level.' I fanned out my hands, willing Tim to accept that I had the inside track on Bram's gnarled psyche. 'That's why he came here, to my home, tonight. He wants to get closer to me.'

'Over my dead body,' said Tim.

We weren't of one mind about my brilliant idea, that much was clear. Tim hadn't liked it when I encouraged Jared Cunningham to publish my name and photo in the *Watertown Daily Times*, either – yet that move had tipped Bram off to the fact that I was living in the Thousand Islands, and brought us within arm's reach of apprehending him. It was a dangerous game we were playing, but it wasn't one I could quit. Bram made sure of that tonight. The push-and-pull between us was getting so intense I feared it could only end with the loss of a life, but every time he got close, my chances of nailing him increased tenfold. He'd already made contact. I suspected he'd want that again. 'I'm not saying I'm going to offer myself up as a sacrifice. I'll do it someplace safe, and I'll be armed.'

'What? What are you saying? You want to use yourself as *bait*?'

I exhaled and closed my eyes. When I opened them again, I held his stare. 'He was here, Tim, right here in this room. He knew I'd be coming home soon, and that I'd likely be alone. If he wanted to take me a second time, or brandish a knife and eviscerate me on the living-room floor, there wasn't much stopping him. Instead, he bought me a fucking snack cake and pointed me in the direction of his next crime. I know it sounds crazy,' I told him, 'but if I ask him to meet me, I think he'll come.'

'No, Shana. No way.'

'I can't tell him to call. He knows we'd put a trace on it. He's too smart to agree to that.'

'If you ask to meet him in person, he'll know it's a trap.'

'Maybe. But he also believes he's too clever to get caught.'

'You're out of your mind!' Tim ground the heels of his hands into his eyes and paced the living room in his mud-dried Carhartt boots. 'None of this makes any sense. There's an entire task force looking for him already. Bram's unpredictable and dangerous. This is a man who slaughtered three innocent women and didn't hesitate for a second to kill a cop, who mutilated a nine-year-old child just to get your attention. I get that he's your cousin. I know he wasn't always like this, and I know you think you understand him. But Shana, you don't. You can't. He's a killer now, a sicko without an ounce of morality who lives to torment you. And you're talking about inviting him out for tea and goddamn crumpets.'

'We'll have Sol and Bogle and the troopers on standby. When I give the signal, they'll come out guns blazing.'

'He'll know. He's smart; you said so yourself. He won't come unprepared.'

'You don't understand.' My eyes had started to sting. I swiped at them and gave my head a hard shake. 'So much of what's happened is my fault. It's *me* he's after, and everyone else is collateral damage. I fucked up, Tim, so badly. In so many ways. Don't you see? This is my chance to make it right, the chance I've been waiting for all this time. You heard what Trey Hayes said. Bram told him about his girlfriends, including one we've never heard of before. In New York, three women dated Bram, and none of them survived. What if the same thing happened to Robyn?' For months now, that name had been gnawing at me like a rat with a scavenged bone. Who was she, and what did it mean that Bram mentioned her to Trey? 'Just because we don't have evidence of other crimes doesn't mean they don't exist.

There could be more victims out there,' I said, 'cold cases involving dead girls who had the misfortune of dating him. Families desperate for answers about their daughters and sisters and the animal who wrenched them from their lives. I'm finally in a position to leverage our history to find out more, map his crimes, and nab that fucker once and for all. Nobody else can do that, Tim. Nobody but me.'

Tim wouldn't look at me. A muscle jumped in his neck. 'You're out of your mind,' he said again, but despite his indignation I could already see him contemplating the idea. And I could see how much that scared him.

It scared me too. Playing decoy for a serial killer might be suicide.

It was also the only play we had.

SIXTEEN

Friday morning. It was pre-dawn, but I was fully dressed, standing in the living room of my rental cottage.

Staring at the body on my couch.

I'd never seen Tim asleep before, and while it made me feel like a bit of a creep, I relished the chance to study him freely. He was sprawled across the sofa like a toddler, one leg bent, arms flung over his head. His chin was tucked against his chest and his lips were parted. A lock of dark hair had fallen over his left eye, and with every breath he took, it fluttered. The lid of the right eye, the one I could see, was the palest shade of mauve.

We'd wedged a kitchen chair under the door handle as a temporary solution to the problem of the busted lock, but Tim still insisted on staying the night – of course he had. Loathe as I was to admit it, I'd enjoyed having a comforting presence in the house. The coffee maker on the counter was prepped and waiting, but I'd decided to forgo my usual, much-needed cup for fear the machine would wake him. I allowed myself to watch him for a few seconds longer. Then, very quietly, I reached for my jacket, inched the chair aside, and crept out the door.

The St Lawrence was covered in a layer of white mist, and it blended seamlessly with the sky to create a wall of soft gray, interrupted only by a cluster of trees that peaked through the fog across the bay. The world beyond my deck looked welcoming and benign. I knew better. I couldn't be sure how soon Bram would get close to the cottage again, but I had my guard up now, and no doubt he knew it. Tim had a friend who'd agreed to change the locks while I was at work, and I'd already placed an online order for a basic home security system I could install on my own. Unless he wanted to put himself at immediate risk, Bram wouldn't come back until he deemed it safe. Not unless he had a death wish.

I wouldn't be so much as using the bathroom without my sidearm, though.

Weapon in hand, I dialed the number my aunt had emailed me. It was way too early to be calling a stranger, but it took half the night for me to muster up the courage and I didn't want to risk losing my nerve.

Olivia Peck picked up midway through the first ring.

'Hello?' Her voice was throaty and toneless.

I may live to regret this, I thought. 'I'm sorry to be calling so early. This is Shana Merchant. You don't know me, but my aunt—'

'Detective Merchant. Or do you prefer senior investigator?'

So she did know me. A few yards away, a pair of ducks sailed across the water, their wings skimming the sleek surface. 'You've done your research,' I said.

'I was hired to find your cousin. I know all about your family.'

'Right.' A shiver swept up my arms. Initially, I'd planned to contact the woman strictly to keep tabs on her progress. Now, I hoped she would serve another purpose. If by some miracle I could convince Bram to meet me, I'd have exactly one chance to eke out every shred of information he had to offer. Why did he kill Becca, Lanie, and Jess? What did he want from me? Why, when he left town, did he never again

contact his family? My singular objective now was to apprehend him, but as soon as that happened his identity would be
made public, and the strain on my family would be unimaginable. They would have so many questions. The least I could
do was provide some answers.

That's where Olivia Peck came in.

'What have you found out so far?' I asked, pinning my
shoulders to the cottage wall. The siding wasn't as frosty as
I'd expected; slowly, the nights were getting warmer. 'Do you
have any leads?'

I half expected her to blow me off or at least insist I call
back at a reasonable hour, but Aunt Fee's PI was only too
eager to talk. 'I've made some headway, yes,' she said after
clearing her throat. 'Before I share what I've found, I have a
couple of questions for you.'

Peck reminded me of a headmaster at a boarding school, a
matronly, no-nonsense type who refused to take shit from
anyone. I could try to steamroll her and dominate the conversation, but I suspected I'd have more success getting what I
wanted if I adopted a passive role. 'OK,' I said. 'Ask away.'

There was a brief pause and a rustling of papers. 'Let's start
with an easy one. Did Abe ever contact you after he left
Swanton?'

That wasn't easy to answer at all. As Bram, he'd abducted
me and sent me cryptic messages. What Peck was after, though,
was news of a letter from one cousin to another. A secret
phone call in the night. 'No,' I said. 'Abe never contacted me
after he left.'

'Would you have told your aunt if he had?'

Any concerns I'd had about the caliber of Felicia's PI were
evaporating like the mist on the water. Olivia Peck sounded
confident and determined. I'd looked her up, and she didn't
have a website, not even a tacky one flaunting decades of
experience and stock images of squinty men with binoculars.
This lack of exposure suggested Peck knew the value of
anonymity. It was likely she relied entirely on word of mouth,
which spoke to her credibility. Good private eyes don't need
to advertise.

'What do you mean?' I asked innocently.

Peck made a sound deep in her throat. 'I've spent quite some time interviewing your aunt. From what I've heard, you and Abe were very close. As a cousin, as a friend, you were loyal to him, no?'

Abe running through a field of purple alfalfa by my side. Tucked into a sleeping bag on my bedroom floor. Eating tender, syrup-drenched French toast with my family. Quick as a wink, I saw it all. After a morning of sleuthing, our bikes would lie discarded on the front lawn because we couldn't get to the cold-damp box of popsicles in the freezer fast enough. There were bad times, too, when Abe refused to go back to his own house, which Felicia's crippling anxiety had transformed into a prison cell. But yes, I had been loyal.

'When we were younger,' I said, 'sure. We grew apart in high school. By the time he left, we weren't close at all.' It was the easiest way to describe the shitstorm that was our final month together. The friction caused by my realization that my cousin's mysteries were far from harmless. He'd brutalized an animal, framed our fellow students and neighbors for crimes they didn't commit, and alienated me from my friends, all so he could hold me in his dark little world. I'd abandoned Abe, and then he'd abandoned me – but not before giving me a physical reminder of the pain my desertion had caused. The scar he'd carved into my cheek with a rusty nail was a brand, a warning that, no matter where we were, I would always belong to him.

Abe had left Swanton. But I'd left him first.

I didn't like the way Peck silently pondered my response. Had we been face to face right then, I wondered if she might see through me. I tried to ignore the fact that she still might.

'What about friends?' she asked at last. 'Who was he close to, other than you? Parents don't always have the best handle on high school friendships. The fastest way to map a social circle is by asking someone who's in it.'

'No friends,' I said.

'Really? None?'

It wasn't accurate to call my cousin a loner since he had me, but Abe was never adept at navigating friendships. He might have shown empathy and compassion as a young child, but by the time he got to middle and high school, those qualities had faded away. 'Abe wasn't very social,' I said.

'I see.'

We'd only just begun to talk, but I wasn't sure how long I could keep up the ruse. On the other end of the line, Olivia Peck was dissecting my every word. Picking through the truth in search of a lie. If I hoped to find out what she knew, I needed her to trust me.

'That's what makes this all so strange,' I told her. 'When Abe left, he was totally alone. We all thought he went to live with his dad in Philadelphia, but of course we know now that wasn't the case. He had no other family there, or acquaintances I knew of. Up until that point, he'd spent his whole life in Vermont. He was sixteen years old, with no job or money – yet he managed to get all the way to Philly and make a new home there. I never understood how he pulled it off.'

The NYPD learned of Becca Wolkwitz's death in May of 2016. Within four months, two more victims, Lanie and Jess, were found as well. Then came my turn. But Bram had fled from Vermont in 2002. That left fourteen years unaccounted for. What I wanted to know, the information I craved with every fiber of my being, was what had happened in between. It was a big leap from maladjusted kid to serial murderer. Without understanding how he made it, I would never understand Blake Bram.

'If you're asking how your cousin survived after he left home, I may know something about that.' The pause that followed was excruciating. 'Russell Loming,' she said. 'Know him?'

I frowned. 'Of course I do.' Loming had been a friend of Uncle Brett's, the bad apple Brett spent all his time with in Swanton. What was Peck doing talking to Russell Loming?

'Loming says Brett used to complain about money. He wasn't good at keeping track of it,' Peck said. 'According to him, Brett made comments about that all the time – I could swear I had a tenner in my wallet, what happened to that twenty, that kind of thing. It's my belief that your cousin may have been stealing from Brett. Just a little here and there, not enough to get him caught. But enough to get him out of town.'

'Abe was twelve when Brett disappeared,' I said. 'He didn't run away till he was sixteen. Why would he start stealing from his father four years before he skipped town?'

That last sentence gummed up my throat so badly I could hardly get it out. Of course my cousin had stolen from Brett. Abe had taken money from our fifth grade teacher's purse when he was just ten years old, and blamed it on a classmate. He'd probably been stockpiling cash for years.

The breeze kicked up, and I drew my jacket tighter around me. Tim was right: I thought I understood my cousin.

I was dead wrong.

'I'm not saying he was planning his departure at age twelve,' Peck went on. 'My point is simply that he had some cash on hand. It isn't particularly hard to buy a fake ID. You know this, I'm sure. Lots of Chinese websites sell them, and did even back then. No mailing address? No problem. Abe could have gone to virtually any college campus and picked one up from a student for a hundred bucks in cash.'

'OK,' I said, 'let's say he bought a fake ID. Where did he go from there?'

'I'm working on that part. The fact that Abe disappeared so long ago makes this harder, but it isn't the first time I've had to follow a trail that's gone cold.'

You and me both. 'Well, I'd appreciate it if you'd keep me in the loop. I'd really like to know where he's been living and working all this time.'

'Sounds like you think he's alive.'

I swallowed hard. 'I guess I do.'

'Good,' Peck said, and for the first time since she picked up the phone, her voice held a semblance of warmth. 'I've worked dozens of missing persons cases, the vast majority of them fruitful. I'm confident I can find your cousin. It's good to keep the faith. These types of investigations can be full of surprises.'

Lady, I thought darkly, *wait till you find out the key to finding Abraham Skilton is me.*

SEVENTEEN

I arrived in Watertown to find Arcade Street cast in an ethereal, rose-tinted light. Dressed in a black karate gi with blue and white accents, Sensei Sam was waiting by the door, hands clamped on his wide hips.

'Two more minutes and you'd be looking at extra push-ups,' he said. His peaches and cream cheeks were high on his face, his mouth yanked up into a sly grin.

'Sorry. Got stuck on a call.'

'This early?' he said as he unlocked the door.

'No rest for the wicked.'

The words sounded ominous, even to me.

When I was on probation, with nothing but time on my hands, I'd been seeing my karate instructor once a week. Somehow since being reinstated I'd doubled my dojo time. It made no sense for me to keep coming back – the drive to Watertown was almost an hour round-trip, plus that hour of class time – but I craved the release of throwing kicks and punches, and returning to martial arts had done wonders for my confidence. Sam went out of his way to work around my schedule, which at the moment only allowed for classes on Mondays and Fridays at six a.m.

Today's session began with the usual warm-up of jumping jacks, crunches, and push-ups, which I finished quickly so we could move on to more productive things.

'You're on fire this morning,' said Sam approvingly. 'What should we work on this time?'

'Self-defense techniques,' I said without missing a beat.

He chuckled. 'We've been doing those for months. You know how to get out of a neck grab, evade a knife, and defend yourself against a club. On top of nineteen combinations, any one of which could be used for self-defense, you've got Combination Thirteen, so you can use your belt as a weapon if you find yourself unarmed. Kempo Karate is *all about* self-defense, Shana. Exactly what kind of techniques are you looking for?'

The ones that can guarantee I come out on top in a fight against a psychopath.

'My concern is response time,' I said, thinking about the previous night and what I would – or wouldn't – have done had Bram still been inside my house. 'I need to be able to react quickly.'

'That comes with time.'

Which is something I don't have. 'Can we speed up the process?' I was fully aware I sounded like an impatient newbie, but I couldn't help myself. 'Any chance you want to teach a one-person boot camp?'

I was joking, but only partly. Sam eyed me with curiosity. 'Why the sudden urgency?' he asked. Sam didn't know about Bram. All I'd told him when I started coming in was that I'd been attacked and was eager to advance my skills after a year-long karate hiatus.

'No time like the present,' I said.

'OK.' Sam locked his hands onto his hips once more. 'You've been at this for a while now. What, six years?'

'Give or take.'

'After that long, students sometimes benefit from going back to basics. Think about all the techniques and combinations you've learned so far. What are they for?'

'To protect myself. So I have the tools I need to react if I find myself threatened.'

'That's true,' Sam said, rubbing his short orange hair with his knuckles. 'But the thing people tend to forget is that fights rarely go according to plan. You may know how to get out of a lapel grab like we practiced.' He took a step toward me and grabbed the fabric of my gi top with both hands, holding me at arm's length. Reflexively, I snaked my hand over and between his arms, grabbed my own fist, and wrenched it upward to break his hold.

'See? You've got that down pat. But what happens if I do this?'

He grabbed me again – but this time, Sensei Sam pulled me forward. With his elbows bent, he held me firmly in place.

Our drills had brought me physically close to Sam dozens of times before. He'd pressed his body against mine to put me in a choke hold, and even flipped me onto my back on the mats. Sometimes I still felt the chemistry that fizzed between us, tingly and warm, but we'd both made the decision to ignore it and focus on the task at hand.

'If I change one thing about the attack,' Sam said, 'you need to change something, too. With Kempo, you don't just learn a technique – you learn all the different ways it can be executed. You have to be ready for anything.'

I didn't think, just reacted, with more speed and power than I would have thought possible. Before Sam could say another word, I'd simulated a foot stomp and mock-raked my nails across the bridge of his nose.

Sam let go of my gi and adjusted my lapels, smoothing them out over my clavicles. 'Good,' he said. 'Very good.' The note of pride in his voice made me blush.

'Ready for anything,' I repeated. Whatever Bram threw at me, I would rely on my training. Adjust my technique. Use what I knew against him.

It felt like I was preparing for battle.

Readying my mind and body for war.

'Breakfast?'

I wasn't much of a cook, but all my life I'd had the pleasure of big, hearty breakfasts in my childhood home, where cereal had been the precursor to eggs and Canadian bacon, fluffy waffles dotted with whipped cream and berries. So when I walked through my front door two hours later with pendulous arms and aching legs to find Tim slicing an enormous omelet in half, I could have kissed him.

'You're a godsend,' I said, accepting a plate and pouring us each a cup of the coffee he'd brewed while I was out.

'How was karate?'

'Invigorating. How was the couch?'

'Same.'

By the time we'd carried our plates to the small kitchen table, we were both grinning.

The breezy atmosphere didn't last.

'I talked to Olivia Peck, that PI Felicia hired,' I told Tim. 'She thinks Abe nicked money from Brett for years and used it to make a fresh start in Philadelphia.'

'OK,' he said cautiously while lifting a forkful of omelet to his mouth. 'And?'

'*And*, if he stole from his dad, maybe he stole after he left home, too. Maybe Peck will find some record of a sixteen-year-old thief with crooked teeth, we'll find out what name he was living under in Philly, and that will lead us farther down the trail.'

'In a city of a million and a half people?' Tim pushed a piece of hair, still damp from the shower, out of his eyes and shook his head. 'Look, I know how badly you want to understand the why and how of his life and crimes, but listen to yourself. You're becoming one of those cliché detectives from *America's Most Wanted*. You know the ones; they're *this close* to nabbing the perp, but they fail to apprehend him and he's never brought to justice for his crimes and they spend the next twenty years letting that eat them alive. The case haunts them their entire careers, all the way through to retirement. By then their marriage has fallen apart, and they hardly know their kids. They're so obsessed, so totally consumed by the lack of closure that, in some tragic, allegorical way, the detective ultimately loses *their* life to the killer, too.'

'Wow,' I said.

His shrug was unapologetic. 'It's the direction things are heading. You can't deny it. Why does it matter how Bram became such a monster? Why can't we just focus on putting him in prison where he belongs?'

Because, I thought. *Because he's blood, and I have to know.*

'Speaking of that,' I said with false exuberance, 'I think I know how we can bait him.'

In Vermont, Bram had communicated with me by letter, an envelope slipped into my parents' postbox. 'I can't say for sure he's been to my mailbox here, but we know he came to the cottage. If he's monitoring my life, it stands to reason he might monitor my mail.'

Tim tipped back his head in frustration and blinked at the

ceiling. 'Fuck,' he said again. 'You're doing this with or without me, aren't you.'

I nodded. 'I have to.'

Exhaling, he shoved his breakfast aside and pushed back his chair. 'Then there's only one way to find out.'

I kept a stack of envelopes and some note paper in the living room. Crouching next to the coffee table, with Tim looking over my shoulder, I started to write. I knew exactly what to say, having drafted and tweaked the message in my head into the small hours of the morning. When I was done, I sealed the envelope, and said a silent prayer.

We hadn't finished eating, yet neither Tim nor I returned to the kitchen table. Instead, we poured our coffees into two of my travel mugs and were out the door.

My mailbox was on East Riverfront, at the mouth of the private drive that led to my rental and a good fifty yards from my front door. I pulled my SUV up next to it and slid the letter inside. I would have liked to turn back, ditch the car and hunker down in the trees for hours or days, whatever it took until Bram showed his face. In order for this plan to work, though, I had to go about my normal life.

And it was time to make a visit to the former mayor of A-Bay.

EIGHTEEN

Picking up where we left off at work after everything that transpired the previous night felt like switching gears on an abandoned tractor brittle with rust. It would be a grind, but we had a job to do, and we couldn't let Bram get in the way of our caseload.

When we didn't find Harvey at Maynard Pope's house, we drove straight into town. Chateau Gris was on Fuller Street, steps from the River Hospital and just a block from busy James Street. Though I hadn't dined there, I'd admired the place since arriving in Alexandria Bay; Maynard Pope had chosen to locate his restaurant inside a two-story Victorian home with a wraparound porch, all of it painted sage green with creamy white trim. The tables inside were dressed with white linens, but according to Tim the food was served on rustic cutting boards, slate platters, and pewter charger plates that highlighted the house specialties.

Filet.

Pork belly.

Chickens stuffed with garlic-studded lemons, roasted whole.

Tim's account of the meat dishes on the menu made my mouth water.

We pushed open the door, and stepped inside.

To my surprise, the restaurant was bustling. Having heard Dori and Courtney's account of the boycott I'd expected it to be deserted, but every single table was full. After months of hanging on by a thread, Chateau Gris appeared to be back in action. The place was warm and cheerful, the air lush with the smell of fennel-spiced sausages. We were greeted by a harried server who seemed perturbed by our request to see the chef-owner. She pointed us in the direction of the kitchen and continued taking breakfast orders, a rivulet of sweat running down the side of her graceful neck.

In the kitchen, a young man in a rainbow-striped skull cap flipped eggs and rotated sausages on a flat-top grill. A meat grinder sat abandoned on a prep counter, surrounded by strings of empty sausage casings, but there was no sign of Maynard Pope.

'He around?' I asked after we introduced ourselves to Pope's sous-chef.

'He'll be back in a sec,' the man said, not taking his eyes off the grill. I was about to suggest to Tim that we wait out front when he elbowed me in the ribs and gestured toward the back of the room.

At some point, the kitchen in the old house had been expanded to incorporate what must have originally been servants' quarters. Now, that space was an alcove housing a table and banquette that faced the prep area, the sort of exclusive chef's table I'd seen people eat at in the movies. An elderly man sat alone, a cup of tea by his side. *The great*

Harvey Oberon, at last. I could see the resemblance to Santa, but only a little. Harvey Oberon had white hair and a beard to match, but both were thin and brittle, and though he might have been a big man once there was a sparseness to him now, too much meat stripped from his frame. His eyes were sunken, his chest hollowed out. He was little more than a jumble of bones. Also on the table was a bowl of dried pasta and a roll of butcher's twine. One by one, with spotted, knobbly knuckles, Harvey worked the noodles onto the string.

'It's great to see you, sir,' Tim said as we approached. 'You're looking well.' Even though I'd never laid eyes on the man before, it was plain Tim was just being polite. I'd been worried he was going to fawn all over the guy, whom he clearly admired, but instead he eyed Harvey with grave concern as if he expected the once-vibrant man to succumb to death on the spot.

'Hello.' Harvey managed a smile. Though he was looking right at us, his light eyes were vacant and glazed. 'Window, or something in the back?'

'Oh, no, we're not here to eat. Mr Oberon, I'm Shana Merchant and this is Tim Wellington. We're investigators here in town. Can we talk a minute?'

The man looked puzzled, but he bobbed his head and we joined him at the table.

'We're very sorry about your daughter Hope, sir,' I said. 'I know this must be a difficult time.'

'Investigators.' Harvey furrowed his brow. His voice was like wet gravel. 'So it was you.'

'I'm sorry?' I said, confused.

'No sympathy, none at all. You bastards hung her out to dry. I guess you're here about the bribes, is that it? I told you yesterday, I don't know a goddamn thing. Throw me in jail too if you have to, but I won't say a bad word against my Hope.'

It was bizarre, watching the man relive a moment from the recent past. He felt it so deeply his lower lip trembled and his hands curled themselves into fists.

'Bad day.'

The voice behind us gave me a start. I turned to see that Maynard Pope was standing in the doorway to what seemed to be a basement storage room. He was carrying a pork shoulder, pink and marbled, on a metal tray, and over his black T-shirt and jeans he wore an apron that had once been white but was now streaked with blood. It was brown in places, vibrant red in others, and there was a smudge of crimson on his cheek so close to his mouth that looking at it made me queasy.

'He has good days and bad,' Pope said, still planted in place.

I wasn't sure how to respond. Even after hearing Pope describe Harvey's mental state, I wasn't prepared for him to appear so lost. I kept picturing the man playing host on one of the islands, greeting his guests as they arrived by boat – a classic motor yacht, maybe, with a starched American flag on a pole at its stern – to join the festivities. I saw him commanding a room of town council members. Glad-handing voters along a parade route. 'Mr Oberon,' I said, looking into his eyes, 'I think you may have mistaken us for someone else. We're homicide detectives. We weren't involved in the corruption case.'

Harvey gave a snort and returned his attention to the dried noodles before him.

'Give us a sec, Harve,' Pope said. He motioned for us to join him by the prep counter, where he set down the tray and kept working on the sausages. The metallic stink of raw pork filled my nose as I watched Hope's widower slap the meat onto the counter and, forearms flexing, work a knife through the layer of intramuscular fat.

'Keeps him busy,' Pope explained of the noodles on the table. 'His doctor recommended it. She calls it a "failure-free activity". It's supposed to help him feel successful. I'm sorry, but if you were hoping to talk to him, your timing isn't great. He's been struggling more than usual since I broke the news about Hope.'

'Would he mind?' I asked. 'Talking to us?'

Pope's mouth twisted. 'Probably not.'

'Then do you mind if we try?'

'Is it really necessary?' he asked as he fed a chunk of meat through the machine.

I didn't want to push Harvey, not in the state he was in. We did have questions, though, and despite his current condition I suspected he'd want us to have the answers if they could help us identify Hope's killer. 'We have some new information we really need to ask him about,' I said.

Pope shifted his weight from one foot to the other. 'All right, but don't expect much. And I should stay with him.' He glanced behind him, at the pass-through to the dining room. The chatter of the diners was punctuated by laughter and the piercing plink of silverware against china. 'I don't have much time. I wasn't expecting it to be so busy, and I've got a ton of prep to do for lunch and dinner.'

'This won't take long,' I promised as Pope wiped his hands on his apron and the three of us joined Harvey at the table.

'A waste of time, is what this is.' Harvey was poking at the noodles with a cracked and yellowed fingernail. In a fit of frustration he swept his forearm across the table, sending dried pasta bouncing across the floor. What must it feel like to be treated like a child at the age of eighty-one? I tried not to let my pity for the man show, and could tell Tim was doing the same.

'I want to let you know, Mr Oberon, that regardless of what happened in Watertown your daughter's a victim now. We're not here to judge her,' I said. 'We're doing everything we can to apprehend the person responsible for her death.'

A trickle of tear slipped from his rheumy eyes. Angrily, roughly, he rubbed it away.

'Did you and Hope talk often?'

'She called me every day.' His eyes swooped to Pope, as if seeking confirmation. Pope gave an infinitesimal nod.

'And did Hope ever mention feeling threatened?'

'Threatened? What do you mean?' Pope asked. But the former mayor had narrowed his eyes.

'Ah,' said Harvey, tapping his temple. 'You're talking about those letters.'

I drew in a breath. 'You know about those?'

'Letters?' said Pope, looking perplexed. 'Who from?'

'We have a statement from a witness who says Hope received a couple of upsetting letters,' Tim explained. 'We're treating them as threats.'

Pope looked aghast. 'What the hell?' he said, palms braced against the lip of the table, but I raised my hand. *Wait. Please.*

'Mr Oberon,' I went on, 'what do you know about the letters Hope received?'

He nudged the remaining noodles around and started rolling one under his thick thumb. 'Someone was angry with Hope about the wind farm. Angrier than most.'

Tim leaned forward. 'Did she mention a name?'

Harvey started to shake his head, but then he froze. 'It sounded like a lady's name to me. Italian.'

'I don't understand this,' said Pope. 'Someone sent my wife death threats and I'm only hearing about it now? Why didn't she tell me?' He looked at his father-in-law. 'Why didn't *you*?'

'Wasn't my place to tell,' said Harvey, 'if she didn't want you to know.'

'We don't have any record of her reporting the letters to the police. And we haven't been able to locate them,' said Tim.

'Our witness believes Hope disposed of them. The man who wrote them claims he had no ill intentions toward Hope,' I put in. 'It's our witness's word against his. Any chance you know what happened to those letters, Mr Oberon?'

'She threw them away. Horrible things in those letters, just horrible.'

Pope looked stunned. 'Are you saying you think this guy had something to do with Hope's death?'

'We're looking into it. It's helpful to know she mentioned the letters to Harvey. It corroborates our witness's story,' I said, 'and suggests the sender wasn't being honest with us.'

'Who is it? Who's the sender?'

'We can't tell you that yet, Mr Pope, but believe me, we're taking these threats very seriously.'

'It's not right,' Harvey said. 'All my ladies, gone.' His eyes brimmed with tears again. This time, they spilled over onto his liver-spotted cheeks.

'Ah, shit.' Pope slumped in his seat. 'The past few years haven't been easy, losing Diane and then Hope. Having all these problems with his health.' He slid a hand onto Harvey's frail shoulder, linking them together in pain.

Pope's words put me in mind of what he said at the house,

about wishing Harvey so wrecked by dementia that he wouldn't have to experience another tragedy. Soon, he might not remember losing his loved ones at all.

But the good memories would disappear with the bad.

'It sounds like you and your daughter were very close,' I said to Harvey.

'She's our only child, me and Diane. Hope's the most wonderful girl.'

'An accomplished adult, too. She had a BA in finance from NYU,' I said, 'isn't that right? And she worked a corporate job after graduating from college?' Tim had found Hope's LinkedIn profile online, but even without the insight we were able to glean from her résumé, we knew a lot from reading recent back issues of the local paper. Cataloguing a person's success was always a popular way for reporters to highlight their faults.

'New York is where we met,' Pope told us. 'We moved here when Natalie was ten. She's back now. Got home last night.' He winced and hung his head. 'She had car problems, otherwise she would have come sooner. She's with my parents for now, over in Chippewa Bay.'

'Natalie's a good girl,' said Harvey. 'Just like her mother.'

'It must have been very stressful for all of you, with the investigation and the charges brought against Hope,' I said.

Pope nodded. 'It was awful. The things they wrote about her – not just in Watertown, but here, too. And after everything Harvey did for them.'

'As mayor, you mean?'

'The beaches, new playgrounds, boat tours to bring in more sightseers – that was all him. He treated every person in this town like family. Isn't that right, Harve?'

'And invited them to parties that were bigger than most weddings,' Tim said.

At the mention of parties Harvey perked up, and when he spoke his jowls quivered like a terrine from the Chateau Gris menu. 'I'm always up for a good party. It gets cold out there, this time of year. We could make a fire, though. Bonfires always draw a crowd. Bonfires and booze and beautiful women.'

The old man looked ready to push up from the table and get the planning underway. Pope gave his sloped upper back a pat. 'There's not going to be a bonfire, Harve. That was a long time ago, remember? There hasn't been a party in years.' Pope let his mouth slip into an anguished smile as he redirected his gaze. 'Some things never change. Harvey has the most amazing stories about those parties, and he'll yak to anyone who'll listen.' He paused as the realization sunk in; it might not be long before those stories vanished, too. 'He never did anything halfway, and every shindig was grander than the last. Diane had to work hard to rein in his spending.'

'Diane always says I have big shoes,' said Harvey.

I looked to Pope for clarification, but he just shook his head.

'Big shoes,' Tim repeated, tilting his head. 'Big shoes to fill, you mean?'

'Diane used to make Hope put her feet inside my slippers. We told her to work hard like her daddy so she could do even more.' The memory lit up the man's face, but the effect was fleeting. 'She dreamed of being mayor herself one day.'

'Is that right?' I asked Pope, who nodded.

'She looked up to Harvey, and she was always interested in helping the community.'

Tim said, 'The apple doesn't fall far from the tree, I guess.'

'Hope didn't mean any harm,' Harvey said. 'She was just trying to help.'

'That's right,' said Pope, as much to his father-in-law as to us. 'Hope made a mistake, but she cared about people. She wanted to provide more reliable electricity, tax relief, another source of revenue for farmers. That wind farm would have done wonders for the community. She would have used that money the developer was offering to transform the city, just like Harvey did here.'

'She didn't deserve this,' Harvey said, sliding a noodle onto the string once more. 'She made a mistake. We all make mistakes.'

I felt sorry for the man, so shrunken now. His vim snuffed out and his wife and daughter – his ladies – gone.

When he looked up from the table, Harvey held my gaze. 'Hope didn't deserve this at all.'

NINETEEN

On the way back to the lead desk, where we'd spend the afternoon documenting our findings and comparing notes with Bogle and Sol, I took out my phone and checked my email. I knew it could be a few more days until we got the results of our victim's autopsy report, and that there might not be much else to learn about her death, but I was ever hopeful. There was nothing new in my inbox from the forensic pathologist.

What I found instead was a message from the Oyster Point Marina in Norwalk, Connecticut.

The marina had been on my list, and I'd filled out the email form on its website contact page Tuesday night. Now, a reply – a long-winded one, at that.

In the off season, most marinas checked their email infrequently, if at all. The owner of Oyster Point, a man named John J. Pearson, wrote that while he normally wintered in Florida, his daughter was about to have her second child and he and his wife were still in town. I'd started every one of my messages the same way: *Apologies for the strange inquiry, but I'm looking for an old friend, and I have reason to believe he may have worked for you.* I offered no explanation for how I knew this – there was none to be had – and didn't identify myself as law enforcement. It was a wonder I'd gotten a response at all.

All the more reason for John J. Pearson's reply to flood my chest with heat. He wrote:

> I think I know the guy you're talking about. He was here for a summer a few years ago. He walked in off the street and said he'd take any job he could get. Didn't know a darn thing about boats, but I liked his enthusiasm. Is your friend's name Seth Williams?

Seth. It was the fake name Bram had used in the East Village, the night he drugged and abducted me. Could it be?

In the driver's seat, Tim was lamenting Hope's fall from grace. 'She was like town royalty once,' he said. 'That family was unstoppable.' I nodded absently as I typed my reply to Pearson. *I have a picture. Is there any way I could stop by to show it to you?* I was reluctant to email the composite sketch that was currently making the rounds of New York State. I didn't want to give him too long with the image, or time enough to do some research of his own. Tomorrow was Saturday and neither Tim nor I were on call.

'. . . that they remember Hope for who she was, instead of what she did. What do you think?'

'Hm?' I looked up from my screen.

'What has you so absorbed over there? Please don't tell me Mom got you hooked on Candy Crush. That woman is obsessed.'

Obsessed. I was getting tired of hearing that word.

That was nobody's fault but my own.

'Hey,' I said, tilting my head in his direction. 'What are you doing tomorrow?'

TWENTY

We left for the coast of Connecticut first thing Saturday morning, stopping once for gas and stale blueberry muffins just north of Binghamton, arriving in Norwalk before noon. John J. Pearson had agreed to meet for lunch at a takeout joint next to the Long Island Sound that was painted buoy-red and smelled of fry oil. We ordered three containers – fried scallops for Pearson, clam bellies for Tim and me – with sides of sweet coleslaw and fries, and settled down at a ketchup-stained picnic table. I could taste salt in the air. Seaweed, too. Norwalk Harbor twinkled beside us, and the joints of the docks knocked against each other with every swell. In the distance, across the Sound, Long Island was a muzzy slash across the horizon.

Did Bram know this view, too?

'Of course I'll come with you,' Tim had said with all the grit of a vengeful cowboy when I told him my plan to drive to the coast.

'It's your whole Saturday. This guy I'm meeting is almost six hours away.'

'I'd cross the freaking Atlantic if that's where this messed-up Easter egg hunt takes you.'

Touched, I'd thanked him, and paid for his lunch.

'How's your daughter?' I asked John Pearson as I bit into a clam belly, its crisp coating giving way to the juicy-firm shellfish underneath.

'She's fine, thanks for asking,' he said through a proud grin. Pearson was in his sixties, with a gray goatee, windswept movie-star hair, and what I suspected was a year-round tan. The guy lived on the water, both in Connecticut and Florida, and it showed. 'Number two is no less exciting than the first. We're all waiting anxiously for the kiddo to arrive. Got any of your own?'

His eyes pinged back and forth between Tim and me as he said it. I had already taken another bite and nearly choked on my roll. I'd introduced Tim as my partner. 'No,' I said. 'I mean, not yet.'

From the corner of my eye, which teared from all the coughing, I caught Tim's smile.

Pearson plunged a scallop into a cup of tartar sauce. 'Why don't you tell me about your friend?'

'He left home – northern Vermont – years ago. I've been trying to track him down ever since.' Better to make this sound like a legitimate search than the vigilante effort it was.

'What makes you think he came here?'

'Process of elimination. He was in New York last year,' I said. 'He spent some time in Philly, too. Somewhere along the way, he learned how to boat.' I thought of Trey, and what Bram said about saltwater. 'I got a tip that he'd worked at a marina, so I've been calling all over the place. You're my first solid lead.'

'You sound like Magnum, PI,' he said as he soaked up the grease from his fingers with a paper napkin.

I attempted a laugh. 'If that's what it takes. He's been gone a long time.' I reached into my purse. 'He might not look exactly like this anymore.'

'Let's have a peek,' Pearson said.

'I had a friend draw this up,' I lied, ignoring the stab of guilt. 'To age him.' I unfolded the paper and handed it over, hoping Pearson wouldn't recognize the image as a police sketch. As he studied Bram's face, I did the same. Even upside down, the drawing was disturbing. It was astounding to me how skilled Bram was at changing his appearance, how easily he could slip into a whole new skin. I said, 'Does that look like Seth?'

I watched with discomfort as Pearson's handsome, lively face morphed into a mask of confusion. What would I do if he recognized Bram? Norwalk was just an hour from Manhattan. The people here got their news from Hartford and New Haven, but they picked up New York stations, too. Pearson might have seen the reports: *Lower East Side Killer Moves Upstate. Abducted Child Saved, Fugitive Escapes.* And here I was, introducing myself as Blake Bram's long-lost pal.

'Wow,' Pearson said. 'No offense to your friend, but it's not the most flattering picture, is it? This makes it look like the guy gained fifty pounds.'

My chest tightened.

'Is it him?' Tim asked, planting his elbows on the table.

'Definitely. He worked for me the summer of 2015. It's the eyes,' Pearson said, gesturing loosely to his own, which were hooded and hazel.

'You're sure?' I said.

'You don't forget eyes like that.'

Behind him – Pearson had insisted Tim and I take the seats overlooking the Sound – a seagull twirled in the breeze. If my math was right, Bram had gone from the marina in Connecticut straight to New York, where he'd worked as a janitor in a residential building for a little over a year. He might have been plotting to abduct me even before he left New England.

'What can you tell us about him?' Tim asked.

I said, 'Did he leave a forwarding address? A cell number?'

'Whoa, slow down.' Pearson squished a lemon wedge over his last battered scallop, popped it into his mouth, and pushed the empty container aside. 'Between you, me, and the seagulls, Seth wasn't exactly on the payroll. I hire a couple dockhands every year, to help people fuel up, greet the owners, and get the boats into dry storage come fall. I usually end up with high schoolers or college kids who are happy to be paid under the table, but sometimes an older guy comes around needing work, and I'll make an exception.'

'What made you want to make an exception for Seth?' Bram, the name he used now, was always close at hand. I'd almost let it slip a few times already. I had to be careful.

'He had a story. I'm a sucker for a good story.' He scratched his thick goatee. 'He told me he grew up near a lake but didn't know much about boats, even though he'd always wanted to learn.'

'That's true,' I said. Or true enough.

'Well, I couldn't bring myself to deny a man a chance to experience life on the water. I asked one of the summer kids to teach him to drive a skiff. He was grateful, and a good worker. At first.'

'At first?'

His expression darkened. 'Look, I don't want to speak ill of your friend.'

'It's OK. I want to know. It could be important for helping us find him.'

Pearson said, 'If you say so. I don't like trouble at my marina. I expect my staff to get along, and I tell them that upfront. But Seth . . . back in the days when we were all politically incorrect, I would have called him a ladies' man. And it wouldn't have been a compliment.'

I felt my pulse flutter. 'What are you saying, exactly?'

'There was this girl working here and, well, he put his hands where he shouldn't. That's really all I know about it, because that's all I needed to hear. I fired the guy on the spot. I've had my marina for seventeen years, I got no interest in getting involved with a sexual assault charge, you know?'

Wouldn't be good for business, I thought, trying hard to

tamp down my anger. At least Pearson had done the right thing by firing Bram. 'This girl. Do you remember her name?'

'I'll have to look that up – but I can access work email on my phone. We exchanged a lot of messages about the situation at the time. She wasn't too comfortable talking about it in person.'

'Was there anyone else?' I asked as he took out his cell and swiped through his email files. 'Any other women who reported inappropriate behavior?'

'You sure you're not a cop?' A wink and a smile. 'Not as far as I know,' he said, 'but none of the girls I had working for me that summer liked him. It was the way Seth looked at them, they said. It made them feel . . . I don't know . . .'

'Hunted.'

'Hunted.' Pearson nodded slowly, holding my gaze until his phone came alive with a buzz. 'Oh.' He looked down. 'It's a text from my wife. Could be about Brielle and the baby.'

'Go ahead,' I said as I started to clear the table. 'We'll clean up here.' After confirming that Pearson would forward me the employee's name and contact information, we thanked the man for his help.

'Sure thing.' He pumped my arm. 'Hey, good luck finding your friend.'

Watching him turn toward his car and, beyond that, his family, I thought, *We'll need it.*

TWENTY-ONE

Kyla Tomlin's apartment overlooked the Norwalk River. We caught her as she was stepping out to meet a friend at a nearby park. Spring was farther along in Connecticut than up north, and the cherry and magnolia trees that lined the city streets were already in full bloom, their heavy blossoms weighing down branches and plastering the sidewalks with pink. I didn't think it likely a young woman would dish to two strangers who approached her on the street, so this time, we introduced ourselves as investigators with the BCI.

Kyla agreed to let us walk with her. She remembered Seth, and confirmed he was the man from our sketch. It had been three years since she worked for Pearson's marina, and she still had nightmares about my cousin.

'I always wondered if someone would show up asking about him,' she said in a bleak tone of voice as she hiked her handbag higher on her shoulder.

'Can you tell us about your relationship with Seth?' I asked.

'It's the classic scenario – which makes me feel like a total cliché. He was cute and sweet. At first. We dated for a few weeks,' she said.

'You dated.' I stared at her for a long moment. 'What did you talk about during that time?'

'Talk about?' she repeated, tipping her head away from us. 'The usual, I guess. Likes and dislikes. He asked a lot of questions about me.' We were passing a tiny white church that looked abandoned, the structure completely at odds with the glass-and-steel apartment buildings all around, but Kyla took no notice. Her attention was solely on us.

'Did he talk about his family?' I asked, and held my breath.

'A little. He said they were back in Vermont. I got the sense they weren't that close. He talked about a cousin. A girl. Her, he couldn't stop blabbing about.'

I swallowed. Nodded. I couldn't speak.

With a sideways glance in my direction, Tim said, 'John Pearson mentioned an incident. Seth did something he shouldn't have. Can you tell us about that?'

Kyla still had one hand locked on the strap of her purse. With the other, she tucked a strand of russet hair behind her ear. 'He fired Seth because of that. Pearson acted like he was doing me this huge favor, but I'd been complaining to him for a long time by then. I'd broken it off with Seth, but he didn't want to accept it. He kept harassing me at work, asking why I didn't want to be with him. Telling me we were meant for each other. He would follow me to my car after work and yell at me, and once he grabbed my arm and shook me. Like, really hard. So yeah, Pearson fired him. But Seth didn't leave me alone.'

We waited for her to go on, listening to the scuff of our boots and shoes on the sidewalk. Close to the river, Kyla's neighborhood smelled faintly of the slime on the stems of week-old cut flowers.

'One night, after being out with some friends, I got back to my place and found him waiting outside. He was acting all shifty. Honestly, I thought maybe he was on drugs. He launched into a speech about how I was making a big mistake, all the stuff he'd said a million times before. I ignored him and tried to go inside, but he pulled me around the side of the building, into the parking garage.'

'What happened then?' Tim asked in a voice soft as goose down. 'What did he do?'

Kyla stopped walking and shook out her arms. 'I should have reported it. I know that. But he'd already been fired, and after that night he just . . . disappeared. I never saw him again. I didn't want to talk about it. I just wanted to forget he existed, you know?'

'What happened in the parking garage? Please,' said Tim. 'It's important.' Next to him, I was trembling.

Kyla bit her lip, dragging her teeth across the skin again and again until she'd shaved off her lipstick and left a purple welt. 'He pushed me up against the wall. He had a knife,' she said, her voice cracking. 'The kind that flips open. He showed it to me. He held it right up to my face and said dating me had been a mistake. That he thought I understood him but he was wrong.'

In New York, Bram's victims had all been stabbed. Jess had more than a dozen distinct wounds on her chest, abdomen, and throat. The nature and pattern of the gashes were consistent across all three victims, but we never managed to find the murder weapon.

'He threatened you,' I said, holding Kyla's gaze.

Her eyes were shiny now, brimming with tears. 'He kept saying he was wrong about me, and that he had to fix that. I swear to God, I thought he was going to kill me. But then this car pulled into the lot. It slowed down to go through the gate, and I guess the driver saw us, Seth holding me up against the wall. He rolled down his window and yelled something,

I don't even know what. Seth got spooked and ran away. The driver started to get out of his car, but I was so scared that I ran off, too.'

Victim accounts aren't always inch-perfect, especially when they describe an event that happened years ago. Upon hearing this story, though, there wasn't a doubt in my mind that had a car not pulled into the lot at that moment, Kyla Tomlin would be dead.

Pearson had told us he usually hired college kids. Like Bram, Kyla was one of his rare older employees. She was in her late twenties when she worked at the marina and dated Seth Williams. She shared other traits with his victims, too. Kyla was Caucasian, with an athletic build. Just like Becca, Lanie, and Jess.

Just like me.

TWENTY-TWO

It was dinner time when we passed the sign for the local mobile home resort – featuring a giant goose pulling a camper, the thing was iconic – and rolled into Alexandria Bay. Even though Tim and I shared the driving duties, we were both bleary-eyed and exhausted. Still, we'd made plans to meet Mac, and we intended to keep them. By six thirty, the three of us had draped our jackets over the bar stools at the Riverboat Pub and were attacking wedge salads, Italian chicken sandwiches, and soda fountain Cokes.

It didn't take long for us to get Mac up to speed on our trip to Norwalk. I'd been routinely feeding her updates on my investigation into Bram's post-Swanton history, and she didn't like the news of his behavior toward his female co-worker any more than I did. On the other side of the bar Matt Cutts, the barkeep, swept over to the nearby sink and began washing beer glasses, twirling each one on an upright brush before transferring them to the drying rack. We waited until he'd moved on again before veering the conversation toward Hope's case.

As I attempted to saw into a hunk of iceberg lettuce without elbowing the sheriff and my top investigator in the ribs, Mac asked after Harvey.

'How did he seem?' she said before taking a long, appreciative sip of her soda.

'Heartbroken. Sounds like they were close,' I said.

'Harvey talked a lot about how Hope followed in his footsteps professionally by going into local politics,' said Tim. 'He made it sound like all the goodwill he built up with this town has been washed down the river.'

I nodded as I swiped a daub of salad dressing from the crook of my mouth, but my eyes had started to roam the room. *Big man with a bomber jacket, sitting at the bar. Older guy alone at a table, keeping his chin tucked into his scarf.* It was always the same routine for me, the same fretful cataloguing of faces as I searched for the one that belonged to my flesh and blood.

'It's sad,' Tim said. 'You'd think people would see things differently after her death, especially with everyone so loyal to her family.'

'Not everyone.' Matt had returned to the sink once more to plunge liquor-sticky hands into the soapy water. 'Sorry,' he said, flushing red as the Rose's grenadine on the shelf behind him. 'Didn't mean to eavesdrop.'

I studied his face. According to Tim, who grew up with him, Matt had been bartending ever since his twenty-first birthday and had considered this place his second home for even longer. The Riverboat was owned by his father, Avery, and Matt had been brought up inside its wood-paneled walls. Even Matt's mother helped out with the business, keeping the books for decades before her death a few years prior.

'Don't worry,' Tim told me. 'You can trust Matt. His family's one of the oldest in town. How's Lisa? And the girls?'

'Good, good,' Matt said. 'Charmaine has four loose teeth right now. I'm thinking of starting a GoFundMe.'

Laughing, I asked, 'What's your beef with the Oberons?'

Matt's forearms were ruddy now, and the air smelled of orange-scented soap. 'Not me,' he said. 'But you hear things when you're behind the bar. It's kind of like being a priest in a confessional, except the congregation doesn't know you're listening.'

Matt's grin, when it finally emerged, creased the skin around his eyes and brought out a dimple on his left cheek, right where his beard began. Though the beard was short, he didn't bother to keep it neat, and whirls of dark hair crept down his throat toward his shirt collar. He was a good-looking man, with the kind of mouth that angles up at the corners even when he's being serious. 'Are you honor-bound to keep their secrets?' I asked. It came out sounding more flirtatious than I'd intended.

Another smile. 'Depends on who's asking.'

Christ. Now I was blushing in front of Tim, which made me want to step outside and jump into the river. I could feel him watching me. Under my shirt, my chest was hot.

Matt had helped out with one of our investigations before. While working the Sinclair case, Tim and I needed to look into Billy Bloom, a trapper who'd been working out on Tern Island the day Jasper Sinclair disappeared. Matt had provided an alibi, helping us knock the trapper off our suspect list. He'd taken Bloom's keys after the man got tanked at the pub, and even called Bloom's wife to come pick him up. Matt Cutts had always struck me as a stand-up guy.

'So what have you heard about Harvey?' I said.

'For starters, he wanted to build a resort, over there on the shore next to Greens Creek.' Matt nodded in that general direction. 'People weren't too crazy about the idea of a big tourist trap, but Harvey was like a dog with a bone.'

'I think I heard about that,' Tim said. 'The place was supposed to be huge.'

'When was this?' I asked.

'Oh, early eighties. People still gossip about it even now. It was my dad who told me. Harvey's plan was pretty ambitious. It would have completely transformed this place.'

'But this whole town's built on tourism,' I said. 'Why wouldn't people want a nice new resort?'

'Big is good, but it isn't always charming. The place was going to be real flashy, with live concerts, maybe even a casino. It took a lot of convincing for Harvey to concede defeat. Listen,' Matt said, 'Harvey did a lot for this town. Every day, I look around and see things he made happen that are benefiting my kids even now. But he had some qualities that maybe aren't so great in a mayor. It's not all about fancy hotels and parties.'

'Ah,' said Mac. 'There it is: Harvey Oberon's true legacy.'

'Did you ever go?' I asked. 'To one of those parties?' Mac was only fifty; if she'd reached legal drinking age in that era, it would have been by the skin of her teeth.

'Too young, sadly,' she said.

'My parents went,' said Tim.

'Mine too,' said Matt. 'Well, my mom anyway. She used to talk about them like they were the highlight of her life. We supplied the liquor, and Mom did the deliveries.'

I felt my eyes widen. 'All by herself?' Based on the crowds I'd seen in Dori's photos, that was no small feat.

'Crazy, right? But Dad didn't like her working the bar alone.' When I picked up my soda and used a straw to stir warped cubes of half-melted ice, Matt reached for a coaster and slipped it under the glass for me. 'She said those years were the most profitable in the pub's history, and I'm sure Dad would agree. You can ask him; he's around here somewhere.' Matt tossed a glance over his shoulder, toward the door to the basement storage room. 'Would you believe someone just ordered a wine slushy? And it's not even tourist season yet. Dad thought we had a bottle of mix downstairs. Anyway,' he went on with a roll of his eyes, 'those parties were a huge scene. But for the people who didn't care to go, putting up a new water tower and repaving the roads was probably more important.'

'Sounds like Harvey was' – I searched for the most diplomatic word – 'strong-minded.' That fit with my impression of the man in his youth.

'Yeah,' Matt said. 'I think Hope was, too.'

'What have you heard about her death?' I asked after Matt offered us a refill on our Cokes. He clearly had a bead on the local intelligence. I loosened up my voice so he'd know this wasn't an interview. *Best to keep it light.*

'People are really shaken up about that,' he said, reaching for my glass with one hand and the soda gun with the other. Then he leaned in closer, and we did the same. 'Most people think it was that guy who did it. Blake Bram.'

The name jolted me like an electric shot, and I felt Tim and Mac stiffen beside me. It was still surreal, hearing Bram's name spoken by someone other than Carson and the task force, and it brought the scope of his notoriety into stark relief. I was used to seeing references in the paper, but this was a different experience entirely. On our side of the bar, where Matt couldn't see, Mac put her hand on my knee and gave it a supportive squeeze.

'What makes them think that?' I willed my voice not to falter.

As the air around our fresh sodas sparkled and fizzed, Matt sighed in a way that exposed his dimple once more and looked over our heads at the windows. They were black now, the view outside masked by the night, but I could still sense the river crammed with all those islands. Eighty miles' worth of places to hide. 'The sheriff knows better than I do,' Matt said with a respectful nod at Mac, 'but before that kid got abducted at Boldt Castle, and before that crazy situation out on Tern, I don't think there'd been a murder around here for at least a decade.'

'This past year has been a real anomaly,' Mac confirmed, echoing her former words. I knew she wouldn't point out that the trouble began when I arrived in town. I also knew nobody blamed me for what, in tiny A-Bay, qualified as a crime spree. The conversation was making me a bundle of nerves all the same.

'Not going to lie,' Matt said as his eyes traveled the room just as mine had moments before, 'I'm freaking terrified. Every guy who comes in here, I study his face and compare it to the sketch they printed in the paper. I've got it right here, behind the bar. Taped up next to Reeba and Charmaine's school photos. My girls get on the bus every day just like that poor kid did, and not a minute goes by that I'm not worried they won't make it home.'

I watched the dark hairs on Matt's forearms pull away from the skin. This was *Bram's* legacy. He sowed terror like seeds wherever he went and luxuriated in watching them take root. 'I don't know what's worse,' Matt said, 'knowing there's a monster out there who's targeting our town, or having no clue what he's going to do next. The papers say he killed three women in New York, but then suddenly he shows up here and snatches a kid? Why? And what about Hope? She doesn't even fit the profile of the women he kidnapped before. He's a psycho who's killing indiscriminately, which is scary as hell.'

Matt's comments surprised me. Praying my voice didn't belie my unease, I said, 'It sounds like you know a bit about him.'

'I listen to those true crime podcasts. You know the ones: people revisiting cold cases, speculating about where the police went wrong. I've always enjoyed that stuff. It's not that much fun lately, for obvious reasons, but I've learned a thing or two about violent criminals.'

Cold cases were of interest to me, too. I contemplated asking Matt for some podcast recommendations, but thought better of it.

'So the people you've overheard talking in here,' Tim said, 'they figure it was him.'

'Has to be. They're calling him the Lady Killer, which isn't very original, but hey, if the shoe fits. I mean, who else would want Hope dead?'

'Well,' I said, anxious to steer the conversation away from Bram, 'that brings us back to your point. Not everyone likes the Oberons, Hope especially.'

'What she did was bad, no question,' said Matt. 'But it's not like she got off scot-free. She was caught, and she was about to pay for her crime. What would be the point of killing her now? And yeah, not everyone likes her family, but that's nothing new. No, it's gotta be Blake Bram.'

I wanted so badly for him to be wrong, not just to allay my own guilt, which had some serious tonnage these days, but for the sake of the community I'd grown to love. At the same time, I was starting to wonder if Tim and I should disabuse ourselves of the notion that we were looking for a new killer. If we were wrong, then all the time we'd spent investigating Val Giovanni had been wasted. It would mean we were looking in the wrong place.

And if we were, then this was a game Bram was currently winning.

TWENTY-THREE

When Tim took a trip to the bathroom and, for the sake of anyone who might be listening, Mac started to talk about getting her 'ancient bones to bed', she and I paid the bill, grabbed our coats, and headed outside. A few minutes later, Tim joined us in the parking lot to confer about next steps. Mac didn't go home, and neither did he. Instead, all three of us passed under the blue-and-white Alexandria Bay welcome sign that, from our vantage point, read: *Come Again to the ♥ of the 1000 Islands*, and headed back to my cottage where I shut the blinds and brewed a full pot of coffee. We had time to kill.

And we needed to finalize our action plan.

The letter I'd slipped in my mailbox, addressed simply to *Abe*, was gone when I checked that morning. The letter had told him to meet me at midnight. At eleven p.m., with an hour to go, we set off for Clayton, Mac in her own car and Tim with me in mine. The fog was back, tumbling off the river and streaming into the road. My SUV cut through it like a hot blade in butter and sent it swirling away.

My eyes were on Mac in the rear-view mirror when she veered off Route 12. Tim and I kept going. When we were close to our destination, I pulled onto a side road. In our headlights, the world outside was the color of a day-old bruise. I turned off the car and submerged us in darkness.

Tim faced me and failed to hold back a shiver. He'd forgotten his favorite off-duty jacket at the pub and had to make do with a down-filled vest of mine, which was too small to zip closed over his chest. I didn't know how he was going to stand being out in the cold tonight.

'I've been thinking,' he said, 'about what you told me in Vermont. That stuff about abandoning Abe. You cut ties with him. You blamed yourself for who he's become.'

'Sounds like something I'd say.'

'Yeah, and it's bullshit. You didn't make Bram what he is. He's a glitch in your bloodline that has nothing to do with you. But that's just one side of the story. His feelings count for something, too. And however he feels about you right now, it's been marinating since he was sixteen years old. That's a long time to be angry, and a long time to be itching for payback.'

Even through the closed windows of the car I could hear the nocturnal refrain of field crickets, singing the same old song. 'Another woman is dead,' I said, 'and there's still a chance he killed her. He left that card for me. He's planning something big. It's now or never. We're out of time.'

To that, Tim said nothing.

I let out a full-body sigh of frustration. My hand was on the gear shift. I hadn't noticed that I'd adopted Tim's quirk. When, surprised, I looked down at it, he did the same. Then he reached over, and put his hand on mine.

I was used to people worrying about me. My parents, and Doug. Carson, when we were together. Tim's breed of worrying was different. He didn't wince when I approached a suspect. He knew I could handle myself on the job. When it came to Bram, though, he thought I played fast and loose. I didn't blame him, and didn't like to see him agonizing over my attitude, either. He cared about what happened to me.

Tim's hand was warm and dry, and though I'd stiffened at his touch, I left my own hand where it was.

'You ready?' he said.

The look on his face was one of abject terror, but he was here with me. We were a team.

I drew in a breath and said, 'Let's do this.'

Tim got out then, but I continued driving a little farther, to park directly next to St Mary's Cemetery. There was no fence separating it from the highway, and it backed up to a copse of trees. I'd spent a lot of time on Google Maps after Bram broke into the cottage, dragging my curser right and left and zooming into potential rendezvous sites. The cemetery fit the bill. I didn't want him anywhere near civilians. Parking lots and back alleys were out. The drive-in, Maxson Airfield, the town landfill – all had a single road leading in and out, and I knew Bram wouldn't chance ensnaring himself. We needed someplace with an escape route – not for us, but for him. So he wouldn't feel hemmed in. He'd be looking at maps, too, maybe even doing some reconnaissance. If he thought I was luring him into a trap, or expected to find a fleet of cop cars waiting at the only exit, he'd never agree to meet.

It was possible, of course, that he wouldn't come either way. There were a lot of *ifs* involved in The Plan: if Bram was still around; if it was Bram who found the letter; if he trusted me enough to show, this night might pan out the way I was praying it would. If not, I might be standing in a cemetery in the cold for a long, long time.

There was another *if*, too. If Bram did come, and he couldn't care less about talking to his estranged cousin, then I might end up dead.

The sky was cloudy tonight, the moon concealed. There were no lights in the cemetery, and I had to pick my way around the graves to find the perfect place to wait. I chose a spot toward the middle, tucking myself against one of the largest headstones I could find. Even through my L.L.Bean jacket – I'd dressed like a civilian, not wanting to remind Bram I was a sworn officer of the New York State Police – the stone was a block of ice against my spine. With every ragged breath I took, I smelled earth and rot and minerals from the monument at my back.

We hadn't accounted for the fog. It was less dense here, farther up river, but heavy enough that I couldn't see more than a few feet in front of me. The same would be true for Bram, but the cloaked view made me uneasy. The last time I'd been close to my cousin, close enough that he could have reached out and touched me, I didn't even realize he was there. The last time I looked into his eyes, I'd been his prisoner. I was a trained police officer, vigilant and skilled at evasion, but he still managed to get me back to his lair, and that was a truth I could never shake off as long as I lived.

When my fingers started to cramp from the cold, I glanced at my watch. *12:08 a.m.*

He was late. Did this mean he wasn't coming? I couldn't

communicate with the others for fear of giving them away, but I knew that somewhere in the thick underbrush, Tim was watching me.

Did Bram know it, too?

I waited, listening to the fretful skittering of creatures in the woods. Letting a velvet-winged moth graze my cheek. Staring unblinking, like a barn owl on the hunt, into the smoky gloom. Five minutes passed, then ten, before I finally heard it. The muffled crunch of dry grass. Movement, somewhere to my right. Was it Tim, coming to tell me the operation was a bust? The fog persisted. I peered into it. Saw nothing.

Then: 'Hi, Shay.'

TWENTY-FOUR

B ram is a featureless ghost and a man of many faces. He's nowhere and everywhere, nothing and all. In New York, he was a young professional on a dating app, with dark hair, blue eyes, and a boyish smile. Then he was Seth from the Irish pub, with an average build and eyes so pale they were almost white. In Watertown and Alexandria Bay he was lumbering and bearish, facial hair like a logger and a cold, black stare.

The man who stepped out of the mist was different still. Between the creases in his brow and his solid gray hair, he looked like he'd aged fifteen years. He'd lost weight since I last saw him, too, giving him a loose, ungainly gait.

Things that had stayed the same: his ears, with a slightly pointed helix, like mine. His voice. It was guttural, but calm. Expressive. Almost cheerful. When he spoke, I heard both teenage Abe and the man who'd held me captive. Both the men I despised and feared, wrapped up in one terrible package.

A finger, pointed at the scar on my cheek. 'Meant to tell you in New York. That healed up nicely.'

I was paralyzed, as stuck as the grave markers around me. We were miles from the nearest town. Bram had to have a car stashed somewhere, but he'd materialized like an apparition. I couldn't believe he was standing in front of me.

I'd rehearsed this part with Tim and Mac, what to ask and how to get the information we needed now that I finally had a chance. I was here for a reason: to stop the trajectory Bram had been on for more than a year. Motive, intention, information on past crimes we might not yet have discovered . . . I needed it all.

I stared at Bram, and said nothing.

'What, are you surprised I came?' When he smiled his eyes – brown this time, like mine – gleamed. 'Thanks for the invite, by the way, Shay. I've been looking forward to seeing you again. And for you to see me.'

What did I feel when I looked at him? I couldn't begin to describe it. On paper, he was still my cousin, but under that smile was a savage. I hated the way he wielded my nickname like we were friends. Like we could ever be anything but hunter and prey to each other again.

Time was wasting. Bram was here, but I didn't know how long he'd stay. The last time we spoke I'd been bushwhacked, caught unawares by an unheralded call. This was different. I'd had time to think. I had to capitalize on this opportunity. It might be the only one I got.

And so, I pictured the faces of the three young women he brutalized with a knife. The rookie patrol cop who left behind a wife and family when Bram pumped four bullets into his gut. I pictured my own face, too, the way it first looked after my cousin slit it open with a rusty nail because I told him that, come graduation, I was leaving him and his twisted games behind.

'I've been wanting to see you, too.' I cocked my head. 'So? What did you think?'

Bram knit his brow.

'Of my new place,' I said. 'Hey, thanks for the Swiss Roll, but I haven't eaten that junk since I was a kid.'

I curled my lip, and held his stare. I wasn't trying to anger him, just throw him off-balance. I wanted Bram to understand that in all things Shay, I still had the upper hand.

'Why did you ask me here?' His voice was gruffer now.

Why did you murder those women? Who else did you kill? What do you want?

These were the questions Tim, Mac, and I had discussed . . . but hadn't I asked them already? Five months ago, when Bram called the station, I'd lobbed them like snowballs, desperate to make a hit. He'd sidestepped every one. He wasn't going to give me what I wanted, I realized now. It wouldn't be that easy. I had to take a different tack.

Sensei Sam's advice was to be nimble. Adjust, and react to my opponent's moves.

'Your mother is looking for you.'

I blurted it. My logic was that I'd appeal to whatever shred of humanity the man had left. At the mention of Aunt Fee, Bram's face shuttered. He watched me through dead eyes.

'She hired a private investigator,' I told him, unwilling to retreat.

'She never cared about finding me before.'

'She thought you were living with your dad in Philadelphia. *You* left *her*, remember? Didn't seem like you wanted to be found. The PI is good.'

'Better than you?'

He meant it as a barb. I hadn't been able to find him, and he knew how long I'd been looking. Always, I had to wait until Bram came to me.

'If she is,' I said, 'if she finds out what name you're using, where you've been living, it's all over.'

Bram smiled.

The arrogance. The gall of smiling after everything he'd done. 'I know what you look like now,' I said, goading him. Every word I spoke made me feel stronger. I was modifying my response, just like my sensei taught me. 'You'll have to change your face again. Find somewhere new to work.'

'What, this?' He gestured at his hair and the wrinkled brow that, when I looked more closely, seemed to have a waxy quality not unlike rubber. 'This isn't me – the latest me, I mean,' he said with a flick of his shaggy head. 'This is just for you.'

I clenched my teeth and savored the flash of pain. 'Give it

up. Do you really want to live this way, hiding in plain sight? Risking discovery every time you step outside?'

Bram shifted his weight, and the mist eddied around his ankles. His eyes twitched in amusement. He was enjoying this. 'But I'm so good at it,' he said. 'And I'm not done yet. We're not done.'

'Not done with *what*?' I said, and immediately felt like I'd been plunged into an ice bath. *The card*. 'Whatever you're planning, don't do it.' My voice cracked. 'Please.'

A look of disappointment washed over Bram's face. 'Don't you see? I know you, Shay, better than anyone. I always have – and you know me. You surprised me when we talked in New York. When I told you all those stories about our time together, you pretended you didn't remember. You played dumb.'

That was wrong. I hadn't been playacting, not at first. I didn't know who he was until the stories started to sound familiar. I did pretend, then, for fear that ID'ing him would give him a reason to kill me.

When I thought back to the experience of being Bram's captive, I couldn't fathom how I'd survived it. Eight days. 192 hours. 11,520 minutes. All that time, I'd been forced to listen as Bram droned on about life back in our shared hometown. He focused on the bad stuff, mostly: his father's departure; the bullying he endured at school; the suffering caused by his mother's mental illness. He talked about the flaws Aunt Fee inflicted – the hack job haircuts, the soiled clothing – and how she tried to convince him those imperfections would keep him safe from the invisible threats she feared would befall him. Bram's appearance had been tarnished, his identity muddled even then. No wonder he was so good at disguises.

'I don't get it,' he said. 'When I tried to warn you about your friend Suze – she was trouble, I told you so and I was right – you accused me of being controlling. Before I left Swanton, you said you didn't like my games. That I *deceived you*.'

I swallowed, my throat bone dry. 'You did.'

'You'd think a girl would learn.'

'What the hell is that supposed to mean?'

He rolled back his shoulders with such slow control I thought

I could hear the grinding of his bones. 'Everything I do, I do for you, Shay – then, now, always. I searched half my life to find you, and look.' His smile was warped, just as twisted as he was. 'Here we are. Together again at la—'

Bram fell silent. Jerked his head to the right. He went rigid like an animal detecting danger. I'd heard it too, a rustling in the grove behind me, right where Tim was hiding. *What the fuck?* I didn't dare turn around, but Bram's eyes darted toward the sound.

'No cops.' He held my gaze. His face was going red, but he didn't look shocked. How much had he deduced about our plan for tonight? 'You wrote in the letter there'd be no fucking cops. You *promised*.'

Bram sounded enraged now. He sounded like an angry child.

'It's over,' I said, unholstering my weapon. Standing my ground. 'I'm placing you under arrest.'

It happened in an instant. Tim burst from the treeline with his sidearm drawn. Reflexively, I turned my head toward him, and in that split second with a crazed roar, Bram lunged. He heaved his weight against my chest and his left hand against my arm. My weapon discharged with an ear-splitting boom as I flew backward. My head exploded with pain. I scrambled to get up, clawing at the headstone. Trying to gain purchase. My vision swam, but I forced myself to my feet.

No sign of Bram. Tim was gone too. I sprinted in the direction I thought they'd bolted. North, toward Clayton. My head ached and I could feel a trickle of blood on my scalp, hot and tacky. I kept going.

'Stop!' I screamed into the night. The troopers were on the road, their vehicles – the 'blue and golds' – screeching to a stop in front of the cemetery.

Bram would head for the trees.

There. Through the fog, a snatch of dark clothing disappearing into a stand of maples. I couldn't tell if it belonged to Bram or Tim. The wooded area that bordered the cemetery backed up to Barrett Creek. Beyond that it was all open farmland and more forest. If he evaded us, Bram could hide out there for hours. Days.

Or he could double back and head for the river.

It was the logical move. There were already boats in the water. He'd fled from us by boat before. If he could reach the river before Tim and I took him down, he could hide on one of the islands, still shuttered for the winter, or go down river back to A-Bay. We would lose him. More than that, he was angry now. I'd betrayed him. And he would retaliate.

But I couldn't stop. Tim was alone out there, and even injured, I was fast. But I'd lost sight of him. I slowed my pace, and listened. Footfalls now, coming from the underbrush. Slapping the short, dry grass.

Moving toward me.

'I lost him. I lost him. *Fuck*. There was a snake,' Tim said, wheezing. Lips pulled back from his teeth. His hair had fallen into his eyes. 'It slithered right over my foot. I'm so sorry – Jesus, are you OK?' When he touched my head, his fingers came away bloody. I shrunk away, shaking my head. Shaking.

We're not done.

As soon as I heard them, I knew exactly what those words would do. They'd burrow into my subconscious and nest there, breeding despair and fear.

They would haunt me until the day Bram was dead.

TWENTY-FIVE

'We had him. We *had him*, Tim.'

I wanted to slam a fist onto the coffee table. Punch a wall. Scream. After all this time Bram was finally within reach, and we'd botched our chance at catching him. The plan should have been watertight. It was devised by three good minds, with a collective forty-eight years of experience assessing and thwarting criminal behavior. We had eyes on those woods, on *him*, with backup seconds from pouncing. And yet, he was gone.

I knew Bram would have a plan of his own. Assembling a team and surrounding the cemetery was my way of mitigating the risk that he could flee. But prior to our meeting, well aware

I wouldn't let my chance to apprehend him slip through my fingers again, he'd done his due diligence. In spite of our preemptive tactics he'd found someplace to stow away, a foxhole so well concealed we'd run right past it. A way to go underground until we withdrew. It was the only explanation for how he eluded us.

We'd spent half the night combing the countryside. The previous fears I'd had about turning up the heat had morphed into a full-fledged nightmare. We'd poked the bear, and now more than ever, we needed him caged. The wooded area surrounding the cemetery, the nearby village of Clayton, the storage facility to the south and smattering of homes within running distance – we'd searched them all, bringing in police dogs. Even after issuing an all-points bulletin and with Tim, Mac, and the state troopers helping to canvass the area, we came up short.

The first thing I'd done upon returning to the barracks was to update Lieutenant Henderson in Oneida. I'd called my old NCO supervisor in New York, too. Neither was happy to be roused in the middle of the night, but my supervisor agreed to pass along my message to the FBI. Agents had been collaborating with the Ninth and Seventh Precincts on Bram's case for over a year, but his reappearance in the North Country upped the ante. Suddenly, there was talk of activating electronic billboards on New York's interstates in the hope that a traveler might spot our fugitive. The extra manpower came as a relief. Coordinating it all wasn't quick. Tim and I hadn't made it back to my cottage until three a.m. It was three fourteen now, and my body still hummed like a struck tuning fork.

Next to me on the couch, Tim knuckled his bloodshot eyes. 'I was so close I could smell him.' His tone was grim. I knew how guilty he felt about tipping Bram off to his presence. Mac and the troopers had been parked half a mile away, waiting for Tim's signal to come careening into battle. If he hadn't made that sound in the woods, Bram would be in a jail cell. 'I'm sorry, Shana. I'm so sorry.'

'Not your fault,' I said, because I couldn't bear to see him agonize over his mistake any longer. We'd tried, all of us. It hadn't been enough. I hiked my stocking feet up onto the couch and, facing Tim, brought my knees to my chin. 'What if we never get him?' There were serial killers who remained at large decades after committing their crimes. The Bible Belt Strangler. DC's Freeway Phantom. The famed Zodiac Killer. The ones that concerned me most were those who kept on taking lives.

Tim's nod was lethargic. He was looking at my feet. They were next to his leg, my toes inches from his thick, jean-clad thigh. 'I think you might know this about me,' he said slowly, still staring down at my socks. 'With you, I feel . . . protective.' I tilted my head, but he wouldn't meet my gaze. 'I used to think it was because of Carson,' he told me. 'I was under his thumb once, too. I know what that's like, how toxic it feels. The psychological abuse . . . I didn't want that for you. Not for anyone, really, but you . . . you'd been through so much already. When you told me about New York . . .' He paused and bowed his head. 'I guess I made a decision. To protect you. No matter what.'

I didn't know what to say. I had sensed this about Tim. He had an innate need to defend people against injustice. No doubt this was why he became an investigator. It was part of the reason I'd joined the force myself, and I felt a similar watchfulness toward Tim. With me, though, his solicitude had felt distinctive, the volume of his attention amplified. I'd grown accustomed to his devotion. I'd come to like it.

But sitting there with him, studying the dark smudges under his eyes and the bristly black stubble on his jaw, dark coils of hair peeking out from behind his ears, it wasn't gratitude I felt for Tim. It was an ache I couldn't name, a desire I didn't know how to sate. It was an emotion I'd never experienced before. And with a jolt of understanding, at long last, I knew.

'Tim.'

He looked up then, and held my gaze. I leaned forward and lay a hand on his thigh. I expected my touch to startle him, but Tim held his ground, searching my face with lips parted and his breath audible in the quiet room. 'You sure?' he said, the words little more than an exhalation. He swallowed twice. Held his body still, as if he feared he might startle a rabbit in the grass.

I nodded, grabbed a handful of his T-shirt, and pulled him toward me.

Musk and pepper. Spearmint and salt. The wet heat of his hands on my shoulders, back, breasts. I gorged myself on his skin and the solid, seamless movement of the muscles beneath it. Rose up to meet him when his hand slipped between my thighs. 'Are you sure?' he asked again, weakly this time, before locking his lips onto my neck.

'Yes,' I gasped as he swept me into his arms.

We didn't say anything more after that.

TWENTY-SIX

I woke up gasping, my heart thundering in my chest. There was a figure standing over my bed, a broad, black mass that cast a shadow on the covers. I could see him. I could *smell* him, the same nauseating amalgam of sweat and synthetic lemons that stung my nostrils every time he lumbered down the basement stairs and stepped into my prison cell.

No. He's not here. You're safe. The vision was a lie. There was no way Bram could get to me. The dream was a memory, nothing more. I'd installed the home security system as soon as it arrived. The front door had been repaired, the windows off the deck locked tight. Tim was sleeping on the couch right outside my bedroom door.

No. That was wrong. Tim was *here*, propped up on his elbow. Staring down at me with a look of deep concern on his face.

'You OK?' Tenderly, he brushed a curl from my cheek. I waited for my brain to catch up. Tim and me. Me and him. How did I feel about that? I wasn't especially surprised to discover there was no place else I'd rather be.

'Yeah.' My voice was raspy, with no more structure than the scratch of bike wheels on rough pavement. I cleared my throat and smoothed down my wild hair, but the moment I sat up, the back of my head blazed with pain where I'd struck it

against the gravestone. 'Ow,' I said as I probed the goose egg
with my fingertips and winced. 'Tim.'

'Yes?'

I didn't want him to think I had any regrets, but after
what happened at the cemetery I was more concerned about
my friends and family than ever. At the same time, seeing
Bram again and witnessing his arrogance first-hand made
me want to defy him. *Fuck his rules*, Tim had said last year,
right after our first kiss. At the time, I'd been too afraid to
agree. Now, the thought that Bram could threaten my relationship with Tim again made me livid. 'We should be
careful,' I said simply.

'We will be,' he replied, and pressed his lips to my hand.

'What time is it?' My bedroom wasn't as dark as it had
been when we finally went to sleep – I blushed at the memory
of what kept us awake – but the seam of light around the
curtains looked thin. It was early. I reached for my phone.
Just past six a.m.

Two hours of sleep. It was going to be a long day.

Tim's mouth contorted into an extended yawn. He didn't
look any better than I felt. His hair stuck up on one side and
was mashed down on the other, but I couldn't tear my gaze
away from him.

'I didn't sleep,' he said by way of an explanation.

'Not at all?'

He shook his head. 'I was thinking about the case. Poking
around the internet on my phone.' A few days ago, I'd assigned
Tim the task of doing some social listening online by checking
keywords like 'Wolfe Island' and 'wind farm murder' on
Facebook and Twitter. Social media chatter sometimes divulged
useful information, and it wasn't unheard of for the internet
to lead us to a perp who couldn't resist crowing about his
crimes. I hadn't intended for him to work all night, especially
not *last* night. 'I think I may have found something,' he said.

'Yeah?' I sat up a little straighter. 'What is it?'

'Hard to say. It's weird. You need to see it for yourself.'

He passed me the phone.

Weird. There was no better way to describe the scene
depicted in the photograph on the blog post Tim had found.

I was so captivated by the objects in the foreground I almost
didn't notice the setting.

'Jesus, is that—'

'A turbine,' Tim said, running a hand through his hair as
he pressed his lips into a frown. 'On Wolfe Island.'

Same ferry ride. Same views. Same turn-off from 95 onto the
paved service road next to the turbine. The drive across Wolfe
Island was familiar, but what we saw when we arrived couldn't
have been more different. Last time, we'd found Hope Oberon's
body slumped against the concrete platform.

Now, the muddy area around the turbine was cluttered with
bloody hands.

They were sculpted from plaster, frozen in myriad pos-
itions. Some pointed their index fingers at the turbine, while
others were balled into fists. All emerged from the ground
like a pack of zombies busting out of their graves. The plaster
was white, and that made the effect all the more disconcerting.
Each hand was dipped in dripping red paint that looked
alarmingly like fresh blood.

Tim had found images of the hands on Twitter. The woman
who'd posted them owned one of the houses nearest to the
wind farm, and had stumbled upon the chilling display while
she was out walking her dog. Instead of calling the police,
she'd uploaded photos to social media, and her post already
had close to five hundred likes. She'd included the hashtag
#wolfeisland, which under ordinary circumstances might have
attracted a dozen social media users a month. Mid-homicide
investigation, the tag was getting a lot more searches.

A length of the barricade tape the Canadians had used to
cordon off our crime scene still fluttered in the breeze. 'It
doesn't look like the hands have been disturbed,' said Paul
Ludgate, who'd beaten us to the scene. 'Same set-up as in the
pics Tim found online.'

'If there was any chance of getting a footwear impression,
we probably missed it, though,' I said. 'Looks like several
other people have been through here already.' There were
tracks all over the place, deep impressions in the muddy terrain.

On the ferry ride over, we'd done a search of our own, and

made a startling discovery. This wasn't the first time a flock of plaster hands had materialized on Wolfe Island. Close to nine years ago, a local blogger had found an arrangement almost identical to the one we were looking at now, sculpted by an anonymous guerrilla artist in protest of the recently erected wind farm. Some hands were made to look like they were throwing stones at the turbines. The message they were intended to send was clear.

'Eighty-six,' Tim said thoughtfully after counting every hand. 'Same number as in the original installation. That's one hand for every turbine here on the island.'

'And this time, they're covered in blood.'

'There were a lot of protests against the turbines back then,' Ludgate cut in. He wore his light hair slicked back today, and it accentuated his prominent features. 'Wolfe Island residents were angry with their mayor.'

The blog post had said the original eighty-six hands disappeared as quickly as they'd come. Ludgate told us there was speculation the mayor himself ordered their removal. The artist never surfaced, not even to take credit when the installation was lauded for its creativity.

'What are the chances the sculptor from nine years ago did this, too?'

'That's definitely possible,' Ludgate said. 'I want to say it's likely we're dealing with a local or someone who lived relatively close. It's not like the hands from nine years ago were national news. Anyone searching for information about Wolfe Island could stumble onto that blog post, though, and there's a lot of interest in this place right now.' He thought for a moment and said, 'Fair to say the perp's within driving distance, yeah? Nobody's taking eighty-six plaster sculptures on a plane.'

'So we're looking for someone relatively local,' said Tim, adding the facts to his notebook. 'We should rule out the woman who found them.'

We were all in agreement about that.

'And the motive?'

'I don't think it's about the wind farm this time,' I said. 'We don't know exactly where the original installation was located, but this is Hope's turbine. The hands point right at the spot where her body was found. Couple that with the timing, and this has to be linked to Hope's death.'

That meant someone had come here, sought out the crime scene, and planted these blood-splattered hands in the ground as a symbol of . . . what? The loss of life that occurred in this place? Their abhorrence of the killing?

Their pride in what they'd done?

'We need to find the sculptor,' I said, peering at the smooth, bleached plaster of the nearest hand. 'Somebody crafted these things expressly for this purpose. Let's make some calls, track down all the artists in the area, both here in Ontario and in Jefferson County. If we find the person who made these things, we just might find our perp.'

TWENTY-SEVEN

As it turned out, there were dozens of artists specializing in sculpture and garden art in Southern Ontario and Upstate New York. On Wolfe Island, though, there was exactly one. Johanna Scott's studio was on Main Street in Marysville, between a bed and breakfast and a fish-themed gift shop. Tim and Paul Ludgate stayed behind to search for additional evidence and keep the scene secure. After I finished interviewing the dog walker, a woman in her seventies who could no sooner have crafted and carried the hands than piloted a tanker ship through the channel, I made my way into town.

I found the artist bent over a potter's wheel at the back of a long, low room. The space closest to the street functioned as a gallery, spotless tables displaying colorful ceramic platters and bowls, but behind a curtain, the work area was lined with shelves caked with residue from the clay. Here and there, objects rested under grubby plastic bags. There was a lush, earthy smell to the place that conjured long-forgotten memories of middle school art class.

Johanna was in her sixties, and had been sculpting for almost thirty years. She'd been living on Wolfe Island for fifteen of those. When I asked her about the original eighty-six hands, her eyes lit up.

'I remember,' she said, abandoning a wet cylinder of clay that looked destined to become a mug. As the clay water dried on her hands it turned them a lusterless gray. 'I went to see them myself. Made it just before they were cleared away. They were quite beautiful, those hands.'

'Any idea who created them?'

'Not a clue,' she said.

My eyes trailed over the concealed objects on the shelves. 'Did you hear they're back? Eighty-six of them, same as before. Only this time, they were made to look bloody.'

I dug out my phone and showed her the photos from the blog post Tim found.

'Oh my,' Johanna said as she dragged her gaze across the screen. Contemplating the photos, she pushed her glasses higher on her nose with the back of a dusty hand. The lenses were splattered with a whisper-fine spray of mud. 'Do they have anything to do with that poor woman who was killed out there?'

'I'm just gathering facts right now,' I said, deflecting. 'Do you know of anyone in the area who does those kinds of sculptures? Someone who might, say, take a commission for a few dozen plaster hands?'

'I know most of the artists around here. But you wouldn't need to be a professional to make these. Life casting doesn't require much artistic skill.'

'Life casting?'

'Creating casts of body parts. All it takes is some silicone and alginate – available at any art supply store – the plaster, and a bucket.'

She walked me through the process: mix silicone and alginate, immerse your hand into the muck, and wait five minutes for the material to set. After that, it was a simple matter of pouring plaster into the mold, waiting an hour, and peeling away the alginate to reveal the body part.

'You can get an incredible amount of detail with this technique,' she told me, brushing her silver-streaked hair away from her face. By now she had a stripe of clay on her nose and another on her right cheekbone. They reminded me of the blood I'd seen on Maynard Pope's face at the restaurant. 'Wrinkles in the hands, scars, even fingerprints are all visible in the clay.'

Fingerprints and scars might prove useful, especially if the creator of the hands and the person who came up with the idea to install them were one and the same.

'Any chance you have a couple of empty boxes I can buy from you?' I asked.

She tilted her head. 'How big?'

'The bigger the better.' After Tim, Ludgate, and I finished photographing the installation, we'd need to collect those hands.

All eighty-six of them.

TWENTY-EIGHT

When we got back to the barracks, we were surprised to see Don Bogle emerge from the building. Tim hadn't even finished parking the car before my investigator was flagging us down – and he wasn't alone.

'Good, you're here. Got a sec?' His voice was rough from all the smoking. At six-foot-six Bogle dwarfed almost everyone, but the way he hovered over the woman by his side seemed especially defensive.

The first thing I noticed about her was that she'd been crying. Her milk-white skin was mottled, her nose shiny and pink. It wasn't until I got a good look that I noticed her eyelashes. She didn't have any. Both eyes were completely bare, and it gave her a stark, haunted look.

'This is Natalie Pope,' said Bogle. 'Hope Oberon's daughter.'

I should have remembered her from the portrait on the wall in Maynard Pope's house. Natalie's hair was pulled into a ponytail as thick as a horse's mane, and it was an impossible shade of auburn splashed with gold, like the light in a Vermont forest on a sunny October afternoon. What was Hope's daughter doing here, in a New York State Police station parking lot?

'What can we do for you, Natalie?' I asked. Bogle's expression gave away nothing.

As a college freshman, Natalie must have been close to twenty, but at the moment she looked about fourteen. 'I'm sorry to bug you. My dad mentioned your names the other day. I didn't know who else to call.'

'Don't be sorry,' I said. 'You look upset. Everything OK?'

'I don't know.' Her shoulder twitched, and she looked away from us. 'I might need help.'

'Did something happen?' Tim asked. 'Is someone hurt?'

The young woman's eyes brimmed with tears. 'I'm not sure. I'm worried about my grandfather. Harvey.'

'OK,' I said, still puzzled. 'Where's your grandfather now?'

'I don't know. My dad's not answering his cell. I called the restaurant and they told me he was out getting supplies. But Gramps isn't there. They said Dad didn't bring him in today.'

Next to us, Bogle continued to stare down at Natalie with concern. I understood now why he'd brought her out to meet us rather than letting us take our time getting inside. 'He left Harvey home alone?' I said.

'I guess so? Gramps always answers the home phone if he's there, though. I've been calling and calling,' she said, 'but he isn't picking up. I went over there too, to check on him, but he didn't answer the door. He's always either home or at the restaurant.'

Given Harvey's condition, her distress rang true. 'Do you have a key to the house?' I asked.

She shook her head, sending a ripple of sunlight through her red hair. 'Not anymore. I've been staying with my dad's parents in Chippewa Bay.' She wiped the back of her hand across her naked eyes.

I scanned the parking lot and, by process of elimination, spotted Natalie's car. 'Would you like us to check on your grandfather? You could follow us there. Maybe he'll open the door this time.'

'OK. Yes, please,' she said with a nod.

She didn't look optimistic.

* * *

There was no vehicle in the driveway at Iroquois Point. I wondered briefly if the garage had been reserved for Hope's car when she and Maynard lived together. I couldn't imagine his colossal Tahoe fitting inside. We waited for Natalie to pull in behind us before approaching the house. It stood as quiet as a tomb.

While Natalie rang the bell, Tim and I circled the home looking for signs of trouble. We found it on the back deck. The sliding doors that led from the living room outside were wide open. Long curtains billowed in the breeze off the water, whipping softly against the cedar siding.

'Natalie!' I called behind me, cupping my hands around my mouth. My mind was in overdrive. There was no sign of Harvey in the yard. In our first conversation with Maynard Pope, he'd told us Harvey once wandered out of the house. That soon he would need full-time care.

That it wasn't safe for him living near the water.

My gaze followed the sloping lawn down to the river.

When Natalie came into view, sprinting around the corner of the house, her father was with her. Maynard Pope looked disheveled. His graying hair was wild. His eyes, too.

'What's happening? They told me at the restaurant Natalie called. Where's Harvey?'

'You tell us,' I said. 'When was the last time you saw him?'

Pope blinked. 'I . . . an hour ago. Two at most. He gave me a hard time about coming to Chateau Gris this morning. He wanted to stay here and watch TV . . . but the restaurant. I'm running out of everything. Is he . . . oh God.' A look of terror crept into his eyes as he noticed the open sliding doors.

'Where is he, Dad?' Natalie said in a tremulous voice. 'Oh my God. The boat.' She ran across the lawn to the boathouse that jutted out into the river, and flung open the door. The structure was empty. Shoes clomping, she raced to the end of the dock and scanned the river. 'I don't see him. Where is he? He can't be out there alone!'

Pope stood on the grass staring out at the water, his mouth gaping like a beached fish. Tim grabbed his arm and gave it a rough shake.

'Is there another boat? A way for us to get out there?'

'No,' Pope said. 'No, there's just the one.'

'Any idea where he went?' I was already dialing the coast-guard. They'd need to do a search and rescue, and they'd need to move fast.

'I don't know,' Pope said, pulling at his hair now. 'I don't know!'

As I waited for the call to connect, I stood at the edge of the river, so close the water lapped at the toes of my boots. The horizon was empty in all directions, the water still.

On the sun-bleached dock, Natalie had started to weep.

TWENTY-NINE

The Alexandria Bay Coast Guard Station was on Wellesley Island, about three miles upriver from Iroquois Point. The response boat got as far as Cherry Island. That's where they located the motorboat registered to Maynard Pope.

It appeared that Harvey had a particular destination in mind. Green Rock Island, we later learned, belonged to a friend of his, and had been the site of many a famed Mayor Oberon gathering. Harvey had gotten close, but by the time the Coasties found him he'd forgotten where the island was and was idling in the middle of the channel, a sitting duck for the freighter ships that used it to travel the river to and from the Great Lakes. Harvey told responders he was late for the Spring Fling Social, and asked if they could get him the rest of the way. They took him to the hospital instead.

'At least he's alive,' Tim said a few hours later as we, too, floated on the river.

'If he wasn't,' I said, 'we might be charging Maynard Pope with negligent homicide.' As it was, we'd left the widower with Harvey. Natalie was at the hospital, too. She blamed herself for endangering her grandfather – 'If I'd insisted on staying at the house from the beginning, this would never have happened,' she'd told us – and had vowed to watch over Harvey from now on. As Tim and I gazed out at the islands in the distance, I found some comfort in knowing Harvey would be taken care of until Pope could hire permanent help.

We'd gone back to the barracks after the debacle with Harvey, eager for an update on the search for Bram, but there had been no calls to the tip line, and nothing new from New York. When our shift was over, we reluctantly headed back to Tim's place. The plan we'd made on Thursday to go boating seemed trivial now. At the same time, we both felt restless and helpless. When Tim suggested we go out on the river after all, I welcomed the distraction from Bram.

His *little runabout* turned out to be a gorgeous antique wooden boat, glossy as a candy and the rich, dark amber of Vermont maple syrup. In his boathouse, he proudly told me it was a sixties-era Lyman made of real mahogany. He'd bought it for a song and restored the interior. Tim had needed a new project after finishing the cottage, which he'd transformed from a three-season shack into a cozy home paneled with knotty pine and stuffed with books. Tim had a lot of projects. I'd never met anyone as motivated, or as determined to find the beauty in things.

And he'd found it again now. In the shallows of Goose Bay, close to Cork Island, the water was calm, not another vessel in sight. The trees that ringed the bay were the kind of colossal evergreens that blanket the rocky shore with rust-colored needles and grow crooked in the strong northern wind. The water was still too cold for algae, and there was none of the usual seagrass wending its way toward the surface, which meant the river was clear as cut glass. I could see almost thirty feet down, all the way to the sludgy riverbed.

My first boating lesson had consisted of an overview of the 'rules of the river' – port to port, red light returning, tanker etiquette – combined with a safety lesson about shoals and currents and some practical facts about the vessel that, down the line, could be applied to operating the police boat. I'd need to take an official course eventually, and would require some additional training, but for the moment Tim let me putter around the empty bay to get a feel for being on the water. What had happened with Harvey drove home the importance of knowing how to navigate the river. I liked the way the steering wheel hummed under my hands, ever at the ready and quick to respond. It made me feel in control. The only thing spoiling the experience was the presence of our sidearms, and the persistent feeling that we were being watched.

'Pope must be beating himself up right now,' Tim said as I turned the boat in slow circles. 'He totally dropped the ball on looking after Harvey.'

'His behavior,' I said. 'Does it strike you as odd?'

'It does, a little. You'd think he'd be used to supervising his father-in-law by now. He did just lose his wife, though. His head must be pretty messed up these days.'

'This kind of thing affects everyone differently,' I agreed. 'I've seen people who lost a loved one to a violent death get violent themselves. Sometimes they lay blame, other times they become catatonic. I've even seen them go about their normal lives like nothing happened.'

'I'd say he falls into that last category.' Tim stretched his arms over his head and yawned. The lack of sleep was catching up with him. With me, too. 'I can't believe he hasn't closed the restaurant. Then again, if he had he would have lost out on a lot of business, and I'm not sure he could afford that. How long can a restaurant sit empty before its owner's forced to call it quits? It's been months.'

'And now, after all this time with no customers, it's packed. Did you see him pumping out those sausages? His days of pawning off unsold meat to family members are over.'

'It's because of Hope's death, has to be,' said Tim. 'Everyone's heard about her murder. People probably feel sorry for Maynard and Natalie.'

I cut the engine and turned to face him. 'I've been thinking about Doug, and my niece Hen.'

Tim nodded, waiting for me to go on. He'd met my brother in Swanton, when Doug had come to stay with my parents following the news of Uncle Brett's death. Henrietta and my sister-in-law, Josie, had remained in Burlington, but I talked about Hen often to Tim.

'If something like what happened to Hope happened to Josie' – the thought made my stomach heave – 'Doug wouldn't let Hen out of his sight. Now, some families are closer than others.'

'Sure,' Tim said. 'But it's almost like Maynard Pope's been trying to avoid his own kid.'

'Natalie lives all the way down in Syracuse. I'm sure she doesn't get to see her family very often. She's traumatized, in mourning – and did you notice her eyelashes? Could be some kind of medical condition, but her hair looks thick and healthy. I've heard of people pulling out their lashes when they're anxious, or under immense stress. She has this frantic energy about her.'

'I'm sure it's stressful to watch your mother get charged with corruption and publicly raked over the coals.'

'All the more reason for her dad to keep her close, don't you think?'

'Yeah,' Tim said. 'I do.'

Somewhere in the near distance, the mournful yowl of a common loon resounded off the water, and both Tim and I looked in the direction of the sound. He was no Val Giovanni, but he knew bird calls: the honks and squawks of the Canada Goose, the frantic squabbling of the snow goose. He knew that geese mated for life. Tim could recognize the arctic species that were getting ready to go north to the tundra, and the warm-weather birds that had already started to return from down south. The loons were my favorite to look at; in the summer, their plumage was checkered white and black, their necks and chests patterned in delicate dots and pinstripes. Their cries, though – those gave me chills. Tim said the mates called to each other, but even now all I could hear was the keening of banshees.

The sort of wails that heralded death.

THIRTY

By the time we got the boat stored way, I was desperate for a hot meal and a cold beer. Neither of us had managed to buy groceries all week, so we made our way downtown. I was no longer concerned with hiding from Bram. Every hawk-eyed law enforcement officer in Jefferson County was looking for him, including the two of us. On top of that, there was little cover to be found. It was Sunday night, and while there should have been at least a half dozen restaurants open, every building we drove past was shuttered and dark. When we saw the lights on at the Riverboat Pub, I was downright giddy.

Matt had a spring training game playing on the big-screen TV, but even so, we were the pub's only customers. 'Where is everyone?' I asked as we sat down at the scarred but spotless bar.

'Haven't you heard? There's a killer on the loose.'

Our increased efforts to locate Bram were all over the news, and the local stations were showing his sketch again. I'd watched a few segments on my phone, of citizens interviewed in their homes. The fear in their eyes had been impossible to miss.

'Seriously,' said Matt, 'the whole town's on a self-imposed lockdown. When I got in a couple hours ago, the only other place open was Chateau Gris. Lisa's none too happy that I'm here, but if I wasn't, where would you two go for your daily dose of good humor?'

'Fair point,' said Tim as he ordered two beers and a couple of club sandwiches. 'Hey, any chance you found my jacket in here last night? Heavy-duty, khaki zip-up?'

'Nope,' Matt said, 'but I'll keep an eye out. Any news on Bram?' He looked sheepish. 'I know you probably couldn't tell me if there was, but Lisa's been so freaking nervous about sending the kids to school tomorrow. I promised I'd at least ask if I saw you.'

'Nothing yet,' I said. 'But you can tell your wife she doesn't need to worry about the kids. We have no reason to believe he would abduct another child.' *A pretty local woman like Lisa Cutts, though . . .*

I pushed the thought aside.

The paper-lined plastic baskets of food were ready in no time, and Matt started rounding up silverware and napkins.

'What's the latest with Harvey?' he asked as he set down our meals.

The question surprised me. It had only been a few hours since Harvey was admitted to the ER. 'Whoever your source is, they're very dialed in,' I told Matt.

'A bartender knows all.' He said it with a wink. The statement was an echo of the one Matt had made the previous night, and I was starting to get the feeling this particular bartender was more clued-in to local gossip than most. But then Matt added, 'Lisa has a friend who works at the hospital. She told Lisa, and Lisa told me.'

'What exactly did you hear?'

'Just that he's getting checked out after taking Maynard's boat into the channel.'

'That's right,' Tim said. 'He gave everyone a good scare.'

'Harvey's usually in here on Sunday nights,' Matt told us. 'Never misses a visit. Hope and Maynard would take turns bringing him by to socialize with his old-timer buddies. Most of them are in the assisted living facility over on Holland. One of the reasons Harvey moved in with Maynard, I guess, to be close to his friends. It's sweet – they'll have a drink and chat about the good old days. I wonder how much Harvey will be able to do that now, if his mind's that unreliable.' He scanned the empty bar. 'Guess they all stayed home tonight. I'm sure they're thinking about him, with everything that's going on. Anyway, I'm glad to hear he's OK. We all are. Hey, Dad.'

Even without the benefit of Matt's greeting, I would have easily identified the man walking behind the bar. Avery Cutts had Matt's same solid build and thatch of dark hair, but his face was clean-shaven, his eyebrows threaded with gray, and he carried some extra weight around his middle that strained against his forest green flannel shirt and dark-wash jeans. When he smiled at us, I saw he had a chip on one of his upper incisors that, despite the eye bags and lines on his face, made him look younger than his sixty-odd years. The barefaced flaw was endearing.

'How goes it, Mr Cutts?' Tim asked. 'Need a hand with those?'

Avery set down the two cases of liquor he'd been carrying and mopped his brow with a cloth from his pocket.

'Nah, he's good,' said Matt. 'No matter how many times I offer, he always says no. He considers this his workout.'

Avery barked out a laugh. 'Do I look like an invalid to you two? And if I've told you once, I've told you a hundred times' – a grin and a wink at Tim; the man's eyes twinkled – 'call me Avery.'

'Sorry,' Tim said as he twirled a fry in a sauce cup of ketchup, 'can't help it. I was raised to respect my elders.'

'Watch it, Tim, or that'll be the end of the free beers.' Matt laughed. 'Rule number one at the Riverboat: never remind my father of his old age.'

'You're asking for trouble, the both of you.' Avery Cutts knelt down to unload a case, but he was chuckling all the while. 'I'm all right, son,' he told Tim. 'Holding up better than some, I expect.'

'We were just talking about Harvey,' said Matt.

Avery's attention was still on his bottles, but he talked as he worked. 'Where on earth could that man have been going in his condition?'

'Out to Green Rock Island, apparently. He was confused,' I said. 'I gather he used to throw some epic shindigs out there. I guess they were on his mind.'

'You know, he was talking about those parties in here last weekend,' said Matt. 'That can happen. Lisa's grandmother had dementia – remember, Dad? She would tell us about stuff that happened decades ago, but she couldn't remember Lisa's name.'

Avery nodded. 'Tough to see a mind go like that.'

'Sure is.'

'I wondered if there might be a connection between Green Rock Island and what happened to Hope,' I said. 'Given the timing of his excursion and all. Were you ever out there?' I asked Avery.

'Nah. I was chained to this bar even then,' he said. 'It was Cora who did the deliveries up until Matt was born.'

'I thought you and Harvey might be friends. You're a business owner, he was the mayor . . .'

'Ah. No. Harvey's five years older than me. Any news about who killed his daughter?'

'We can't talk about an ongoing investigation,' I said, 'but I can assure you we're doing everything we can to find the perpetrator.'

'I'll get those cases of beer, Dad – not that we'll be needing them tonight,' Matt said, and headed for the basement door.

When he was gone, Avery turned to face us. 'I'm sure everyone appreciates your help. Harvey's pretty popular in these parts.'

I inclined my head. 'Is that true?' On our last visit to the Riverboat, Matt had said the opposite.

Avery unpacked the rest of the bottles, sliding some rum into the speed rail, and mopped his brow again. 'Hard to please everyone when you work in local government, I guess.'

'You must be talking about the resort,' I said.

'Were you yea or nay?' Tim asked with a sly smile.

'Bah, it was a long time ago. Doesn't make any difference now. Well, what do you know,' he said, glancing at the door. 'Customers.'

'You're freaking kidding me,' Tim muttered under his breath.

A moment later, Carson Gates and his newly minted fiancée Kelsea were standing in the middle of the pub.

Same sparkly blue eyes. Same dark goatee woven with silver. The smell of him, the colorful socks peeking out from his pant legs – he wore pressed slacks; I had never once seen the man in anything as informal as jeans – assaulted my senses. For a moment, it was as if the last five months hadn't happened and I was at his mercy again, as helpless as ever.

It was Tim who brought me back to the present. 'Five minutes,' he hissed through his teeth. 'Give me five minutes with the guy in the parking lot out back.'

'Get in line,' I said. I hadn't seen Carson since I learned from Tim that he'd been talking about my treatment, and I was itching to get him alone.

'Well, would you look at this,' Carson boomed from the center of the room. He slipped an arm around Kelsea's waist and pulled her to his hip. 'An impromptu reunion with old friends. Are you two here on official police business, or is this, you know . . .' He sucked his teeth. 'Pleasure.'

Every single seat in the room was open, yet Carson pulled

out a stool for Kelsea right next to me. As he took off his coat and waited for his future bride to do the same, Kelsea caught Tim's eye and they exchanged a meek smile. This was going to be torture. Already Tim's neck was flushed.

It was the first time I'd seen Tim and Carson together, and I didn't know what to expect. Carson had committed some serious acts of vandalism as a kid, and pinned them all on Tim. His behavior had almost cost Tim his future career in law enforcement. Tim got along well with just about everyone, but with Carson, he was done.

Matt was back. When Tim drained his beer, Matt immediately poured him another. He didn't just have his finger on the pulse of local gossip. He could read a room, too.

Grudgingly, Tim said, 'I guess congratulations are in order. When's the big day?'

She had the face of a child, Kelsea did. It was soft around the edges, with oversized eyes that made her appear to be in a constant state of awe. She did her best to play that down with cat-eye make-up and some sort of highlighting powder I gathered was supposed to create the illusion of cheekbones, but when she looked at Tim those big eyes were still round as coins. She opened her glossy mouth to speak. Carson beat her to it.

'Late summer,' he said, sitting down next to her. As he spoke, he gathered up the ponytail from her back and rearranged it over her shoulder. The act felt proprietary. This woman belonged to him, and he wanted us to know it. 'We plan to find a new place first. Fresh start, and all that.' He shot me a look. 'Actually, we've got our hearts set on an island.'

I'd heard this about Carson, way back in November. Private islands hardly ever went up for sale. Carson didn't often take no for an answer.

Tim said, 'And how's that working out for you?' Behind the bar, Matt unloaded a case of beer while Avery looked on. Both men were smirking.

'We have several prospects, actually,' said Carson, but there was color in his cheeks now, a light sheen on his brow. 'What about you two? You must be very busy these days. Another homicide on your watch.' He shook his head. 'Horrible news about that crooked official.'

'She had a name,' I said.

'Right. Hope, was it?' He snorted. 'How ironic. So how's the investigation going?'

'You know we can't talk about that.'

'Two vodka tonics,' Carson said, ignoring Tim's reply. 'But for the love of God, Matt, not the cheap stuff. Remember when we used to drink that, Timmy? That speed rail garbage?'

Beside me, Tim went rigid. Looking at him askance, I could see him trying to work out an escape plan, and coming up short. It wasn't getting late. There was nowhere else he needed to be. Tim's hand was wrapped around a fresh pint of Stony Creek Cranky IPA. He had no valid excuse for leaving now. And Carson knew it.

'We used to come here all the time,' Carson told me. 'Isn't that right, my guy?'

'I'm not your guy,' Tim said.

'I'd say we were, what, seventeen the first time we ordered beers at this bar? Whoops.' Carson fixed his gaze on me. 'Probably not something I should share with a *senior investigator* or these fellas might lose their license.'

Matt's expression clouded and his eyes darted to his dad. Avery's mouth was pressed into a deep frown.

'We had good times, though,' Carson went on, oblivious. 'Except when Timmy would get the hots for my girl, which happened way more often than it should have.' He paused to glance in my direction. The look he doled out was not kind. 'Speaking of which, you need to give us some space.'

Kelsea blushed scarlet. As for Tim, he stared dumfounded at Carson. 'We were here first. There are ten empty tables over there. Have at it.'

'That's not what I mean,' Carson said, 'and you know it.'

'I really don't.'

'You've been following us.'

Tim's jaw dropped. 'What?'

'Look, it's over between you and Kelsea,' Carson said. 'You need to accept that, and you need to move on.'

'And *you* need to stop accusing me of something I didn't do.'

'Whoa,' I said, lifting my hands from the bar top. I was sitting right between them, and their negative energy crackled like a live wire. 'Cool it, OK?'

Carson said, 'Downtown. Today. We *saw* you.'

'That's it,' Tim said, and got to his feet.

Matt was already halfway around the bar by the time I yanked Carson out of his chair. 'Outside,' I said, ignoring the look of horror on Kelsea's face. 'Now.'

'What the hell? You can't—'

'*Now.*'

'Wow.' Carson looked from me to Matt, whose outward fury matched Tim's. Even Avery, behind the bar, radiated aggression. 'You know, I've been meaning to follow up with you, Shana. Do a mental health check. Clearly I'm too late.'

'You son of a bitch,' Tim growled. Matt grabbed him by the arm and held him firmly in place.

Without looking back, I sunk my fingernails into my ex-fiancé's arm and dragged him out the door.

The air outside smelled fresh and clean, like green grass and clear water. I drank it in and tried to calm down. 'How dare you,' I said.

'How dare I what?'

'Treat Tim that way, talk shit to Matt and Avery, break patient confidentiality – take your pick. You've been bragging about treating me to Kelsea.'

'*That's* what you're upset about? Mea culpa, OK? So I told a few people I got you through the trauma of your abduction.'

'A *few people*?'

'Look, I'm building a private practice from the ground up. You're one of my most successful case studies – at least, I thought you were.' Eyeing me, he said, 'Honestly, now I'm not so sure.'

'And how are you going to build a practice if I hold you liable for the unauthorized disclosure of medical information?'

'Calm down,' he said, but he looked less assured. 'I didn't reveal anything we talked about; all I did was mention you were associated with Bram. Your entire precinct knew that already. You can't tell me they're still keeping that under wraps.'

'I'm pretty fucking sure they are. Do you have any idea

what could happen if this gets around town? If people find out I'm the nameless woman Bram abducted in New York, I'll lose my credibility. We're in the middle of a goddamn manhunt, Carson. No one's going to believe I can apprehend Bram when he already got the better of me once.'

'You're overreacting,' he said. 'It'll be fine.' But the skin on his neck was gooseflesh now, pink and bumpy.

'Spare me your platitudes. It isn't just the locals I'm worried about.'

He gave me a curious look. 'What . . . Tim? Did you not tell him what happened to you?'

'Of course I told him.'

'And the sheriff knows, too. So, you see? It's fine. If it makes you feel better, I really don't think people care as much as you think they do.'

Back to the old routine of Carson planting seeds of doubt. 'You're leveraging a murderer's infamy to shore up your own reputation. What you're doing is wrong, and it's dangerous.'

Behind us, the creak of old hinges. Tim and Kelsea stood in the doorway with a beer-scented, slightly fusty wall of heat wafting out from behind them. For a moment, I thought I could see what had brought them together in the fall. In the span of minutes, both managed to rein in their emotions. For our part, Carson and I were fully prepared to scream ourselves hoarse.

'Well, this has been fun . . . said the masochist to the sadist.' Carson took Kelsea by the hand and planted a kiss on her powdery cheek. 'Next time let's do dinner, yeah?'

He was still chuckling when they disappeared, arm in arm, around the corner.

'You OK?' Tim placed a hand on my arm. 'You're shaking.'

'Oh, that's just the blistering rage.'

Tim didn't return my smile.

'Gaslighting is Carson's favorite form of entertainment,' I said. 'Why would he stop now? Someone should tell Kelsea what kind of person he is. The way you told me.'

'Think she'd listen?'

I didn't know, but I hoped she would. Just like I hoped Carson would listen to me.

THIRTY-ONE

O n Monday morning at ten a.m., Paul Ludgate called with a report about the plaster hands. All eighty-six of them had been put under a microscope, and his analysts were at a loss. There were no differentiating markings that they could see, and no indication the artist had notable scars or wore an unusual ring. The fingerprints didn't match any in Canada's criminal database, and we didn't get any hits on our side of the border, either.

'Where does this leave us?' I asked Paul over the phone as I massaged a kink in my neck. I had cancelled my karate class with Sam to catch up on sleep, but with Tim still staying at the cottage it was another late night. Not that I was complaining.

'My team did some pretty extensive canvassing, and based on statements they took from residents in the area the hands turned up sometime between Tuesday and Saturday,' he said. 'I'll check with border patrol again. That's only helpful if the person responsible came from the States, but it's worth a shot.'

I suggested that we try more social listening, too. 'Maybe the perp will show their face to take credit, or someone who knows where the hands came from will fess up,' I said. 'In the meantime, I want to keep looking at Val Giovanni.' I wasn't ready to assume Bram was our man, mainly because I still didn't understand why he'd single out Hope, not when she was so different from his past victims. It seemed prudent to exhaust other possibilities. 'Giovanni's passport was used at the border that night. He threatened the victim. He has a strong alibi, but it's still possible he has an accomplice. We've got those natural fibers from Hope's car, too. Not sure where they fit in yet.'

'Any other threats to the vic that we know of?' Ludgate asked.

'There are plenty of people in town who were angry with her. But again, why kill her now when she was about to be sentenced? There's something else going on here, some other motive that hasn't surfaced yet.'

When I ended the call, Tim spun his desk chair to face me. 'You know, there is someone else we haven't looked into.'

'Yeah?' I said. 'Who's that?'

'Hope's husband.'

Maynard Pope. The thought had crossed my mind. 'The Husband Did It' had given rise to an entire cottage industry of T-shirts, emblazed with the adage and marketed to fans of airport novels and true crime podcasts. Considering more than half of all female homicide victims in America were killed by their partners, Tim's point wasn't without merit.

'His behavior's been strange, I'll grant you that,' I said. 'First, he packs his grieving daughter off to his parents' place, then he leaves Harvey unattended for hours – and after acknowledging the man needs round-the-clock care. What possible reason could he have for killing his wife, though?'

'She moved out,' Tim said.

'A year ago.'

'She committed a crime that made an enemy of the entire community. That must have been humiliating for him.'

'But again, that was months ago. Why kill her now?' I chewed the inside of my cheek as I thought about the savage nature of her death, catching the flesh between my molars. I'd been doing that a lot lately, and it had become a difficult habit to break. The places I'd gnawed were inflamed, making it easy to fret them all over again, and as a result the inside of my mouth was a mess, crosscut with hidden scars.

We'd been to see Maynard Pope twice already, and found no evidence that he was involved in Hope's murder. He claimed he had no knowledge of Val Giovanni and his threats. At the same time, he'd been with Hope the day she disappeared. He knew exactly where she was going, and when. He'd even confessed to being a regular Wolfe Island visitor.

So: means, and opportunity. But where was the motive? *What's in it for them?* was the first question I asked when investigating a crime. Motive wasn't meant to be shoehorned into a feeble theory, and at the moment the theory that Maynard Pope killed his wife felt puny enough to fly away in a light breeze.

'He hasn't given us much to work with,' I acknowledged. 'Maybe we could come at this from another angle. Dig a little deeper into his life with Hope.'

'The daughter,' Tim said at once. 'Natalie.'

'Right. She may not have been around much this past year because of school, but she probably knows her father better than anyone. Maybe she can give us some insight into Maynard and Hope's relationship.'

'What is it they say about the sins of the father?'

'They're visited upon the children. If something weird was going on with her parents,' I said, 'there's a good chance Natalie knows about it.'

THIRTY-TWO

We returned to Iroquois Point to find Natalie alone. It was sunny out, the sky flecked with wisps of cloud, and the breeze lifted the ends of my hair when, with no answer at the front door, we circled the house. Sitting on the back deck, Natalie startled when she saw us but seemed grateful for the company. The restaurant was back to being open every day, her father working his usual long hours. Harvey, for his part, was watching a TV program in the family room.

Our timing was spot-on.

Natalie's hair was braided today, as neatly twisted as a dock line, and she'd set up a laptop on the outdoor dining table. 'Distraction,' she told us with a half-hearted shrug as she tucked her hands into the pockets of a pilled orange fleece. 'My profs said I shouldn't worry about any assignments right now, but I can't sit around doing nothing.'

'How are you holding up?' I asked as Tim and I joined

her at the weathered teak table. For the second time, I marveled at Natalie's bare eyes. Had she plucked out her eyelashes one by one over time, or all at once? Did it start when her mother was charged with corruption, or had she been at it for years?

The young woman rubbed her freckled nose. 'I'm OK. It just feels so surreal, you know?'

'I know.' Violent death had that quality about it. It was jarring, its horror impossible to fathom. 'What about your grandfather?' I asked, chancing a glance at the lake. The door to the boathouse was closed now, and there was a padlock near the handle that hadn't been there before.

'He's better,' Natalie said. 'He's having what my mom would have called a good day. The whole thing doesn't seem to have fazed him at all. Dad and I, though . . . we may never sleep again.'

I nodded, but I was picturing Pope casually running errands while his mentally-impaired father-in-law went for a joy ride on the river.

'He must feel awful,' said Tim. 'Not that he's responsible.'

Well done, Tim. I leaned forward slightly, awaiting Natalie's response.

'He does feel bad,' she said. 'We had a long talk about it last night. The restaurant hasn't been doing so great lately. I think he just got caught up in the excitement of finally having a full dining room again. He went straight there after Gramps was discharged from the hospital, and stayed until almost midnight prepping for today. There was still more to do this morning.'

'Busy guy,' I said. 'Natalie, your mom and dad. Did they have a good relationship?'

Her breath hitched. 'Sure. Why do you ask?'

'Well, she moved to Watertown.'

'For work,' Natalie said firmly. 'It was the only way she could get a job in local government. She really wanted that, always has – I remember her talking about it even when I was little. She wanted to do what Gramps did. Fix up a town, make it better.'

'And your dad supported her?'

'Yeah. Of course.'

'What about your mom?' I asked. 'Did she support your dad?'

'With the restaurant, you mean? Totally. Opening Chateau Gris was a dream come true for him. He's a really talented chef – he went to culinary school in France, and worked at a really good steakhouse in Murray Hill before we moved here from New York – but he always wanted to open his own place. It was hard in the city, though. Rent was super high, and the restaurant scene is so competitive. It was Mom's idea to come here.

'I remember when she started talking about it,' Natalie went on, 'because it totally freaked me out. I didn't want to leave my friends. I was, like, nine at the time. I really liked my school. I knew it had always bothered Mom that we lived so far away from family, though. One day, when Dad had a tough shift at the restaurant, she told him that if we moved upstate he could work for himself, and every hour he spent in a kitchen would be for us.'

'That's a strong argument,' said Tim. 'And it's definitely cheaper to run a restaurant up here.'

'Right. Dad realized that pretty quickly. We moved eight or nine months later. Dad got lucky and found a job at the TI Club right away.'

Lucky is right. In true North Country style, the Thousand Islands Club wasn't as posh as some yacht clubs on the East Coast, but it was impeccably groomed and offered surf and turf and salmon piccata galore.

'It took a couple more years before they had enough money to open Chateau Gris, but they would never have been able to save up as fast living in the city,' Natalie said. 'And Gramps helped him out with the financing, too. He was so excited about bringing gourmet cooking to town. Dad always says it was worth the wait. When he opened the restaurant, it was an instant hit.'

'That's true,' said Tim. 'It did seem to take off right from the start.'

'Yeah. When the summer residents heard an upscale place had opened in town, they all wanted to check it out. It's been popular with the Canadians, too. They boat across the river from Rockport. Some come all the way from Brockville or Kingston.'

'Your dad must have a strong ad campaign,' I said.

'Not really. That's all thanks to Gramps. He's pretty well-connected from when he was mayor. He told everyone about it.' A flicker of a smile. 'He'd even stop strangers on the street. He loves the restaurant almost as much as Dad does. And Dad's obsessed with the place.'

'It must be a lot of pressure on your dad,' I said. 'Owning a restaurant. Did your parents ever argue about that?'

Natalie turned her head toward the wide expanse of glistening river. She brought her fingers to her right eye, froze, and plunged her hand back in her pocket.

'I mean, it can be stressful, even with the help from Gramps,' she said. 'They took out a second mortgage on the house when they bought that old building downtown, and it needed a lot of renovations. Dad gets upset sometimes about the debt he racked up over these past few months. And he works so hard – he practically lives at the restaurant. That's why I was staying with my other grandparents in Chippewa Bay.'

'Natalie,' I said gently, 'you didn't answer my question.'

Her chest juddered under her fleece when she exhaled. 'Things weren't that great between them this past year or two. It's part of the reason Mom moved to Watertown. Dad tried to make it up to her – that's why he agreed to keep an eye on Gramps – but then Gramps got worse, and Mom . . . well. You know.'

It was Tim's turn now. 'Why do you think your mother did what she did in Watertown?'

'Honestly?' Her expression was pained. 'I think she saw Gramps's mind going and panicked. Like, she realized she didn't have much time left to show him what she could do.'

'To make a big impact on a small community, you mean,' said Tim.

'Yeah.'

'How did your dad react to that?'

Natalie picked up the end of her braid and brushed it against her face, back and forth. She was self-soothing. Her freckled cheeks were blotchy.

'Not well,' she said. 'They had to spend all this money on lawyers for her, which Dad was super stressed about – and then all of a sudden people stopped coming to Chateau Gris. At first Dad thought it was the season. It was a really rainy October, even before that big nor'easter, and people were hunkering down at home. But things got worse and worse. Mom told me there were days when Dad wouldn't get a single customer. She said it was her fault. She thought people were punishing her.'

'Word got around pretty quickly, I guess,' Tim said.

'Yeah. People just stopped coming. Everyone, all at once.'

In other words, Maynard Pope had been blindsided. It didn't matter how respected and connected Harvey Oberon had been. His daughter committed a crime, and just like that the community's loyalty was washed away.

Tim said, 'That must have been really hard on your parents.'

Though she nodded, Natalie couldn't bring herself to speak. 'I think,' she said at length, 'if this hadn't happened to Mom . . . I think they would have split up.'

Kids always know more than their parents want to believe. They think they're fooling them, but children see everything. Drink it all in. Those two words – split up – made everything click into place. Hope and Maynard's living arrangement hadn't made sense from the start. I could buy that she rented an apartment for work, but opting to reside in Watertown even after her illegal activities were exposed, and she was fired from her job? That never sat right with me. She must have had another reason to stay away. Here it was.

Hope and her husband had been on the outs. She humiliated him. Her actions had threatened his business.

But she was gone now.

And where Maynard Pope's business was concerned, Hope's death was a godsend.

THIRTY-THREE

The sun was a warm hand on my back, the air soft and light, but as we interviewed Natalie, she couldn't stop shivering. It might have been the grief. More likely, she knew that in the context of a murder investigation, what she'd just told us about her father didn't bode well for him. Tim suggested she grab a coat from inside. We had just a few more questions, he said. Almost done.

And then, we'd need to have another talk with Maynard Pope.

No sooner had Natalie disappeared through the sliding doors than I heard the pop and crackle of tires on the driveway at the front of the house.

'Perfect. Let's catch him before he goes in,' I said. Ambushes could do wonders for helping us ferret out the truth. When we rounded the corner of the low house, though, we found Pope's car sitting empty.

'Mr Pope?' Tim called. Had he rushed inside the house? If so, our conversation with Natalie was most certainly over. I wondered how he would react when she revealed what she'd confessed about the restaurant and his life with Hope.

'Should we knock?' Tim asked, heading for the front door. Halfway there, he stopped short. A noise. The clatter of metal on concrete. It had come from the garage.

'Mr Pope?' It was me who called this time. I raised my voice a little, but kept my intonation even. There was a stirring deep in my stomach that I didn't like. It felt like a warning. The automatic garage door faced the driveway, but the structure also had a side door closer to the house. 'Let's take a look,' I said, crossing the lawn toward it.

With Tim by my side, I eased open the door.

At first I didn't understand what I was seeing. The interior of the garage was dim and damp, in chaos. Bikes, bins, and waterproof boxes were stacked halfway up the walls, the exposed beams discolored by time. On the ceiling, a bed of nails. They'd been driven into the roof above, their sharp ends winking in the beam of light from the open door. What held my attention, though, was the folding table pushed up against the far wall. It was partially covered in newspapers, splayed open to blanket the surface. The newspapers were splattered with blood. On one side of the table Maynard Pope stood frozen, more paper balled up in his hands, his face gray and still as a river stone as he took in the sight of us.

'Stop right there, Mr Pope.' My mind was buzzing. I took a step toward the table. I could smell it now, through the damp wood and termite rot, the same dusty, earthy smell that permeated the walls of Johanna Scott's studio. My eyes darted around the room. Under the table, two buckets coated in a silvery residue. Dirty rags. A sealed paint can with a dried drip extending downward from its rim. It was all there.

Everything needed to mix and mold plaster body parts dipped in red.

'Dad?' Natalie burst into the garage, eyes ablaze.

'Get out of here,' her father said, but his daughter's hands were drawn up to her mouth.

'What are you doing? Dad, what are you doing in here?'

'Not one more word,' said Pope.

'I'm going to need you to step outside. Both of you,' I said. Tim herded them out the door while I fumbled for my phone. *Ludgate. Bogle. Sol.* I'd need to call them all, get a forensic team over here to take samples. There was no question, though, that this place was the source of the eighty-six hands.

I was still trying to process what that meant when, as I stepped from the dark, musty garage into the sunlight, I saw that Tim was no longer standing with Natalie and Pope. Instead, he was back at the front door. On his knees.

I'm no expert on natural fibers. I couldn't tell jute from seagrass to save my life. Even so, I knew exactly what Tim was doing on that stoop. The mat, the same one we'd stood on numerous times upon visiting the house, was so parched by the harsh island weather that the woven strands of material – tiny ropes, really – were virtually shredded.

As I looked on, Tim brushed some pale fibers from his shoes, and the wind carried them away.

THIRTY-FOUR

There was a ticking coming from the radiator by the floor. Every few seconds the tapping started anew, sharp and intermittent. The air in the interview room was stuffy and hot, so dry that when I lowered my hands to my lap my fingertips snagged the polyester of my pant leg. The situation didn't appear to agree with Maynard Pope, whose forehead shimmered with sweat. Whose eyes flitted between Tim, me, and the table like he didn't know where to look. The fabric under the man's arms had slowly grown three shades darker than the rest of his tight-fitting shirt, and a nerve next to his left eye was twitching. His distress was so thick I could practically smell it.

As for me, I felt more confident than I had in months.

The past two hours had been a whirlwind. A sample of the fibers from Pope's doormat was rushed to the forensic scientist who'd processed Hope's sedan, and I was prepared to bet a month's salary that the sisal was a match. Meanwhile, I'd assigned Solomon the task of looking into the family's insurance plans. His report had been enlightening. Maynard Pope didn't have a policy under his name – but Hope did. Far as Sol could tell, she'd signed a contract with a local insurance agent shortly after losing her job and the coverage she had through the City of Watertown. The new policy had a payout of $750,000. The primary beneficiary? Hope's husband.

When asked about the insurance, Pope insisted the policy wasn't his idea. His wife was terrified of dying an early death due to the loss of her mother, and wanted to make sure Natalie would always be taken care of. But as the old proverb goes, whoever profits from the crime is guilty of it, and as we questioned Pope about the evidence in his garage, I couldn't shake those words from my head.

'I told you,' Pope said after Tim prodded him yet again, 'I've been patching some walls. It's an old house.'

Snapshots of the hands punching up through the earth around the turbine were fanned out on the table. I pushed them toward him. 'The red paint on the plaster. It's a particular shade, verging on crimson. The same color as the paint on your front door, along with the near-empty can in your garage. Can you explain that?'

'The front door needed touching up.'

'Seems like an odd time to be thinking about home improvement, Mr Pope.'

'My wife was murdered a week ago, detective. Should I be out golfing?' He'd been aiming for sarcasm, but the comment landed heavily and made him sound heartless. Pope squirmed in his seat. 'I don't know anything about these hands,' he said, shoving the photos away. 'What you saw in my garage is all perfectly innocent. You're wasting your time.'

My expectation was that Maynard Pope would confess. There was no way the materials and paint we'd seen in his garage weren't related to the plaster hands found on Wolfe Island. And yet, Hope's husband continued to deny the connection. The first time I showed him the photographs of the sinister exhibition, his head tilted in a way that had surprised me. Now, he wouldn't even look at them.

I wondered how Natalie and Harvey were faring. We only had one interview room, so Don Bogle had taken them to the conference room next door. The space was mainly used for coffee breaks and meals, and it was a good stretch more comfortable than where we were now. I'd asked Bogle to keep Pope's family there until Natalie could get in touch with her paternal grandparents. At the very least, that enabled us to make sure Harvey stayed safe. The walls were thin at the barracks, though, and every now and then, over the song of the radiator, I could hear Natalie crying. There wasn't much of a difference between sorrow and dread, at least not physiologically. Both hurt in equal measure, tightening around our guts like a noose on a neck.

Pope winced when his daughter's sobs broke through the noise, but still he said nothing. Until we found indisputable evidence linking him to Hope's death, my theory about her killer was pure speculation. I was reaching, desperate to gain purchase. Investigators solve crimes by gathering evidence, evaluating it with a critical eye, and slotting together the puzzle pieces. Forcing knobs into holes they don't belong in isn't particularly effective, but there are plenty of times when I have to give them a nudge.

In other words, I needed a foothold. A way in.

'It's been a long few months, hasn't it, Mr Pope? Can't have been easy,' I said, 'watching the customer base you've worked so hard to build get eroded by something beyond your control. Hope committed a crime. You shouldn't be the one who has to pay for it.'

'It's Hope who paid for it,' he said without delay. 'She's dead because she happened to piss someone off who's not right in the head. Where's the guy who sent those threatening letters, huh? *That's* who you should be talking to.'

'Did you argue with your wife, Mr Pope?'

My question angered him. He unfolded his arms and balled his hands into fists. Squeezed until his knuckles were white as bone. 'I loved my wife. Ask anyone.'

'We asked your daughter,' said Tim. 'She said you hadn't been getting along.'

'You leave Natalie out of this.'

'You can't tell me you weren't upset when that scandal in Watertown threatened to obliterate your business,' I went on. 'Hope's crimes were like a poison that seeped into this community. To the restaurant, they were toxic. Did you finally find an antidote, Mr Pope? A way to reverse the damage? Business is strong again. Isn't that right?'

He folded his arms, heavy as joints of meat, and stared straight ahead.

I said, 'Let me tell you what I think happened. When word got out about what Hope had done, your restaurant suffered. You lost customers, even the faithful ones. Even the ones you considered friends. For the sake of your family – to keep up appearances and protect Natalie – you tried to be supportive of Hope. You brought her groceries so she didn't have to leave the house, and had her over for dinner. You couldn't very well leave her when she was going through the hardest time of her life. Your family was maligned enough already.

'But the stress became too much to take. Every day, you went to Chateau Gris and tried to think of a way to fix things. The tables sat empty while the mortgage on the building and the invoices from your suppliers ate away at your profits. Eventually, you grew desperate. You and Hope had grown apart. And the only way you could imagine the restaurant bouncing back was if Hope, and the scandal, were gone.'

'No.' Pope's voice was hoarse. 'What Hope did caused some problems. Was I happy about it? Of course not – and neither was Harvey. He gave the best years of his life for this town, made a name for himself that should have lived on forever, and people still look at him like this is all his fault. But I would never – I *could never* – hurt the mother of my child. I loved her. We all did.'

His eyes went glassy. He was thinking of motherless Natalie one room over, and poor Harvey who, thanks to Pope's carelessness, the family almost lost as well.

I softened my tone, made it extra gentle. 'You weren't in your right mind. You were distraught. Panicked, even. And then you found out about the threats.'

It was the only explanation. If Maynard Pope was guilty of murder, he had to have known about Val Giovanni.

But Pope said, 'I told you, I had no idea about those.'

'You'd never heard of Giovanni?' Tim asked.

'I'd heard of him. He was in the newspaper a bunch of times. I didn't know he wrote any letters to Hope.'

'Hope never mentioned him? Not once during all of her visits?'

'No.' His face went slack. A beat, then two. 'She may have mentioned a protestor once, but I didn't—'

'Is that when you came up with the idea to kill Hope and frame him?' I said.

There was panic in Pope's eyes now, pure animal fear. 'No. No way. That's insane.'

Was it? No matter how I looked at the situation, I could only see Pope's beefy hands around Hope's neck. The materials in his garage were damning. Pope's marriage had been troubled, to the point where Hope had chosen not to live with him even when given the chance. Even with business picking back up, Pope's finances were floundering. And then there was the matter of a hefty life insurance payout.

'The supplies in your garage suggest you went to Wolfe Island over the weekend to plant those hands,' I said. 'Did you use Giovanni's passport for that, too? You might as well tell me, Mr Pope. Any minute now, our law enforcement partners in Canada will be calling with a report of exactly who came through Port Alexandria, and when.'

I wasn't lying. We'd been expecting that call from Paul Ludgate all morning. If a resident of Wolfe Island was responsible, we might never track the perp down. If it was someone from the mainland of Ontario, Ludgate might be able to find them through a ferry ticket purchase. My money was on an American, though. Someone who already had a stolen passport on hand.

'I–I didn't do what you think I did. I didn't kill my wife.'

'I need to remind you,' I said, 'one of my investigators is searching your house as we speak.' Mac had a friend who was a judge, and it had taken less than an hour for him to sign the search warrant, during which time a trooper stood by the Pope residence to safeguard any evidence that might be hidden inside. Tim and I had agreed on what Sol should look for. Val Giovanni's passport was still missing. 'Given your current financial situation, that life insurance policy is a pretty strong motive for killing your wife. If we find Giovanni's passport, we'll have enough evidence to merit a first-degree murder charge. But if you confess,' I told Pope, 'and tell us everything we need to know about Hope's death, you might not have to spend the next sixty years in prison.'

I let my gaze trail to the room next door.

'I didn't kill her,' Pope cried once more.

There was a folder on the table, next to the photographs of the hands. I'd made a point of keeping it closed, but now I extended my hand toward it. I stared at the folder for a long time before opening it. It contained a set of photographs far more savage than the ones I'd shown to Pope already. Images straight out of a nightmare. I looked up at Tim, half expecting to find an appeal for mercy. His gaze was cool and constant. *It's the only explanation*, I told myself again.

I flipped back the cover. Hope's body, in that purple coat, looked like an oversized rag doll left out in the rain. Forgotten. Forsaken. I nudged the photos toward him.

Maynard Pope blinked at me, agony writ large on his face. He knew what awaited him on the table. His gaze drifted away from mine to settle on the photograph. He was shaky when he reached out to expose the other pictures in the pile. There was a close-up of Hope's face, and he lifted it from the table with the utmost of care, running the tips of his fingers over her ashen cheek. His own face crumpled then, his shoulders began to shake, and he uttered a sound that was so full of anguish my whole body went cold.

A muted, drawn-out buzz sprang from my jacket pocket, which I'd draped over the back of my chair. I pulled out my phone, glanced at the display. 'That's them,' I told Tim. 'The Canadians. Last chance, Mr Pope.'

His eyes still on the photos, he shook his heavy head.

'We're going to take this call,' I said with a nod in Tim's direction. 'And when we come back, I want the truth. All of it.'

Without looking at him again, I shoved back my chair and headed for the door, Tim close beside me.

'Jesus,' he wheezed when we were in the hall. 'I can't believe you did that.'

I had already hit the answer button, but I pressed the phone against my chest as my face arranged itself into an open-mouthed stare. 'I looked at you!' I hissed under my breath. 'You seemed fine with it!'

'I didn't know you were going to do *that*!'

'We were getting nowhere. What choice did I have?' As I said it, though, my gaze was drawn back to the interview room. Through the window I could see Pope had folded his arms over the photographs and buried his head between them. I felt nauseous and heavy, like I'd swallowed too much water. *He's guilty*, I reminded myself. *He did this to her. He has to live with that.* Still, his profound misery was almost too much to bear. Turning my back on the door, I scrubbed my face with a free hand and brought the phone to my ear.

'Paul,' I said, clearing my throat. 'Sorry. What have you got?'

'Border patrol got back to me with the latest report on crossings. We got a hit on a US passport.'

'Giovanni,' I said at once, eyes on Tim. It was all coming together. Ludgate was about to tell us the stolen passport had been used a second time to cross onto Wolfe Island. Combined with everything else, it would be more than enough for us to bring a murder charge against Maynard Pope. The case would be closed by dinner.

'It wasn't Giovanni's passport,' Ludgate said, jolting me from my reverie.

I faced the window again. Watched Maynard Pope's back quake while Tim watched me. 'Then whose was it?' I asked. *Who else could it be?*

Paul Ludgate took a breath. 'Ah hell, I hate to say it. It was Pope's daughter. She took the ferry there and back, and spent an hour on the island in between. We've got her car on camera. Natalie Pope planted those hands. And I, for one, would like to know why.'

THIRTY-FIVE

The only thing worse than not having a single lead on a homicide case is watching a case fall apart. And watch I did as, bit by bit, the evidence we had against Maynard Pope ceased to exist. I barely had enough time to tell Tim the news about Natalie before Sol called to report there was no passport, or any other suspicious evidence, at the Pope family home.

We'd gone back into the interview room then, and I had put my questions to Pope plainly – starting with why we'd found fibers from his doormat in the driver's side footwell of Hope's car. Pope said that Hope had lingered on the mat upon her last visit, the day she was killed. Harvey hadn't wanted her to leave, and had followed her outside.

I asked again about the paint and plaster, too. Reluctantly, Pope explained he'd found remnants of the sculpture work the previous day. He knew right away it was Natalie who left the mess behind. She'd always been creative; she was an art major at SU. She'd had ample opportunity to work in the garage while Pope and Harvey were at the restaurant.

Initially, he'd assumed she had started a new art project to get her mind off her mother. It was only when he read about the plaster hands online that he realized what Natalie had done. Whether a Wolfe Island resident had leaked the discovery to the media or a reporter stumbled onto the dog walker's tweet, I didn't know, but the eighty-six hands made the news, and Pope had seen the reports just that morning. They speculated the sculptures may have been left by Hope's killer. Confused, and concerned that Natalie could be implicated in the crime, Maynard Pope had driven straight home to talk to her. When he saw our car in the driveway, he panicked and tried to conceal the evidence.

Everything that followed had been a desperate bid to keep his daughter safe. Pope knew the hands would look suspicious to the authorities, and didn't want us finding out his daughter was responsible. He couldn't stand the idea of Natalie being dragged into her mother's homicide investigation and pummeled by the press. He felt guilty enough about his estrangement from Hope and keeping Natalie at arm's length for fear that she might find out their relationship was on the rocks.

All of this, Maynard Pope relayed to me with a stricken, tear-streaked face. He was a man transformed, an empty sack, every ounce of machismo wrung out of him by grief. I believed him. There was just one thing about the man that continued to nag at me, and that was Hope's hefty insurance policy. But as Pope was quick to point out, he didn't really need the money. The restaurant was busier than ever.

We were all in the interview room now: me, Tim, Natalie, and her dad. I had removed the photos of Hope's body from the table, but I couldn't pack away my shame. I'd jumped to conclusions, pushed too hard too soon. Not only had the theory I'd lobbed at Pope not stuck, but it had slid down the wall to the floor with a sickening splat. I'd exposed Hope's husband to images that would haunt him for the rest of his life, and there was no taking that back. All I could do now was go easy on his daughter and get Hope's family out of here so they could start to heal.

Natalie Pope hadn't killed her mother. Tim and I knew that. Ludgate did, too. She'd been in Syracuse when Hope's body was identified, and hadn't arrived in town until a day and a half later. At twenty years old and slender, Natalie lacked the brute strength needed to fracture a trachea. It did surprise me that she'd thought to pack her passport after learning of her mother's demise, but Tim noted that the Pope–Oberon family made regular trips to Canada, and Natalie's parents had no doubt trained her to be prepared. No, I didn't believe Natalie had anything to do with our homicide case, other than muddying the waters.

That didn't mean her actions were without purpose.

So we listened, Tim and I, as she explained everything.

She'd been fourteen years old when the eighty-six hands appeared on Wolfe Island for the first time. She was fascinated, both by the anonymous hands and the notion that a few bags of plaster of Paris could make such a powerful statement. 'That stuck with me,' she told us. 'As soon as Dad said Mom was found by a turbine on Wolfe Island, I remembered.'

'What you did threw us way off track.' I shuddered to think how close we'd come to charging her father with murder. 'Didn't it occur to you that we'd make a connection between the hands and your mother's death?'

'Yeah,' Natalie said. 'And that's exactly what I wanted.'

'I don't understand. Were you trying to send a message to the person who hurt her?'

'The message wasn't for the person who killed her,' she said darkly. 'It was for everyone else. Like the father I saw at the grocery store when I was home for Christmas. He had a toddler in his cart, and he kept trying to make the kid laugh. You were with me, Dad, remember?' She dragged a hand across her nose, her hairless eyelids aquiver. 'He was buying all the stuff for homemade cookies, flour and brown sugar and three kinds of sprinkles. He looked like a good guy. Except he kept sneaking glances at us, staring like we were a couple of freaks – and when we passed him in the aisle, he backed up so far he almost knocked over the cookie cutter display.'

Maynard Pope took Natalie's hand in his and clutched it hard. His gaze flicked to her naked eyes, now a watery shade of pink, and remained there.

'Those hands were for Mrs Bremmer,' Natalie went on, 'who used to be one of Mom's closest friends but wouldn't walk on the same side of the street as her after the first report about the scandal aired on TV. Mom told me a ton of stories like that, of all the people who were supposed to be her friends but turned on her without a second thought.'

She drew in a breath and collapsed her shoulders. I wondered if she had a therapist in Syracuse, or access to a grief counselor she could talk to. She would need one.

'The community,' I said gently. 'You think all those people have blood on their hands.'

'*Of course* they do. I'm not saying what Mom did was right, but she had good intentions. Nobody wanted to believe that, though. No one would listen. If they'd been more understanding and given her a little support, the articles wouldn't have been so awful. Mom said there were reporters crawling all over town looking for quotes about her, and people were happy to give them. Every single friend and neighbor who got interviewed threw her under the bus. Mom even called a few of them to ask why they did it, how they could stoop so low. She was a *good person*, always helping people and volunteering. She wanted to remind them of that. And you know what? They wouldn't even pick up the phone.'

'Oh kiddo,' said Pope, folding his daughter into a hug.

Was that how Natalie saw the community she'd grown up in, the people her family had been close to? Were they all heartless traitors to her now? The town where she'd spent the past decade, the place she considered home, would be forever tainted.

When Hope's acts of corruption went public, there had, in fact, been a few people who came to her defense. I recalled that Mac had to field a lot of phone calls from locals who were convinced investigators had it wrong. Courtney and Dori weren't among those who ostracized the woman either, but I had a feeling that, overall, Natalie was right and Hope had been roundly dismissed. *No*, I thought. *It was worse than that.*

They'd put Hope through a meat grinder, and used what was left as fodder for chinwag. Pope told us as much the first day we met him. Hope hadn't even bought her own groceries, for all the rude remarks she'd have to field. *Gossip. Nasty stuff.* The bloody hands were a brave young woman's way of showing her community exactly how she felt about its fickle conduct.

I felt sorry for Natalie. I knew what it was like to be gossiped about. For a moment, my thoughts came to rest on Swanton. How would my parents, and Aunt Fee and my cousin Crissy, survive there once Bram's identity was publicized? They'd be shunned. Shamed. Or worse. There would always be neighbors who'd assume bloodlust ran in the family and refuse to live with the people who raised a predator of the highest order.

What then?

'That must have taken a lot of courage for your mother to confront those people,' I said, banishing all deliberations of my hometown from my mind.

'That was Mom,' said Natalie, extricating herself from her father's embrace. 'She could do anything. She got a new job, her dream job, after being out of the workforce for years. She found this amazing economic opportunity for Watertown, and all anybody cares about is that she made one mistake.'

I didn't like the acrimony in her words, or the idea that this experience could turn her so bitter. 'I'm sure that's not true,' Tim said in a sympathetic voice. 'People disappoint us sometimes, but I bet a lot of those folks will come around.'

'Yeah, to ogle the family of a murder victim.'

'She's right,' Pope said sadly. 'It's not everyone, but there have been more customers taking selfies and trying to get candid photos of me this past week than I can count.'

'In time they'll forget,' Tim said, ever hopeful. But Natalie's expression had grown surly.

'Yeah, right,' she snorted. 'This isn't the first time our family's been shut out.'

I turned Natalie's words over in my head. Tim's brother J.C. had called Harvey Oberon a legend. By Courtney and Dori's account, the former mayor was a beloved fixture in the town. He played Santa Claus, for God's sake. The man was practically a saint.

'Anyone who projected blame onto Harvey will come around eventually,' I said, feeling her out.

'It's not that,' said her father. 'She's talking about the resort.'

Once again, decades after the fact, the resort was a point of contention. There had been some opposition to it; Matt said as much at the pub. I hadn't gotten the impression that the project resulted in Harvey's constituents leaving him out in the cold.

'That was a long time ago, wasn't it?' I asked.

'Doesn't matter,' Natalie replied. 'People still harp on it. Gramps still talks about how rude some of the older folks are to him.'

Pope gave a nod. 'People loved Harvey when he was hosting parties and throwing money at waterfront beautification, but when it came time to do something that would really make a difference and pump a ton of money into the local economy, he couldn't get a buy-in. That resort was supposed to be the crown jewel of A-Bay, but some people were convinced it would lead to overcrowding. They didn't want to see the village commercialized. So Harvey backed off,' he said with a sigh, 'and a couple years later, a gorgeous new resort opened up in Clayton. Guess who's got the lion's share of the tourist money now?'

I'd never considered that Alexandria Bay could lack for tourists. In the summer, the riverfront town was stuffed to the gills with visitors, all of them throwing money at the souvenir shops and ice cream stands. At restaurants like Chateau Gris. When I stopped to think about it, though, nearby Clayton had the more expensive hotel rooms. It was Clayton where luxury cruise ships from Montreal docked so passengers could experience small-town living in the beautiful Thousand Islands. I'd been in Clayton myself last July, eating fried perch at the Thousand Islands Inn with Mac, when one of those boats deposited more than two hundred well-off travelers from France in the middle of town.

'Big shoes,' I said thoughtfully. 'Harvey said he and Diane used to tell Hope she had big shoes to fill.'

'That's part of the reason why she went to Watertown,' Maynard Pope said. 'To do what Harvey couldn't do here.

The hotels Hope planned to get built would have created a lot of new jobs – just like that resort would have here in A-Bay. The revamped hotel would have attracted more tourists, too. With the donation from Green Wind, she could have put Watertown on the map.'

I turned to Natalie. 'And you're saying some people still hold a grudge against your grandfather for a decades-old project that didn't happen?' If that was true, maybe there was someone around who hated Harvey enough to kill his daughter.

'Small towns have long memories,' Natalie said, sounding older than her years.

Once again, my mind flashed to Swanton. 'You're right about that.'

'Everything Mom did, she did for Gramps,' said Natalie, 'and the people who live and work in Watertown. I'm sorry if the hands screwed with your investigation. I was just so fed up, and I didn't know how else to show them their actions had consequences.'

It was an astute remark, made by a girl wracked with grief, and I knew it would stick with me until our investigation was over. A single unpopular act could transform a persona completely.

It might even become a motive for murder.

THIRTY-SIX

B ack when I was still in training in Albany, I used to picture what my life on the force would be like. I imagined myself stalking the streets of neighborhoods that turned ruthless and cruel at night, spackling the chipped corners of society and clearing out depraved killers like trash from an alley. Back then, I craved the terror of facing them full-on and yearned for the mind-numbing exhaustion it would bring. It didn't take long for me to discover that, in reality, the majority of my time on the job would be spent doing one thing.

Paperwork.

Tim and I did loads of it that afternoon, cataloguing everything new we'd learned. We didn't come up for air until after three p.m., and by then I was mentally spent. I was also famished. I'd barely eaten over the past few days, and didn't think it likely that we'd finish our shift on time, so at my suggestion we ordered a pizza and sat down in the conference room to eat.

'We've got nothing,' I said as I gathered up a droopy, extra-cheesy slice and guided it into my mouth. 'No evidence of value. No witnesses. No suspect. So who the hell killed her, Tim? *No*,' I said through a second oily mouthful. 'No way.'

Tim hadn't said a word. He'd barely had time enough to draw a breath. But I knew exactly what he was thinking.

He set down his slice, and wiped his chin.

'Hope's body was brought all the way out to the wind farm to make it look like the murder's linked to her job,' said Tim. 'The killer impersonated an average citizen and crossed the border wearing a disguise. You can't tell me this doesn't have all the earmarks of one of his psycho games.'

I used my free hand to knead my forehead. *Could it be?* We'd spent the last six days following leads that any investigator would have deemed legitimate, but our efforts had been fruitless. Try as I might to dredge up an alternative suspect, I could only think of one. If Tim was right, and Blake Bram had masterminded all of this, then we were merely cattle in an abattoir, turning circles on the kill floor. Waiting for the butcher to finish us off.

I pondered that as I took another bite. 'It doesn't feel right. The card said Eel Bay. What does that have to do with Hope's murder?'

'More misdirection? The bastard lives to send you on a wild goose chase. He's the one who convinced you those cards mean something by leaving them in your bag last fall. Maybe that's a trick too, and you're reading too much into them.'

I didn't want to concede to Tim's point. At the same time, there was only one person around who we knew with certainty was capable of killing Hope. If my suspicions were right, he'd been in the area for months, long enough to keep up on the local news. To hear about the scandal. To note Val Giovanni's public presence, and track the man down. Bram had proven himself adept at burglary when he broke into Mac's house last year. Accessing Giovanni's isolated farmhouse and filching his passport would be a walk in the park for a man like him.

I'm not done yet, Bram had said at the cemetery. *We're not done.*

'There is another possibility,' I said, unwilling to give in.

'Yeah? What's that?'

'The resort. Look, I know it was decades ago that people butted heads with Harvey, but you heard the Popes. Neither of them even lived in town in the early eighties – hell, Natalie wasn't even born yet – and they're still worked up about the backlash against Harvey. And then here comes his daughter, attempting something similar in Watertown.'

'So, what, someone's been holding a grudge against the Oberons for close to forty years?'

'Stranger things have happened,' I said. 'Small towns have long memories, remember? You said yourself the Oberons were like small-town royalty. And where there's royalty, there's always someone waiting to usurp the throne.'

The phone on the conference room table rang before Tim could reply. Grudgingly, I dropped my pizza to my plate and answered.

'Shana?' Don Bogle rasped into the receiver. 'We've got a situation out here.'

'Oh, *come on*,' Tim said when we arrived in the building's small lobby.

Carson Gates was standing next to Bogle, and he looked pissed.

I cocked my head at my ex and delivered a scathing look. 'What, no Kelsea this time? I thought you two were attached at the hip.'

'Kelsea,' Carson said, 'is at home, and I'll have you know she's very upset. If this is your idea of a joke, Tim, it's not funny.'

After sending Bogle back to the lead desk, I turned on Carson. 'What are you talking about?'

'He's been following us,' Carson said, thrusting an extended finger in Tim's direction. 'Kelsea saw him outside the apartment again last night, lurking in the trees by the parking lot. Peeping through the windows. Kelsea had the blinds open. She was changing. I'm here to file for a restraining order.'

It was all I could do not to burst out laughing. Next to me, Tim was stoic.

'You're out of your mind,' he told Carson. 'I wasn't anywhere near your apartment. Not last night, not ever.'

'You're a fucking liar.'

'Hey.' I stepped forward and glared at Carson. 'Are we gonna have a problem here?'

'Oh, nice,' Carson said. 'You come to the police for help and get treated like a criminal. I know it kills you that I'm with Kelsea now, but you need to get over it, Tim. Move the hell on.'

'I couldn't care less what Kelsea does, and I'd sooner gouge my eyes out than *peep through your windows*. Jesus.' Tim was nose to nose with Carson now, his shoulders drawn back, muscles tense. 'All I've wanted my whole life is for you to leave me alone. Do you seriously think I'd hang around your place to spy on you?'

'On *Kelsea*. I do, and I'm telling you to *cut it out.*'

That last word was accompanied by a shove. The heels of Carson's hands sent Tim stumbling backward. When Tim looked up from the floor, his eyes were two shades darker and there was more vitriol in his expression than I knew him to be capable of. 'I wasn't at your place,' he said again in a voice that was low and dangerous.

'Bullshit. I saw you. You had on the same jacket you wear around town.'

'Wait.' I pushed my way between them. 'What did the jacket look like, Carson?'

'It was khaki. It had a zipper. Don't try to tell me it wasn't him.'

'It wasn't,' I said. 'That wasn't Tim, Carson, because Tim was at my place last night.'

I took some satisfaction in watching my ex's jaw drop.

'That sounds about right,' he said. 'Low self-esteem and fear are the two biggest drivers of toxic relationships. You two deserve each other.'

'It's time to go,' said Tim, ushering Carson out the door.

'He's an asshole,' Tim said when he was gone. 'Always has been, always will be.'

'I can vouch for that. But listen, what he said about your jacket—'

'Geeze, Shane. I don't even have that jacket anymore.'

'I know. It's been missing since Saturday night. And yesterday – and then again today – Kelsea saw a man she thought was you lurking outside Carson's apartment.'

'You don't think . . .' Tim blanched. 'Bram's targeting Kelsea?'

Hearing him say it made my stomach rise. There was no time to dwell on the appalling realization that Bram could have been in the bar with me that night, watching with excitement while I scrutinized the faces of all the other men. 'I don't know. But we know the guy out there wasn't you. Seems like a pretty big coincidence that whoever it is has your same jacket. It's been, what, almost a week since Bram broke into my cottage. Almost forty-eight hours since I pissed him off at the cemetery. We don't have another explanation for what Kelsea saw. I think we have to assume it's him.'

Horror-struck, Tim said, 'We have to warn them.'

Tim hadn't been privy to the photographs of the three women Bram killed in New York, or stood in an autopsy suite with Jess Lowenthal's mangled body. He knew the victims had been stabbed, and that it was grisly, but their bloodless faces and dead eyes didn't haunt him like they did me. That didn't mean he couldn't imagine what Bram might do to Kelsea Shaw, or how quickly her name could be added to his macabre list. Tim understood the kind of person we were dealing with the day he saw the gash Bram left on an innocent nine-year-old's cheek, the same child from whom Bram had wrenched a live tooth mere days prior. Neither of us wanted to picture sweet Kelsea gutted like a smallmouth bass, but in that moment, for both of us, it was hard to imagine her any other way.

'Where does she work?' I was already reaching for my cell phone.

'She's a physical therapist at Evolution PT.'

'Go there,' I told him. 'Stay with Kelsea until we can figure out what's going on.'

'What about Carson? He's not going to like me tailing her.'

'Leave Carson to me,' I said as I dialed the sheriff. 'Mac? We've got a lead on Bram. We think he was outside Carson's place today, watching Kelsea Shaw through the window. Tim's going to find her. I'm headed to Carson's now to look for witnesses, and I'll dispatch the on-duty troopers. Can you help?'

I listened as she told me she'd round up some additional officers and meet me at Carson's apartment.

We didn't have much time. If Bram had already chosen Kelsea as his next target, he could come for her at any moment. Suddenly, in my mind's eye, I saw the card. *Eel Bay*. The apartment I'd shared with Carson, the one he still lived in, was five minutes from Eel Bay by car. Did that mean something? Was the card intended to lead me to Tim's ex?

Another thought began to calcify in my brain. Tim and Kelsea's relationship had been short, but it ended on amicable terms. Tim cared for Kelsea. She was a friend. Had Bram chosen her because he wanted to hurt someone who meant something to *me*?

Tim was already out the door by the time it occurred to me to call the Riverboat Pub. Matt had been there when Tim's jacket disappeared, but I didn't have high hopes that he could help us. He was already on high alert about Bram, and even though the pub had been jam-packed I had a feeling he would have noticed a stranger. Matt had said his father was around that night, though. For the moment, he was our best shot.

'Mr Cutts,' I said when Avery picked up. 'Just the man I was looking for. It's Shana Merchant.'

I didn't waste time explaining the situation. 'Any chance you saw a guy loitering in the bar after we left? About five-eleven, two-hundred-thirty pounds, possibly with gray hair and beard to match?'

'Saturday, you say? It was pretty busy that night.'

'I know. It's a long shot, but did you notice anyone unfamiliar or sketchy?'

'Can't say that I did,' Avery told me. 'Does this have anything to do with Hope Oberon?'

I hesitated. I didn't want to scare the man by telling him I suspected Blake Bram had been in his bar. There was a chance he'd report back to Matt and Lisa, and they were nervous enough already. 'We'll see,' I told him simply.

'Sorry I can't help. There's a lot of information to process with a case like that, I guess.'

'Yeah,' I replied. 'Especially when it spans close to forty years.'

Thanking the man, I ran back to my desk to get my own jacket and set off for Carson's apartment.

THIRTY-SEVEN

I was pulling into the parking lot, already eyeing the trees where Carson said Kelsea saw the man she thought was Tim, when my cell phone rang. Olivia Peck's name was on the display. I hadn't thought much about Aunt Fee's PI since my meeting with Bram. I'd been so on edge, preoccupied with Hope's case and a string of dead-end leads, that I'd all but forgotten the woman's pursuit. I couldn't imagine what she was calling to say.

'Got a second?' She asked it as though I were a friend she called up for a chat all the time.

'It'll have to be quick. I'm in the middle of something relatively urgent.' That was putting it mildly.

'You'll want to hear this,' Olivia Peck said.

In all the time I'd been hunting Bram, more than a year of scrutinizing his behavior and trying to make sense of our past together, there was one question I kept returning to. Abraham Skilton had committed the most brutal of acts, nightmare-inducing atrocities only an utterly depraved human could perform. It had taken me a long time to accept it, but on paper, my cousin had all the characteristics of a future killer. He'd been teased and bullied as a child, an experience known to produce aggressive fantasies. His relationship with his mother was strained. Abe didn't have an Oedipal complex, at least not that I was aware of, but Freudian theory hypothesized that bad things could happen if a person failed to achieve autonomy with their mother. The mothers of serial murderers tend to be overprotective and controlling, and that was Aunt Felicia to a tee. Her anxiety had stoked his fears and eroded his ability to follow social conventions.

Then there was Brett, who vanished from Abe's life quite literally overnight. One study I'd read found sixty-six percent of serial killers were raised in a home where the dominant parental figure was the mother. My cousin showed no empathy for his victims, not even when they were grade school class-mates he'd framed for stealing money from the teacher. His urges to inflict harm on others went unchecked. He was quick and calculating, erratic and unkind, and those traits had been left to fester.

A few years ago, when I was studying criminal profiling, some scientists got together and analyzed the brain matter of homicide offenders. Neuroimaging scans were used to deter-mine whether the make-up of their brains was inherently different from that of law-abiding members of society. What they found was that murderers had less gray matter – fewer cells, neurons, and glia – in the area of the brain linked to emotional processing and behavioral control. There was no doubt in my mind that, on a basic anatomical level, Bram lacked the substance needed to feel for anyone. At least anyone other than me.

It had taken a long time, but I'd finally accepted my cousin's behavior wasn't my fault. I knew how Abe became Blake Bram.

My question now was what he did afterward.

'First off,' Olivia Peck said, 'he hasn't made this easy.'

'No,' I said flatly. 'He hasn't.'

'Let me walk you through my process. Abe was a minor when he left home, just sixteen years old. His first stop would likely be a shelter. The kid's gotta sleep and eat, right?' When I didn't answer, she went on. 'We know exactly when he left home, so I called around to all the shelters in Philly. Worked my contacts.'

'Mm.' I'd done the same, to no avail.

'I happen to know someone in Trenton who helped me get the lay of the land. There are only a few emergency youth centers for Abe's age group. I looked at the ones closest to the bus and train stations. We're talking hours of research, entire days dedicated to phone calls.'

I waited for her to go on.

'Now, some of the shelters that were around in the early 2000s have closed down, but there's this one place that's operated consistently for sixty-odd years, mainly servicing runaway teens. It offers on-site medical care, educational support, and counseling. Good place to land if you're a kid with limited options. I talked to one of the counselors there – ex-counselor, I should say. She lives in the suburbs now, raising a few kids of her own. In my experience, civilians are generally under the impression that PI's have similar authority to the police. They think they have to cooperate with us. I take full advantage of that misconception. Anyway, she remembered him.'

'Wait.' My heart slammed against my ribs. 'You found him?'

'Let me explain. I showed her a school photograph, and she identified the boy she'd worked with as Abe. These counselors, they try to help kids find a long-term living situation. Minors are often placed with family members, if that's a safe and feasible option. Abe told her things were rough at home and that he couldn't go back. He insisted he had no other living relatives. That was problematic. But the bigger issue was his mental state. She was worried about him. He was aloof and moody, more so than most. In the end, he didn't stick around for long.'

'She remembered all that, after so many years?' That was ominous, to say the least.

'She did. There's a reason. I need to warn you, what I'm about to say won't be easy to hear.'

'Tell me.'

I listened as Peck drew a breath through her nose. 'OK. There was a girl at the shelter that Abe took a shine to. Kid named Robyn.'

A pit opened up in my stomach and I stood at the edge of it, flailing. *Robyn.* The girlfriend Bram told Trey about. Here she was at last.

'Robyn was about his age—' Peck went on.

About my age, then.

'—And according to the counselor, they became fast friends. But Robyn was friendly with other people, too. Seems like Abe might have been jealous of that. Here's the reason the counselor remembered Abe, one kid among the thousands who walked through her office door. Close to a week after he arrived at the shelter, Robyn died on site.'

No.

'She was just fine when she went to bed. Next morning, she was no longer breathing. Things like that didn't happen too often, and given shelters are in the business of keeping kids safe, there was a sizeable investigation. The autopsy showed signs of suffocation, and the medical examiner told the shelter manager she was likely smothered with a pillow. It was foul play through and through. By the time the report came back, though, Abe was long gone.'

No, no, no.

When she spoke again, her tone was deadly serious. 'Abe was new to the shelter, but the girl who was killed . . . they were inseparable. When he got possessive, Robyn complained to the counselors. She died that same night. The police looked for him, of course, but they never found him. I think I know why. The name he gave the counselor at the shelter was a fake. He told them he was Abraham Merchant. Bram, for short.'

If I hadn't already been sitting down, wedged into the driver's seat of my stuffy parked car, my knees would surely have given out. He'd used my name. All this time, as I'd combed the entire East Coast for the false identity he was using, the answer had been right on my own police business card. He'd tried to bind me to him in innumerable ways when we were young, dragging me into all manner of brutal diversions. When that failed, and I left Swanton anyway, he linked us by name.

'Bram Merchant,' I said, sluggish and close to retching. If that's who he'd been, who he thought he was, maybe the name could lead us to him. 'Did you . . . have you . . .'

'That trail went nowhere. There's no telling how long he

used the name, and since it's a false one there are no government records for me to leverage. That counselor in Philly,
though, she had one more useful tidbit to share. She remembered Abe had talked about someday moving to New York
City. I don't know what he did for the ten-plus years after he
left the shelter. Stayed in Philly, maybe, or traveled around.'
    Connecticut, I thought. *He lived in Norwalk, next to the
Sound.*
    'Somewhere along the way he must have acquired a false
ID like we talked about, and used that to find work and
housing,' she said. 'Not knowing anything about that identity
makes my job pretty tough. I worked with what I had. The
name Bram Merchant isn't very common. When I searched
for it, I found three things. The first was an abandoned Twitter
account. The second was a Facebook page belonging to a
motorcycle enthusiast in Indonesia. The third is why I'm
calling you now.'
    The starkest memory I have from nineteen months ago, after
I was admitted to the hospital following my escape from Abe,
is the IV. I had been dehydrated, in shock, and the nurse was
gentle with the needle. I hadn't registered so much as a pinch,
but I felt the rush of cold fluid flow through my system, an
uncanny sensation akin to being dunked in cold water but
somehow remaining perfectly dry. I experienced that surge
again now as my blood pressure plummeted. There was an
icy river running through my veins.
    'When you search the name Bram in conjunction with New
York City,' Peck said, 'you get news reporters, dozens of them.
They tell a very grim story, about an unnamed female detective with the NYPD who was abducted by a serial murderer
from Swanton, Vermont. A man who goes by the name of
Bram. You knew.' There was no astonishment in her voice,
none at all. This was information she'd had time to process.
When had she made the connection? How long was she sitting
on this bombshell?
    What did she plan to do with it?
    'He held me captive.' My voice was weak when at last I
spoke, my vision blurred. 'I didn't know who he was for a
long time. It was just us in that basement, him with his stories

and me listening. Waiting. Expecting to die like the other three women.' *No. Not three. There were even more.* 'He didn't tell me he was Abe. I think it was some kind of test. Eventually, I figured it out on my own. I don't know if I passed or not, because one day a rookie cop got suspicious and came down to the basement. Abe killed him,' I said. 'He killed those women, and then he killed that cop and took off. I had a chance to stop him, and I couldn't do it. I've had to live with that ever since.'

'And you didn't say anything to Felicia. All this time, you never told her Blake Bram is her son?'

'How could I?' My face was wet and hot, my whole body burning with shame and crackling with fury and fear. 'Abe is a monster. He's pure evil, and what he's doing out there? It's about me. He's harboring some sick obsession. Looking for a way back into my life. I don't know how to stop it. I want to, so badly. I fantasize about killing him, and it's the best fucking feeling in the world, but then an image of him at five years old, or ten, or twelve, with that humiliating haircut and those terrible teeth, shoves its way into my head, and I'm a kid again, laughing with him until my ribs hurt, and I have no idea how to reconcile those feelings. I'm committed to enforcing the law. I swore to preserve human life. But I kept this to myself. I did, and that's on me, and all I can do now is pray we find him before someone else dies. I'm doing everything I can. I'm out looking for him right now. I'm doing my best. He's my cousin.'

The tirade spilled out of me like water from a lock. Every truth and fear I'd held back since the minute I realized I missed my chance to apprehend Bram in New York burst free. It was shocking and shameful, even to my own ears. What did Olivia Peck, a freelance detective who'd come into my family's life blind and somehow managed to track down an elusive mission-oriented serial killer, think of me now?

It didn't matter. All that mattered was finding Bram.

It was a long time before Peck spoke again.

'I'm sorry,' she said. 'For what you've been through. It's unimaginable. But Shana, your aunt hired me to find him.'

'I know.' I slid my fingers into my hair and seized a handful of it, squeezing until my scalp hurt.

'It's been fifteen years. She doesn't know if her son is dead or alive.'

'I know. But we're so close to finding him. And when I do, maybe I'll finally understand. I need to give her answers. All of us . . . we need to know the full scope of what he did, and why.'

Another stretch of silence. Peck said, 'I have to write up my report. I'm a slow typer. It's going to take a while. A couple of days for sure.'

The breath I'd been holding slipped through my lips like a sigh. 'A couple of days.'

'Yes.'

'OK. Thank you.'

'Hey, Shana?' she said, dropping the formality.

'Yeah?'

'Be careful.'

When she hung up, I sat in silence. I sucked air through my nose and held the breath in my lungs. Every now and then, I still found myself revisiting the breathing exercises Carson taught me to cope with stress. It would take a lot more than some mindful exhalations to help me now, but it was a start. After a minute, I felt my heart rate slow.

Smothered. Bram had smothered a girl my same age. While I was starting my senior year of high school back in Swanton, my cousin was in Philadelphia taking a young woman's life. By all indications, Robyn was Bram's very first victim. It was so much ghastlier than I could have imagined.

I couldn't – wouldn't – let it get worse.

I reached for the door handle and stepped out of the car. Aside from a couple of parked vehicles, the lot outside Carson's apartment complex was deserted. I'd heard Carson had actual office space now; no more working from the coffee shop to a soundtrack of clinking cups and the shriek of hot milk steamed by an industrial machine. It looked as though he'd gone back there after leaving the barracks. I didn't see his car in the lot.

Tim had eyes on Kelsea. For the moment, she was safe. There were troopers on the way to help search the area surrounding the complex and canvass the neighborhood.

Someone had to have seen Bram. What he looked like now, what he was driving. We'd find a witness before Olivia Peck talked to Aunt Felicia. And then we'd find Bram.

I drew another deep breath, and headed for the trees.

They provided perfect cover for a creep who wanted to see through Carson's windows; I had a feeling Kelsea would never change with the blinds open again. I crunched across the dry tufts of grass and ochre pine needles that littered the floor of the thicket, crouching every now and then to study the ground. Up ahead, a small piece of paper that I took to be a receipt was caught in a bush. In the breeze, it undulated like the body of an albino eel. If Bram had indeed been out here, there was a chance he'd left something behind. The receipt was worth a look. As I stepped toward it, something exploded behind me and a stream of ice-cold air whizzed past my face.

Something struck the tree immediately to my left with such force that a chunk of bark leapt from the trunk and cuffed me in the arm. Splinters rained down like jagged confetti as I dove to the ground, rolled to my right, and withdrew my sidearm. *What the hell?* This was no home defense handgun I was dealing with. Someone was shooting at me with a fucking shotgun. I couldn't believe it. What was going on here? Had a hunter taken a wrong turn and mistaken me for a deer? I was in the middle of town, wearing a jacket with the words *State Police* slapped on the back. Who in their right mind would shoot at a cop?

Bram. He was furious with me for deceiving him. There was no more hiding the fact that my team and I were actively looking for him, or that we'd been achingly close to a successful capture. But if it was Bram out here with me now, why attack in broad daylight at the same site he'd just fled?

As I dug my back into the coarse trunk of the nearest tree and contemplated how to deal with the situation, a second shot rang out. This one stripped the bark off a red oak to my left, leaving a baseball-sized hole behind. Blood pounded in my ears like a drumbeat. The noise was deafening. Drawing my elbows toward my chest, I steadied myself and spun around to take aim.

The shooter was gone.

THIRTY-EIGHT

We searched the area for hours, interviewing more than a dozen neighbors and pedestrians in search of a sign pointing to Bram, the shooter, anything that could help us catch a goddamn break. There were only two witnesses we deemed promising enough to connect with our forensic artist, but whether or not Bram knew he'd been spotted, it was likely he'd change his appearance again.

In the meantime, Tim had sent Kelsea to stay with a friend and posted a trooper outside her house in case Bram came looking. Carson insisted on staying home, in part, I believed, to antagonize me. I'd relayed our suspicions about Kelsea's peeping Tom, but Carson was disbelieving, then furious, and we'd argued for ten minutes before I reached my breaking point and hung up. I was no longer his fiancée, not beholden to him in any way, and I had better things to do than listen to him moan about my inability to protect the good people of A-Bay.

After my call with Olivia Peck, I was more anxious than ever. That Bram continued to succeed at evading us troubled me to my core. In a village as small as Alexandria Bay, at a time of year when visitors were scarce, he should have stood out, but he'd proven he could skirt the periphery of the community without being seen, bide his time, and strike without warning. I figured he was holed up in an abandoned building somewhere, or possibly camping in the woods. The BCI, and the sheriff's department. The NYPD, and now the FBI. Dozens upon dozens of law enforcement professionals were involved in an operation that, if successful, would lead to Bram's capture and expose him as my blood relative. But I worried we wouldn't see him again until he wanted us to, and if that was the case, two days wasn't going to be enough time to end this.

That evening, Tim and I went back to the barracks to review everything we knew. I was convinced the answer to Bram's whereabouts was right in front of us. In November, when he took Trey, he'd chosen a location that, in retrospect, should have led me straight to him. One thing about my cousin: he didn't leave his opponent unarmed. He never did enjoy an easy win, so he equipped me with the tools I'd need to challenge him. There was no reason to believe he'd changed his ways.

It took longer than it should have for me to remember my laptop, and the file I'd been keeping there. It included facts I'd learned about Bram in New York, and avenues of inquiry I'd managed to eliminate. Tim suggested the information might be worth revisiting, that it behooved us to look at the data with fresh eyes. He was optimistic, and I was desperate. Together, we drove out to my cottage.

'The computer,' Tim said as we hummed along the highway, 'and whatever else you need. In and out – and I'll come with you. We can look over the file at my place. We're sticking together from now on.'

It hadn't escaped my attention that Tim had scarcely left my side since my return from the woods. He'd been protective before, but the attempted shooting had him completely spooked. 'OK.' I brought my hand to my holster, finding comfort in the sidearm's grip. 'In and out.'

'Gah, my phone.' He reached awkwardly into his pocket with his right hand while steadying the wheel with his left. 'Would you mind?' he said, tossing me the device.

'It's your mom. Speaker?'

'Please.'

I hit the speakerphone button, and Tim greeted his mother.

'Sorry for the late notice,' Dori said, 'but I've got extra pork chops, and I thought of you. J.C.'s eating at a friend's house and didn't think to tell me until the last minute. Any interest in coming over? There's plenty for the both of you.'

The way Dori made it sound like Tim and I were a package deal gave me a small thrill. He must have felt it too, because when he reached over to brush his fingertips against my knee, a flush crept into both of our faces.

'That sounds great,' Tim told Dori, 'but it's going to be another late night for us.'

'Darn. Well, I suppose they'll be just as good for lunch tomorrow. I'll drop them off at your place in the morning. How are things going?'

'As well as you'd expect, considering we haven't made an arrest.'

As Tim took a left turn off Route 12, I noticed the trees that lined my road were getting greener. It would be summer before we knew it, a whole new season. Would I be spending it chasing Bram?

'Anything I can do to help?' Tim's mother asked.

Any chance you've got a psychotic killer living in your garden shed? 'Thanks for the offer,' I said, 'but at this point all we can do is exhaust every lead we've ever had.'

'I've been thinking about Hope a lot,' said Dori. 'Feeling guilty, I suppose.'

'Guilty?'

'She wasn't treated very well around here. I guess that's normal, really. Forgiveness is a thing some people struggle with. It's easier to stay angry and hold a grudge than to accept someone's mistake. Hope was one of us, though, and a big part of this community. I should have done more to help her.'

'Don't beat yourself up,' I told Dori. 'You can't force people to forgive and forget.'

'Maybe not, but I wish I had done more to defend her, even if that just meant reminding people Hope was their friend. Maybe that would have made her last weeks on this earth a little easier. Life's just not fair, is it?' she said. 'Hope gets herself in trouble by trying to make her father proud, and Harvey can't even appreciate the effort. And the irony is, he would have loved what she was trying to do. Not the bribes, of course, but the spirit of it all. If Harvey was in his right mind, maybe she would have confided in him. He might have tried to talk her out of it then, or at least been able to commiserate. He does have first-hand experience with turning half a town against him.'

I couldn't help but think Dori was right. Harvey may not have broken the law, but he'd been bullheaded about projects that didn't sit well with much of A-Bay. Father and daughter had a lot in common.

I picked at a loose thread on my jacket, winding it around my nail and watching my fingertip swell bright pink. As soon as I released the pressure, the color went back to normal. 'Maybe I'm wrong,' I said. 'Look how people pivoted when they found out what happened to Hope. They went from boycotting Chateau Gris to filling every chair. Sure, there may be some rubberneckers there, but there are honest folks who see a family in need of help, too. It could be we're not giving them enough credit.' I hoped that was true. There were just a few days left until sentencing for Sejal Basak, Freddie Keening, and Jim Hathaway. Hope wasn't around to receive her punishment, but her cohorts were. I had to wonder how the locals would treat them after judgement day had come and gone.

'You know, I think you're right,' said Dori. 'They would probably have forgiven Hope eventually, once her wrongdoings weren't as fresh in their minds. Lord knows they forgave her father worse.'

'I still don't get it,' I said, thinking of the resort. 'Tourists come to the Thousand Islands every summer. They're always going to need a place to stay. Surely a new hotel would have only helped the town. Which side of that argument did you fall on, Dori?'

'What argument is that?'

'The resort,' Tim said. 'The one Harvey wanted to build back in the early eighties. Matt Cutts told us people were angry with him for pushing the project as hard as he did.'

'Oh. The resort.' She spoke haltingly. 'To be honest with you, I hardly remember that at all. I guess there was a difference of opinion about it. I was referring to Harvey's affair.'

My eyes met Tim's. 'Affair? What affair?'

'Oh.' Dori sounded embarrassed now. 'Please don't think me a gossip, Shana, it was so long ago . . . but back in the party days, Harvey spent quite a lot of time with Cora. It wasn't exactly common knowledge, but for regulars of those parties it was fairly obvious what was going on.'

'Cora,' Tim said. 'Cora *Cutts*? As in Matt's mother? How long ago was this?'

'That was in the early eighties too, maybe even late

seventies. Cora did the liquor deliveries out to the islands while Avery tended to the pub, and she usually ended up sticking around for a while. She was a beautiful woman, lively and effusive, and Harvey . . . he was more than ten years older than her, but he was a charmer, and well-liked by the ladies. They became close, and then . . . well. I saw them slip into a bathroom together more than once. I wasn't the only one.'

'Mom.' Tim's eyes had widened. 'Why didn't you tell us this before?'

And how had we not heard about it? In a small village, where rumors grew and multiplied like buds on a tree, Tim and I should have encountered the information long ago. Except, who else was there to reveal it? Harvey's wife was dead. Maynard and Natalie Pope wouldn't have shared such shameful news about their beloved Harvey, not with us or anyone else. It was entirely possible they didn't even know about the romance. Hope may have been aware of what was going on – she would have been in her late teens or early twenties during the party years – but she wasn't around to tell us. The only people we'd spoken with over the past week who might know were Matt and Avery Cutts, and I couldn't see them admitting to something so disgraceful either.

Dori let out a laugh. 'What possible reason would I have for talking about that?' she said. 'It was decades ago. Ancient history.'

'It's evidence of a potentially fraught relationship between the Cutts family and that of our victim,' I said. 'It could be relevant.'

'Oh. Oh, I'm sorry. I didn't know. I didn't think.'

'Who else knows about this?' I asked, working to keep my voice steady. Beside me, Tim's fingers buckled against the steering wheel. 'It's important.'

'Gosh,' said Dori, 'I guess I don't know for sure. My friends Sylvia and Maria would, I think. They were at most of those parties too. Their husbands might, I suppose, but it was so long ago . . .'

'Did Avery and Cora ever divorce?'

'No,' she said. 'No, they were still married when Cora passed away a few years ago.'

'So it's possible Avery and Matt only found out recently,' I said.

'What does Matt have to do with it?' said Tim.

Damn. I hadn't realized there were drawbacks to Tim being buddies with half the town, too.

I thanked Dori for the information and ended the call before turning back to Tim. 'I know you guys are close,' I told him, 'but it might be worth checking into both of them. We should call in the morning, feel them out about their family's connection to the Oberons.'

'I guess it can't hurt,' said Tim, but I was quite sure that it did hurt both him and his mother to imagine anyone they considered a friend could become a killer.

THIRTY-NINE

P ast seven o'clock, we were settled at Tim's kitchen table, Tim staring at my laptop screen and me working my cell phone. Armed with the knowledge that Bram had used my last name after leaving Swanton, I'd put in another call to my old precinct.

The old team had news for me, too.

'They hired him in November. He works part-time. Most days, he's alone in the shop power-washing boats and spiffing them up for the season,' said Sergeant Mateo De La Cruz. I listened, slack-jawed, as he told me the FBI had received a tip about a man who was a match for several of Bram's physical and behavioral characteristics. The proprietor of the auto and boat restoration business in North Hammond, New York had driven past one of the FBI's billboards on his way to see family in Syracuse, and the image on the screen held enough of a resemblance to his awkward, quiet employee to warrant a call. 'Owner says the guy, name of Jason Willis, gave a place over in Brier Hill as his address.'

Brier Hill was a hamlet up near Morristown, five miles or so from North Hammond. De La Cruz told me there was a team of agents on the way to the house already. 'If he's there,' he said, 'we'll find him.'

Jason Willis was obviously a false identity, but the address, that might be real. As I processed this information, I could feel the walls of Tim's little cottage closing in. It had been months since my last counseling session with Gil Gasko of the New York State Police's Employee Assistance Program, and during that time I'd had my house broken into, met my abductor and long-time tormentor face to face, and dodged a shotgun blast aimed square at my back. For the most part I'd managed to keep my head, but I worried my cool wouldn't last. *Are you able to identify your core stressors?* Gasko used to ask. The answer was yes – and they currently had me surrounded. *Do you know the self-help strategies for avoiding a panic attack?* I did. But as I registered the telltale signs once more – clammy skin, a tingling in my hands and feet, stomach pain and nausea – I feared I wouldn't be able to keep the fit of terror at bay. Breathing exercises and refocusing my thoughts wasn't going to cut it anymore. My life and the lives of the family I loved were about to be in shambles.

Tim's hand slid across the table to find mine. 'All good?'

'I don't know. This is it,' I said. 'The FBI, they'll end this.'

He studied my expression.

'It's hot in here. Come on, let's get some air.'

When he handed me my jacket, my hands trembled so much it took three tries to get my arm through the sleeve.

Violet hour on the river. Summer sunsets were the darling of the locals, spectacles of purple and neon orange so vivid they verged on obscene and seemed to last forever before melting into an equally dazzling band of burnished gold. Tonight's sunset was softer, the colors more akin to Easter eggs dyed with onion skins, but it gave the water a pink hue that I found soothing. I followed Tim down the steep staircase that led from his deck to the boathouse, and together we boarded the Lyman. Without preamble, he put out his hand for my Glock, and stored both our sidearms in the cubby by the controls. Then he started the engine, backed out of the boathouse, and turned the wheel over to me.

The water, the silence, it was just what I needed. I used to think spring was all movement and noise, bursting blossoms and cheery birdsong, but the air on the river was hushed, the water a level plane. It was still cold enough that the fish were sluggish, moping down near the riverbed, and every now and then Tim would catch a glimpse of one and rattle off the species like some freshwater pundit. Carp. Walleye. Smallmouth bass. All around the edges of Goose Bay, the fading sun leached the color from the trees and turned them black. It gave the impression that we were surrounded by a ring of dark walls, but somehow that didn't bother me. Now that we were on the river, I could focus on the whoosh of the water against the hull and the brisk air streaming through my hair. I was feeling better by the second.

Just for a moment, Tim closed his eyes. 'They call it a dead wind when it blows directly at a boat like this. Opposing its course. Ease off the throttle a little,' he said from his station next to me. When I hesitated, he guided my hand. 'You're doing great, Shane.'

I nodded, savoring the residual heat of his skin, and looked out past the fenders tied tight to cleats on the gunwale at the last beads of sunlight shimmering on the horizon. The water wasn't pale pink anymore, but a deep, inky black. I turned the wheel and felt the boat arc through the water. Spray from the wake showered me with cold mist.

'What happens when we get him?'

'What?' Tim said. The wind was in our ears, and I'd kept my voice soft.

'When we catch Bram. What happens then?'

Tim's gaze grew tender. 'Then it's over. You get your life back. Think of what it will be like when he's in prison. No more looking over your shoulder, or worrying about your family and friends. After all this time, you'll finally be free.'

I wanted to believe it. But my freedom was contingent on my cousin being stripped of his. My fear, the biggest, blackest one of all, was that no matter what happened to him, my link to Blake Bram would be everlasting.

'It's getting dark, and there are some shoals out here,' Tim said. 'We should probably head back.'

I stepped aside so he could take the wheel and maneuver us back into the boathouse, a process I had yet to learn. *You'll get there*, Tim had told me. *You're a quick study, Shana.* According to him, I'd be driving the police boat by Fourth of July weekend. Almost exactly one year after I first arrived in Alexandria Bay.

Tim had the foresight to switch on the exterior boathouse lights before we departed, so the structure was visible even in the semi-darkness. He slowed our speed, and I felt the boat sigh and settle in the water. Already, my mind was turning to what lay ahead. An evening spent alone with Tim in his one-bedroom cottage. The heat of his body next to mine.

We were fifty yards away from the wide boathouse door when I caught sight of something on the shore. The staircase leading up to Tim's cottage was built into a steep, rocky hill, where bent evergreens fifty feet in height grew up between toothed boulders. It was movement that I'd noticed. Right behind one of those towering trees.

'Hey,' I said to Tim, raising my hand to point at the dark figure on the shore. My arm didn't make it past my hip. With a thunderous bang, the windshield on Tim's beautiful Lyman exploded in a shower of glass.

'Fuck!' I dropped to the deck, yanking him down with me. 'Are you hurt? Talk to me!'

Dazed, he patted his chest and face. No holes. That was good. There was a gash on his cheek from the glass and blood trickled down to his chin, but it didn't take him long to recover.

'Bram,' he said. The word took the shape of a growl.

'I didn't see. I don't know.'

What I did know was that we were up the creek. At a higher elevation, the figure on the shore had a distinct advantage. Tim reached for the cubby where he'd stored our sidearms, but the man had a shotgun, and plenty of trees to use as cover, while we were fully exposed. We were trapped between the boathouse and the shore; there was no way we'd have time to turn the boat around before the shooter took aim once more.

Swim for it, I thought, my flight response strong. If we

abandoned ship, we could use the vessel for cover. Make a
call from the water and wait for help. But the water tempera-
ture still hovered around thirty-seven degrees Fahrenheit,
according to the thermometer on my own dock. I checked it
often, counting down the days until I could swim. Tim and I
might last a minute in the river before cold shock kicked
in and we started to hyperventilate. Hiding in the water or
swimming for the opposite shore was not an option.

'I'm going to talk to him,' I said.

'Talk to him? He's trying to kill us!'

'What choice do we have? Look at us. We've got nowhere
to go. Don't shoot!' I yelled, raising my hands.

'Don't do this,' said Tim, his voice desperate.

I locked him in my gaze. 'He'll talk to me.' *He has to.*

Tim's face twisted with fear. But he brought his sidearm
level with the shattered windshield and with a curt nod turned
his attention to the shore, ever closer as the boat drifted.

I didn't know what to expect, whether the man who emerged
from the trees would be the guy with the baseball cap who'd
stalked me in Sam's dojo last fall, or the grizzled old timer
from the cemetery, or – worst of all – the boy from my childhood in Vermont. What I saw didn't match any of those
descriptions.

What I saw was Avery Cutts. Matt's father. Tim's friend.
My brain struggled to put it all together, to make the connections that must have been there but felt tenuous even now.
'Tim,' I said weakly, but he saw now too, his face a jumble
of emotions. It hurt to look at him.

'What the hell?' He shook his head like a kicked dog and
squinted as if trying to regain his bearings. To make the pain
of what he was witnessing go away.

'I'm sorry,' I said. 'I'm so sorry. How do you want to handle
this?' The situation was grim. If it had been Bram standing
on the shore with a gun, I might have stood a chance at
de-escalating the situation, but Avery? I had no clue what this
man was thinking.

But I knew why he was here.

Everything Dori said came flooding back to me. My own
comments about the Cutts family and Cora's adultery did, too.

I'd wondered aloud how long Matt and Avery knew about the affair between Harvey and Cora. And here was Cora's husband, armed and on the attack.

I'd given us away over the phone, when I called the bar from the barracks and unwittingly revealed that the scope of Hope's case had expanded to include events that were decades old. *It spans close to forty years*, I'd told Avery, not considering that he could be a suspect. Not thinking at all. If Avery knew we were investigating the Oberons' past in A-Bay, he knew we were closing in on the affair. On him.

'Tim,' I said, prodding his arm. Mouth agape, he had lowered his gun. The presence of the shotgun meant Avery was likely the shooter from Carson's apartment, too. Twice now, he'd taken aim at me. I didn't doubt he'd do it again. The only other option was to send in Tim. Tim, whom Avery had treated like a second son. But Tim was halfway to catatonic, unable to process the truth.

Buckshot, I knew, was most effective at close range. We were still more than thirty yards away from where the man stood. At the same time, I'd heard stories of hunters who could make a kill with a shotgun at a hundred yards, and I didn't like those odds. In the last few minutes, the Lyman had floated well past the entrance to the boathouse and was listing toward the shore and the man with the gun. We were running out of time.

'This can't . . .' Tim's face was alarmingly blank. 'He can't . . . this doesn't make any sense.'

'Do you want me to talk to him? Tim?' I grabbed his arm, gave it a shake. He wouldn't look at me. *Fuck.* I couldn't count on him right now. The dialogue we were about to have with Avery Cutts was crucial. I reached into my pocket, took out my phone, and slapped it into Tim's hand.

'Call Mac and the troopers,' I said. 'Tell them to hurry. *Do it.*'

When at last he started dialing, I turned to face the windshield.

The shotgun was still pointed our way. The man who held it tight against his shoulder was all in black, with a dark cap pulled over his head. Avery Cutts was dressed like a man on a mission. He was dressed like a killer.

'Avery!' I called, still crouched next to the wheel. In the bay, my voice held no heft and echoed feebly before fading away. Broken glass crunched and popped under my boots as I readjusted my weight. 'Avery, it's me, Shana Merchant. It's Shana and Tim.'

For a second I wondered if he'd answer me at all, or if he would just keep on blasting. His eyes were narrow, his arm steady. At length he called, 'I know who you are.'

'Talk to me, Avery. Put down that gun, and let's talk.'

'There's nothing to talk about.'

'Come on, Avery. Put it down.' I could sense the tension in Tim's body beside me. He'd finished placing the call and regained his senses enough to take aim at his friend's father, but I knew there was a chance that act alone had leached every ounce of mettle from his body.

Think, Shana. I had to stall. With any luck it would be less than ten minutes before the on-duty troopers arrived. A lot could happen in ten minutes' time.

'Talk to me about Cora,' I called.

Avery took a step back, stumbling a little on the rocks. Even at a distance, I could see the disquiet in his face. His cheeks and neck were red. 'He took her from me,' he said.

'Who took her, Avery?'

'Harvey. That bastard took Cora from me, and I didn't even fucking know it.'

'I can't do this,' Tim said suddenly. 'Matt and Lisa, Avery's grandkids. If he takes another shot . . .'

'Then you'll do what you need to.' I said it under my breath, and prayed that I was right.

Returning my attention to Avery, I said, 'We don't know anything about Harvey and Cora. Put down the weapon, and let's talk about this back at the station.'

After a long moment, Avery dragged a hand across his brow. 'They used to meet up at the parties.' His voice echoed too, and it sounded pained, like those mournful loon cries. 'I supplied the booze for him and his friends and stayed behind to run the pub. And all the while he was fucking my wife.'

'How did you find out?' We were ten yards away from shore now. I barely had to raise my voice.

'He told me. Harvey *told* me,' Avery said through a grimace. Harvey came to the Riverboat every Sunday, Matt had said. To reminisce with old friends, buddies from town who'd likely attended those parties, too. 'Fifty years we've been living blocks away from each other, and he hid it from me, and it took until he lost his goddamn mind for me to find out. He talked about her like she was still alive. Like the bastard was about to go meet her on one of the islands.'

Green Rock. Was that why Harvey had tried to get out there? Did he think he'd be meeting Cora Cutts nearly forty years after the fact? I believed what Avery was telling us. Harvey had done the same thing at the restaurant, sinking into the past with such abandon that Pope needed to remind him to come up for air. 'What did he say, Avery? What did Harvey tell you?'

'It wasn't a one-time thing. It went on for almost five years, until she got pregnant with Matt.' A sob caught in his throat, but he choked it back and tightened his grip on the shotgun. 'They'd meet up in those fancy island houses, with all those people right downstairs, while I was back on the mainland working my ass off trying to keep the pub and my family afloat.' He spat the words, furious now. 'He said he fucking loved her.'

What was it Harvey had told us? *All my ladies, gone.* It had seemed like a strange way to refer to his wife and only daughter, but then, he hadn't been. Harvey had three ladies: Diane, Hope, and Cora Cutts.

How many minutes had gone by since Tim called the barracks? Five? Six? 'What did you do, Avery?' I had to keep him talking.

I listened with horror as, through gritted teeth, he said, 'He took her from me. So I took someone from him.'

The realization arrived like a hail of bullets. All at once, with those six words, I understood everything. Hope's death had nothing to do with the wind farm, or her marriage, or the resort Harvey had pushed for all those years. This was payback, plain and simple. *Sins of the father.* It was all I could do not to shake my head. Tim had it right. The thing of it was, we'd been looking at the wrong damn father.

'Hope,' I said. 'You took Hope from him.'

'She was as selfish as Harvey. She didn't care about anyone else. She deserved to die.'

'You made it look like her death was about the wind farm. About her crimes.'

'There were plenty of those.'

'You framed Val Giovanni.'

A smile now, crooked and cunning. 'Harvey told me about him, too. Hope would talk about Giovanni to Harvey, how the guy was pissed at Hope about the project. He threatened her. Sounded to me like a man who'd hold a grudge.'

'So you stole his passport and impersonated him? You took a big risk, bringing Hope into Canada.'

His smile slipped. 'Would you have believed Giovanni killed her if I didn't?'

Would we have? Hope's body was dumped on a wind farm, and the symbolism of that was hard to deny. Without evidence that Giovanni had crossed the border, though, we couldn't have linked him to the crime. Avery Cutts had taken care of that for us. He'd made Giovanni his scapegoat, and made it easy for us to distrust a man who, by all appearances, was the ideal suspect.

The boat rocked a little as Tim shifted his weapon. Any minute now, our troopers would come tearing through the trees that encroached on Tim's cottage. But Avery Cutts was still holding a gun. We were too far away to disarm him, and he'd just confessed to murder. If that fact hadn't sunk in yet, it would soon, and I hated to think what he'd do when it did.

'Talk to him, Tim.' The two men had history, and a common love for Matt. Avery couldn't be so far gone that he'd think of Tim as a threat. Could he?

Tim gave a tentative nod. Setting his sidearm on the seat of the captain's chair, he raised his hands, and I covered him.

'Mr Cutts?' Tim attempted a chuckle to remind Avery that, just last night, they'd been trading jokes at the bar. The man's face remained stony. 'Avery. Put that thing down, OK? Jesus, don't you know it's rude to point a gun at a lady? I'm sorry about what happened with Cora and Harvey. That's not right, not at all, and you didn't deserve it. What you're doing here, though, it won't change anything.'

Avery said nothing.

'Why don't you put that gun down and give us a chance to get this boat docked. Think about Matt and Lisa. Reeba and Charmaine.'

Avery's face crumpled. 'Matt can't know. Not any of it.'

But he will. What Avery did to Hope, Harvey's affair with Avery's wife, Avery's bid to incapacitate me at Carson's apartment – it would all get out. Would it mean the end of the Riverboat? Would Matt and his family be run out of A-Bay? These were transgressions I wasn't sure any town could forgive.

But Tim said, 'We'll see what we can do. OK, Avery? Come on.' His voice was beseeching. 'Put down the gun. We don't need you getting hurt out here. As long as you've got that weapon pointed in our direction you're threatening officers of the law, and that gives us the right to respond with deadly force. We don't want to hurt you, Avery.'

The Lyman had just about reached the shore. We were in the shallows now. The water would come up to my thighs once my feet were swallowed by the silky silt that coated the riverbed, but we could wade to land from here.

'We need to get to Avery before the troopers do,' I said quietly. 'If they see him with that shotgun . . .'

'We're coming in, Avery,' Tim said with a curt nod. 'We'll work this out together. We're lowering our weapons. I want you to do the same.'

Avery took a quivering breath. Slowly, he began to lower the barrel of the shotgun toward the ground.

Tim was quicker to exit the boat than I was. With his strength and long limbs and comfort level with the Lyman he was out and in the water in a flash, long before I'd so much as slung my leg over the gunwale. He closed the distance between him and Avery just as quickly. Tim was mere feet away from the man now, and Avery looked defeated, ready to give in. We had him. It was done.

The snap of a twig was what I heard first, the sound so

innocent it might have gone ignored had it not been followed by the thump of footsteps. My heart sunk as I realized we were too late. The troopers would assess the situation and deem Avery – Avery, who'd heard the ruckus too, who was raising his shotgun once more and spinning toward the sound – a threat to be neutralized. From my position, teetering on the side of the boat with one leg dangled over the water and the other hovering above the deck, I watched it all play out with a horror that, to this day, remains ineffable.

A flurry of movement.

Figures colliding.

Two gunshots, loud as cannons, that nearly stopped my heart.

'*No*.'

The boat rocked violently beneath me as I lost my balance and tumbled into the river. I floundered as my clothes sucked up the water and towed me down. It filled my mouth too, mossy and ice-cold, so that it took too long to get to my feet and drag myself to shore. Too long to lope toward them, my limbs wrapped in sodden fabric, dead weight that shaved off precious seconds and trapped me in a horrible dream.

'No!'

I dove to the ground next to Tim's body. Heaved him onto his back and searched his face. He was white. The shock of the buckshot to his body had drained all the blood from his face. Now, it pulsed out from between his fingers, which clutched at his shredded right thigh. Tim's forehead was creased, his face contorted in agony. The entire leg of his jeans was soaked with blood and it clung to him like a blanket, wet and oil-black.

'Fuck. *Fuck*.' With trembling hands, I tore off my jacket and wrapped it tight around his leg. 'Hang on Tim, help's coming. Help's on the way.' My words were a plea and a prayer.

It wasn't until I looked up to try to make sense of what happened that I saw Bram.

FORTY

He towered over me where I was sprawled, limbs akimbo, next to Tim. His hair was the chestnut brown of his youth, cut the same haphazard way Aunt Fee used to do it, with pieces sticking out where they shouldn't. It made him look like a mangy, rabid animal. Dangerous. He was dressed in a flannel shirt with a frayed collar, jeans with stringy white knees. Avery's shotgun was clutched in his hands.

My eyes trailed from the shotgun to Avery, sprawled on his back in the dirt. His chest was in tatters, the fabric and flesh a nest of red snakes. The man was dead.

It had happened so quickly. What had I seen?

Bram, bursting from the trees. Throwing a punch at Avery that spun him halfway around.

Bram, snatching Avery's gun.

But no, that was wrong. Avery had held onto the shotgun a split second longer. He'd seen a man, a stranger, coming at him. Avery had taken aim. And when Tim – realizing, seizing his chance at last – lunged at Bram, Avery had fired.

It was only then, when Tim lay bleeding on the ground at the hand of an old friend, that Bram snatched the weapon and obliterated Avery's chest with a spray of twelve-gauge lead shotshell.

'Run,' Tim said weakly. He was staring hard at Bram, who I now saw was holding Tim's sidearm, too. Had Bram wrested it from Tim's hand after he was injured? Nothing made sense.

Slowly, Bram lowered the shotgun, and raised the Glock.

Tim's chest rose and fell beside me, his breaths increasingly shallow. My hands, the same hands that had stroked his body, his prickly cheeks, eyebrows like velvet ribbons under my thumbs, were hot and sticky with his blood. I shivered, my cold, wet clothes impossibly heavy and the skin underneath rough with goosebumps, so tight I felt vacuum-sealed. All the while, Bram watched me.

Willing my knees not to buckle, I got to my feet and lumbered away from Tim's body.

Bram gestured at Tim's leg. In a voice devoid of emotion, he said, 'That looks bad. Sorry I couldn't get here sooner. I was tied up.'

'Shana.' Tim again, pleading with me. '*Go.*'

But Bram said, 'She's not going anywhere. Are you, Shay?'

'You killed him.' My mouth was packed with dry gauze, my tongue swollen to three times its normal size. My voice, though . . . it didn't so much as waver. 'You killed Avery.'

'Is that his name? All I know is he was threatening you. If I hadn't come, you'd be the one dead. I saved you, Shay.'

I felt like I was breathing through a straw with lungs shrunk down to raisins, but I forced myself to meet his gaze. 'What do you want, Abe? Why are you here?'

'Abe.' He smiled a little. 'I've been waiting a long time to hear you call me that.'

'Why wouldn't I? You're still him.' I spoke the words slowly, concentrating hard on keeping my body still. 'You'll always be Abe to me.'

It was what he wanted to hear. I had to believe that. Nothing else about my cousin was a foregone conclusion. Nothing but this.

He'd forced me back to Swanton to get closure on his father's death. He'd recast us in our childhood roles as if nothing had changed. Every interaction I'd had with Bram since he reappeared in my life, whether direct or indirect, had mirrored our relationship as kids. Last year, when he wanted to coax me into unravelling the mystery he devised, he'd asked *Wanna Play?* When he broke into my cottage, he left me a childhood treat to prove he still knew me. Everything he did seemed to indicate he was stuck in the past. *Our* past.

It had been years since Adam Starkweather and I last talked about mental disorders, but I could still hear the psychological profiler's voice in my head as he described the condition I now knew with certainty had befallen Bram. If I was going to take Bram down, it wouldn't be by force. If I stood any chance of winning this fight, I had to apply what I'd learned from Adam and manipulate his psyche.

Just like Carson had done to me.

I took another step away from Tim. *He's just a colleague*, I thought, trying to channel the message to Bram. *Some guy from work.* My cousin was jealous and irrational, and he had Tim's sidearm. I needed him focused on me.

'You came back for me,' I said. 'Didn't you, Abe?'

'It wasn't easy, going all those years without seeing you. Being alone.' He eased back into the banter, his gaze fastened to mine. 'You don't know how hard it was. I had to find you.'

I blinked, and for a second I was back in the Irish pub where Bram, masquerading as Seth, knocked my beer into my lap. Before he slipped Rohypnol into my pint and steered me into a cab and locked me in the damp cellar of a prewar apartment building, we'd spent all evening chatting about favorite restaurants, novels, how we took our coffee. Our conversation that night had been effortless, just as if we'd known each other all our lives. Because we had.

'And you found me in New York.' I had to keep him talking. I'd pushed too hard at our last encounter. Bram didn't want Senior Investigator Shana Merchant. He wanted his cousin, Shay.

'Your precinct's website had your photo and name,' he said. 'I followed you. Watched. I had to find the right way for us to reconnect.'

The approach he'd settled on was murdering three women in and around my neighborhood. Knowing I was the only detective in the Ninth Precinct, he could be certain I'd try to hunt him down, and when I did he made me his captive. This was the method my cousin had chosen for rekindling our relationship.

On the ground, Tim moaned. He'd lost so much blood. Where the hell were Mac and the troopers?

'You missed me,' I said. A salty glob of bile crept up my throat, so vile I feared I wouldn't be able to force it back down.

'Of course I missed you, Shay. *God.*' He waved the gun in frustration before training it back on Tim. 'You're my best friend. My family. You're the only one who understands me.'

But I hadn't, not soon enough. If I had I would have stopped him long ago, before he punched a knife between those

women's ribs and carved a comma into a little boy's flawless
face. All I really understood was that he'd always wanted me
and that, right now, he had me.

I looked down at Tim, bleeding out on a soft bed of pine
needles. I ached to reach for him, to hold him again, but I
resisted. He needed first aid, and fast. A person could bleed
to death from a gunshot wound in five to eight minutes, and
Tim's face was already deathly pale. The listlessness I saw
there filled my stomach with cement. I looked up at my cousin.
Swallowed hard.

'I missed you too, Abe.'

He smiled, but there was something not right about his eyes.
They had glazed over. He sighed heavily. Said, 'I owe you an
apology. I know this last year hasn't been easy for you.'

An apology? I gave a timid nod.

'You were hurting. I never wanted that. A game is a game,'
he said cryptically. 'It wasn't right, what he did. Not fair.'

I didn't follow. For the life of me, I couldn't parse his
meaning. *He?* Was he referring to himself? Did he have a
dissociative identity disorder, too? Was he experiencing some
kind of bipolar episode? His sentences had become chaotic,
and I was picking up something else from him now. What was
it? Dejection? Remorse?

Could it be?

I was still struggling with what to say next when my ears
perked up. The doleful wail of sirens, distant but getting closer.
Intensifying with each passing second. Bram's eyes widened
and I felt mine do the same. On the ground, Tim raised his
head a little, and I looked down at him once more. His skin
looked so much like Hope's had on Wolfe Island that my
stomach heaved. *Hurry*, I thought. *Please.*

'Ah,' Bram said as he cocked his head. Turning Tim's gun
over in his hand, he gripped it hard and repositioned his finger
on the trigger. 'I didn't want it to be this way. I had so much
more planned for us. A whole life together.'

'Abe.' My throat was on fire and my fingers twitched as I
reached toward him. There was a high-pitched buzz in my
ears, the thump and whoosh of my heartbeat inside my head.
'Abe, don't—'

The sirens blared now, filling my ears, the side of Tim's cottage awash in red light. I heard the staccato slam of car doors. Muffled shouts.

The gun hovered above Tim. Bram steadied his hand.

I whimpered Tim's name.

'Shay,' Bram said, the word like an exhalation.

It was almost entirely drowned out by my scream.

The shot went off with a crack like two rocks slamming together at full force. Instantly, the piney air filled with the stink of sulfur and blood. I dropped to my knees. I could hardly hear my own keening through the wringing in my ears. I could feel, though, dread so intense it threatened to destroy me.

That, and the hot splatter of blood across my face.

'Shana!' Sheriff McIntyre bore down on us. 'Holy hell – we need help over here!' she shrieked above my head. Then, to me: 'We got here as fast as we could.'

It hadn't been fast enough. Tears streamed down my face and into my mouth, the taste alkaline on my tongue.

'Shana,' she said again, harder this time. Insistent. She grabbed my shoulder, gave it a shake. 'Stop. You have to stop. It's over now.'

It's over.

FORTY-ONE

Trust is a trickster. We convince ourselves it's safe to give up and give in. Pin our faith on someone we love who would never, ever betray us. I didn't trust Bram. I hadn't for a long time.

But that day, I should have.

'It's about love,' Adam Starkweather told me, all those years ago. 'Not necessarily romantic love, but a fixation on someone that creates in the obsessor the need to protect or control. These individuals crave intimacy. That sense of being bonded. They believe their feelings toward the object of their affection are exceptionally rare, that they alone possess the power to understand and care for that person. Obsessives like to believe they know more about the object of their infatuation than anyone else.

'At its core it's an attachment disorder, with qualities of addiction. It tends to manifest in individuals who suffer from delusional jealousy – inventing falsehoods about the object of their love, believing their love is mutual when it isn't. Defending the loved one without invitation, and often going to extremes to preserve the relationship. And attachment disorders often start in childhood.

'In other words,' he'd said, looking me straight in the eye, 'they cling to the one relationship they've got like their life depends on it. The intensity of those emotions don't fade with time. To the contrary, time can make such feelings more pronounced. Turn them into an itch beneath a cast, or sutures just starting to heal. Something to pick at until it bleeds.'

Obsessive love disorder. In movies, OLD is romanticized. Viewers swoon when a handsome bachelor follows the female lead home, or dupes her into agreeing to a first date by some adorable means. In real life, it isn't nearly as much fun.

I'd suspected Bram's condition for some time, having caught glimpses of it in New York. Everything he'd done since then was consistent with my theory. Bram always loved me – I loved him too, once – but this was something more. Obsessive actions, possessive behavior, the need to control me by holding me captive and, later, monitoring my every move were symptoms I'd witnessed in my cousin time and time again.

In the end, it's what killed him.

The room at River Hospital has a view of Heart Island. Sun streams through the window and across the clean blue floor. In the bed, he squints.

I rub the sleep from my eyes, and smile.

With the exception of the time he spent in the OR, I haven't left Tim's side since the ambulance brought him here from Goose Bay. Even though most of the pellets missed him – the surgeon said a direct shot to his femoral artery would surely have been a death knell – the process of extracting the lead from his body, stitching him up, and completing the blood transfusion took time, some of the longest hours of my life. But Tim is stable now. And although he's looked better, in the swath of sunlight from the window the eyes under his endearingly thick eyebrows are crystalline.

'You're awake,' I say.

'Didn't want to miss anything.' He stifles a yawn and winces as he repositions himself in bed. 'Our debriefing sessions are my favorite.'

I laugh at that. 'There's plenty of time for me to fill you in.' It had been just me and Mac closing the investigation this time, and we'd done it over the phone, recording everything that had transpired and conducting what I'd come to think of, somewhat ironically, as a post-mortem. We'd had two cases to contend with: Hope Oberon's, and Blake Bram's.

Hope's had been straightforward, in the end. I explained to Mac that, at some point, we'd suspected Hope's killer was using misdirection to throw us off track. For a while, we even thought Bram was responsible for her death. There were enough similarities between the killer's behavior and Bram's to confuse us. We'd been right in thinking the turbine was a means of distraction. It was Avery Cutts who'd played us though, not my cousin.

'We were close,' I'd told Mac from the hospital hallway, my eyes on the door to Tim's room while I paced. 'There was a time when we thought Maynard Pope used Giovanni's passport to frame him. Right theory, wrong man.'

'I still can't believe it,' she said. 'I've known Avery for years. He seemed like a good man.'

'Maybe he was. Before he turned bad.'

It isn't that simple, of course. People aren't good or bad, generous or selfish, thoughtful or inconsiderate. Most people, I've learned, are as deep as the river, and you can find all manner of unexpected things in the weeds.

When it came to Bram, things were a bit more complicated.

De La Cruz had left me a couple of voicemails. The address Bram gave his employer turned out to be legit. He'd been renting a ramshackle house from an elderly woman thrilled to have a tenant who didn't complain about the peeling paint and dilapidated roof. The task force had already found evidence there linking Bram to other homicides. He didn't have much in the way of material possessions, but in his search for my replacement he'd kept a book of names, every one of them crossed off. In addition to Robyn, Becca, Lanie, and Jess, there were more than a dozen. De La Cruz was hopeful the list would help investigators solve countless cold cases.

Bram had made time for another crime before he took his life. While Tim and I were out on the water, before Bram showed up at the cottage, he'd paid a visit to Smuggler's Cargo. It was the same cheap souvenir shop where, five months earlier, he'd planted the message that launched a panicked hunt for both my uncle's killer and Trey Hayes. The shop had served a different purpose on the day Bram died. Armed with a canister of gasoline and a lighter, both of which he abandoned on the street out front, he'd set Smuggler's Cargo, its racks of Thousand Islands T-shirts and its pirate-themed snow globes, aflame.

Several people witnessed the act of arson, and our unit had been flooded with calls. The fire was the reason Mac and the troopers hadn't been able to respond more quickly. With our unit diverted, Bram had more time at the cottage, with me.

And that had nearly cost Tim his life.

'When he pointed that gun at Tim, I thought . . .' I'd stopped walking then to gather a jerky breath, my boots squeaking on the hall floor.

'I know,' Mac said, her voice strained. 'I thought the same thing. Had my sidearm out and ready to take him down.' She sighed. There was nothing more to say. In a single swift movement my cousin had brought the weapon to his own temple, and fired.

It was only after I knew Tim was safe at the hospital and would make a full recovery that I started to realize what that meant. By the time the sun rose on A-Bay the next morning, my cousin's name headlined every news broadcast and report in the county. By noon, the bulletins had gone national. I wondered who was first to leak the really juicy bits. Despite her ambition, I didn't believe Olivia Peck would betray me after the conversation we had, but there had been a fair number of EMTs outside Tim's cottage to witness me in a fugue state, blathering about my cousin's suicide. It had only been a matter of time.

'Room-temperature tap water?' I ask now, passing Tim a Styrofoam cup.

'Yum,' he says with mock enthusiasm. 'My favorite vintage.' He studies me for a moment. 'I was thinking, maybe once I'm out of here we could get a glass of wine sometime. Maybe grab dinner at Chateau Gris.'

'I think I'd rather stay in.'

Comprehension dawns slowly on his sun-washed face, and Tim's eyebrows waggle. 'You're the boss.'

Gingerly, I lean over the bed and kiss him. Tim's lips are warm and soft, at once both new and as comforting as a dog-eared paperback. He relaxes against me, and we stay that way for a minute, nose to nose. I feel his mouth turn up into a smile. Mine does the same.

I don't know how I'm going to deal with what's coming. There's so much I still don't understand about Bram and why he did the things he did, and I can't imagine how I'm going to explain his actions to my family.

At least I know I won't be alone when I try.

Between the cafeteria food, the hospital room showers, and my need to never leave Tim's side again, I haven't been back to my cottage in a couple of days, and my absence shows. When I roll to a stop in front of the mailbox at the mouth of the private drive that leads down to the river, I find it's overflowing with flyers and bills.

I scoop them up and toss the pile on the passenger seat to sort through later. I'm just here to pack a bag. Tim gets out of the hospital today, and I've offered to stay with him. It'll be a while before he's comfortable on crutches, and he'll need some help. We're both taking a sick leave to rest and recover. To heal.

Gravel pops under the tires of my SUV as I meander

down the lane. Beams of spring sunlight break through the increasingly leafy canopy of trees above, scattering my car hood with tinsel. When the light gets in my eyes I think of Tim back at the hospital, and my chest grows so hot I have to crack a window.

I park next to the cottage, gather the mail, and clomp up the stairs. As I'm fumbling with my key chain, looking for the right one, my cell phone rings. I set down the mail on the arm of the nearest Adirondack chair. It's Mac calling. Immediately, my mind goes to Tim. He was fine when I left him a few minutes ago. Could something have happened? An infection, or something worse?

With my heart in my throat, I answer the call.

'Shay,' she says in a way that sends a chill straight down to my toes. There's a long, agonizing pause. 'Oh, honey. I'm so sorry to have to tell you this.'

It was Sol who received the call. A summer resident had returned to his cottage to open up for the season, sweep out the cobwebs and enjoy a few weeks of cool, quiet nights before the rest of the vacationers come streaming in. His annual routine included flipping over the canoe he stored under a tarp next to the water. He'd dragged it over to the dock and was about to tip it in when he noticed something in the river. He called the village police in a panic. And they called the BCI.

'The coroner thinks he was in Eel Bay for a couple of days,' Mac tells me. 'Multiple stab wounds to the chest. It's likely he was dead before he hit the water. Kelsea says she hasn't seen him since Monday, when she went to stay with that friend in Watertown. She was keeping her distance until he let off some steam. They'd had an argument. He was convinced you and Tim were trying to break up his engagement. He didn't believe what you told him about Bram being a threat.'

Wobbly. I feel wobbly, and weak. I sink into the chair, scattering the mail across the deck. It's illogical. Impossible. As I listen to Mac describe the waterlogged playing card that was found in Carson's pocket, the pulp swollen and paper peeling so all she could make out was the word *Bay*, my eyes drift down toward my feet.

There's an envelope there, tucked between a Price Chopper flyer advertising S'mores sticks and one for the local Kinney Drugs. My name is written on the front. Not Shana, but Shay.

I reach for it with unsteady hands and slide my finger under the flap. There's a folded slip of paper inside. The writing doesn't match that of the notes Bram left for me last fall. This is a childish scrawl, tentative and scruffy, as if penned with a non-dominant hand. It's Abraham Skilton's writing, when he was in second grade.

I stop Mac mid-sentence. She doesn't ask questions. I clutch the paper in my hands, and start to read.

> Shay. Did you figure it out? Solve the clue? It felt like fate, when I found that particular card. Eel Bay. It's perfect. I know what he did to you. Nobody treats Shay that way.

I picture Carson Gates, a person I once loved and who Kelsea loves now, bloated in the river, his dark hair swirling around his face and those silly novelty socks blackened by silt. The image makes me gag.

> I tried. I looked for someone else, for years and years I looked, but nobody came close to replacing you. No one else could love me the way you did. Some didn't even try. They only cared about themselves. Their looks, their perfect lives. Their other, better friends. It had to be you.
>
> I didn't play fair. I know that now. All I ever wanted was for you to come back to me. But I get it. There's no going home, not really. No way to get back to where we were before it all went to shit. I know about the FBI, and that they're close. So, I'm conceding. You win, ding ding, applause. And here's your prize: I'm fixing things by getting rid of the two men who hurt you the most.

I suck in a breath as I picture him raising the gun to his head, and the horror that followed. The blast. The blood.

There are just four words left.

Good game. Love, Abe.

I look up from the letter and realize I'm crying. Sobs, hawked up by the lungful, rack my body like a boat in a storm. I cry for Carson, and all the lives that were lost because my cousin knew I liked to play detective. For the girls Abe murdered in his senseless search to replace me, whose families still don't have answers. I cry for Abraham Skilton, who lost his life to Bram too, and my family, who'll be tied to a monster for the rest of theirs.

When I finally pry open my burning, swollen eyes, I see the river. The water is a mirror glinting in the sun. The St Lawrence is wide, and deep. Familiar now, but still a mystery too. Traversing it could be perilous.

But I can see the other side.

ACKNOWLEDGMENTS

I finished writing this book during the pandemic, when uncertainty seemed to be the only constant, and the steadfast support of the following people was a lifeline in a very strange storm.

Thank you Marlene Stringer for your continued guidance and faith, and Kate Lyall Grant and Rachel Slatter for wholeheartedly embracing this series. I'm so appreciative of the entire Severn House crew, especially Natasha Bell, Anna Harrisson, and Martin Brown.

Where would writers be without subject matter experts? Thank you, Sheriff Colleen O'Neill, for answering my endless questions about law enforcement in the North Country (any mistakes here are mine). Thanks also to John Brandy, Deborah Colson, K.J. Dell'Antonia, Elle Desamours, and Marc Maier for your knowledge and willingness to share it.

To my early readers Leila and Karl Wegert, Carol and John Repsher, Michelle Sowden, and Dorinda Bonanno, along with graphic artist Jessica Burnie, you rock. Much love to Barrett Bookstore, Finley's Fiction, The Little Book Store, Darien Library, Abby Endler, Sloane Bernard, and Sonica Soares.

Though most of our time together has been virtual (so far), I'm immensely grateful for the generosity of the mystery and thriller writing community. Special thanks to Sarah Stewart Taylor, Joanna Schaffhausen, and Charlie Donlea.

To the artist who sculpted eighty-six hands and planted them on Wolfe Island in 2009, thanks for the inspiration, wherever you are.

Finally, to my family: you put up with long hours and late nights on the laptop, listen to me ramble on about plot ideas, endure side trips to bookstores, and never complain. There are no words to describe my gratitude and love.